# STOKER RULES

## DAN PEREZ

*STOKER RULES*

Copyright © 2025 by Dan Perez All rights reserved.

No part of this book may be used or reproduced in any manner whatsoever, stored in any retrieval system, or transmitted
in any form by any means – electronic, mechanical, photocopy,
recording, or otherwise – without prior written permission of the
author. Brief quotations embodied in critical articles or reviews
are allowed.

This is a work of fiction. Names, characters, businesses, organi-
zations, places, events and incidents are either the product of the
author's imagination or are used fictitiously. Any resemblance to
actual persons, living or dead, business establishments, events, or
locales is entirely coincidental.

Cover art: Lesia S. (germancreative)

Author photo: David Lam

Contact info: www.dans-books.com

ISBN: 978-1-953740-02-1 (hardcover) 978-1-953740-01-4 (pa-
perback) 978-1-953740-00-7 (eBook)

# ACKNOWLEDGEMENTS

Thanks to my incredible fiction coach, John Yearley, for his thoughtful and incisive help. He helped me immensely with the outlining process and kept me focused and doing my best during the writing.

Thanks to my editor Dale Prasek, whose critical eye really helped me improve some big-picture stuff with the book.

Thanks to hypnotist extraordinaire Anthony Jacquin for above-and-beyond help of the highest caliber.

Thanks to Rima Bonario for her amazing, inspirational involvement in the development of the book. Thanks to David Brashear for his insightful friendship and support, as well as his coaching on kung fu. Thanks to Lynn Swayze-Hall, fiction colleague, hypnotist and marketing maven, for identifying some really important changes the book needed.

Thanks to my beta readers: Rima, Lynn, Jordan Sprague, Jill Lien, Richard Castaneda, Lindsey Short, and my fine friend Sarah Shults. You helped me shape the book and let me know how I did.

Thanks to Dr. Richard Nongard for his enduring friendship, and for his unflagging help, encouragement, and support, and to all the wonderful folks in Richard's Twelve Week Book classes.

Special thanks to Brian Upton, whose in-depth critique of a different writing project some years back prompted me to work diligently and seriously to improve my craft.

Thanks to Bram Stoker, whose enduring vampire tropes inspired me to write this book, and for *Dracula* itself, which became the reading equivalent of comfort food as I worked on this book. Thanks to Stephen King for writing *Salem's Lot*, which I reread numerous times while working on my own modern vampire tale.

Heartfelt thanks to a remarkable group of people (too many to mention here) who came to the rescue when things in my personal life took a serious turn for the worse during the writing of the book.

Finally, thanks to Thor, a pup rescued from a roof in the aftermath of hurricane Harvey in 2017. He's an adult now and is very patient when his dad trots off to the coffee shop to get some more writing done.

*This book is dedicated to the memory of two men who passed too soon: my real uncle Maxie, whom I wish I had known better, and my father, Alex John Perez.*

# CONTENTS

# 1
— · —

J ennifer was face down on a yoga mat in the back of the van. The husky man had already zip-tied her hands behind her back. Now he was zip-tying her ankles together. Duct tape covered her mouth. She had tried to struggle but he was too strong.

An icy chill spread in her gut as he slammed the van doors shut. The only light came from the instrument panel up front and a single dim light overhead.

Suddenly he was close to her. "I got you now. You ain't going nowhere now."

His rough hand caressed the nape of her neck, and she whimpered through the tape. "Pretty blonde hair you got there." She shivered.

"I got a place out in the woods," he said. "It's cozy. Just perfect for you and me. You could stand outside and scream your lungs out and nobody'd hear you. Nice and secluded."

He slid his hand down her back, inch by inch. Her muscles tensed.

"Pretty dress. Musta been going to the club to meet your girlfriends, huh? I got a lot of pretty things for you to wear out at my place in the woods. And some naughty things, too. Can't wait to see you in 'em."

He moved her bound hands up, away from her buttocks. She made a sound and tried to push them back down, but he wrenched them up until she cried out.

"You need to get this: you're my obedient little fuck toy. You do what I want you to when I want you to or you get hurt. So are you my obedient little fuck toy? Nod if you are." Jennifer sobbed through the tape. *Why is this happening to me*?

He wrenched her arms up again and she cried out. "Are you my obedient little fuck toy?" he growled.

She nodded. He lifted the hem of her dress to expose her buttocks and panties. She tried to remain still, as if that would somehow help. He caressed her buttocks. He leaned close to her ear. "That's my good little fuck toy," he whispered. She was rigid, her eyes wide, gasping through her nose.

"They're never going to find you," he whispered into her ear, caressing her buttocks and thighs. "It's just gonna be you and me every night. Every single night. Weekends too. I think you have a pretty good idea of what I'm going to do with you. And I'm gonna do it over, and over and—"

As he kept whispering and it got uglier, she closed her eyes and thought of her boyfriend Ben. He was so gentle and loving. Would she ever see him again? Would he even want her after this guy was through with her? An icy black cloud roiled inside her gut.

Suddenly there was a tortured sound of tearing metal from behind and she flinched. The man's hand was gone as he turned and cried out, "What the fuck?"

She twisted and craned her neck in the dim light. *This might be my only chance to escape*. She managed to roll over in time to see the husky man being dragged out of the van by his hair by a thinner man in dark clothing. They vanished from view, and she heard a muffled cracking sound and a strangled, glottal cry, followed by silence.

Alexandru Stoica dragged the heavyset man—dead weight now that his neck was broken—into a nearby alley. Mosquitoes buzzed in the hot, humid late-July air. A slick of stinking liquid waste had leaked from a large green dumpster nearby. Though his hunger for blood was strong at this point, Alex frowned. *Can't feed on this guy.* He was dead and livor mortis had begun; all his blood was surely settling to the lowest parts of his body. Too difficult and too exposed even on this lonely bit of street. Alex lifted him like an average person would lift a small child and stuffed the body through the open door on the side of the dumpster. The body dropped into the stinking fluid with a dull splat.

He jogged back to the van, its doors still open. The blonde woman had wriggled around, and her head was closer to the doorway. Her eyes widened when she saw him.

"It's okay! I'm here to help you," he said, pulling the fake badge and ID from his jacket pocket. He flipped the leather case open and flashed it in front of her face. "Marco Bellinger, HPD undercover. You're safe now."

She relaxed and tried to say something through the tape.

He replaced the badge in a pocket and said, "Here, let me help you."

With fingers that could bend half-inch steel rod, he gently broke the bonds on her wrists and ankles. Then he gingerly removed the tape from her mouth.

"Oh God, oh God," she said, trembling and breathing rapidly.

*Panic attack*, he thought. "Breathe slowly," he said. "Breathe in on a mental count of seven and out on a mental count of eleven."

She shook her head, too agitated to listen. "Heart racing," she said, still gasping for breath. "Am I dying?"

*No choice*, Alex thought. He willed his pores to emit the charisma pheromone, and she grew calmer. He helped her get out of the van and she looked at him with a smile on her face. "That's better. Thank you for saving me."

"This is a rough neighborhood to be alone in, male or female," he said.

"I was going to meet my girlfriends at Club Santeria. It's a block or two from here. Uber driver got confused and was acting weird, so I made him let me out. Out of nowhere that guy grabbed me."

"My car is this way," he said. "Let's get you home."

She nodded happily. "Okay." Alex sighed.

City lights swept past as he drove through the night. The illuminated skyline of Houston was visible against the night sky in the distance. Alex's red Miata convertible had the hard top on. In the passenger seat, the woman—Jennifer Codie was her name—sat calmly. She turned to him and said, "Never saw a cop drive a car like this. It's nice."

"I'm off duty. I saw the guy closing the van doors, but I caught a glimpse of you in there as well."

"Are we going to the police station?"

"Not tonight, Jen. Just home. I will fill out a report at the station later. And someone will come by for a statement in the morning. You've been through enough tonight."

That seemed to satisfy her, and they drove down U.S. 59 in silence. Following the female voice prompts on Google Maps, he exited on Buffalo Speedway and drove north. When they neared her neighborhood, he pulled over to the curb on a quiet, shady street. "It's just a block or two up there," she said.

Alex gritted his teeth. His hunger simmered beneath his ribs. *Have to hurry up*, he thought. There was a moment of weakness as he shut the car engine off. It disgusted him, but it was there just the same. That *need*. Unlike her dead captor, her blood was young. Untainted. Fresh. Alive.

"What are we doing?" Jennifer asked.

"You've been through a bad experience today," Alex said, regaining his composure. "I bet you'd like to forget about it."

A tear rolled down her cheek. "Yeah. Those things he said—" She sniffled.

Alex pulled a gleaming dollar coin from his jacket pocket and held it out in front of her, just above her eyeline. "Focus your eyes on this coin."

Since she was still under the influence of the charisma pheromone she went into hypnosis very quickly. The hypnosis session was brief and powerful. James Wilcox, the most successful hypnotherapist in the United States, had taught him. Alex had used a false name and had paid Wilcox well. Alex smiled through his hunger at the thought of a vampire having to learn to hypnotize. Dracula just had the innate ability. But that was a Stoker rule.

There was another challenging moment as she sat in trance, eyes closed, her face relaxed. With the car engine off, he could hear the warm fresh blood pulsing through her carotid arteries. He remembered another young girl, nicknamed Jellybean, on a beach in Malibu decades ago. He'd fed on her with the stars scattered overhead and the sound of waves crashing in the distance. The *taste*!

"You're safe with me," he murmured, more to himself than to her. Still in trance, Jennifer slowly nodded. But she wasn't. Alex gritted his teeth against his hunger, against his weakness. *You're no better than that guy with the van*, he thought. *A predator*.

Feeling desperate, he used a trick Wilcox had taught him. Mindfulness. He stopped fighting the memory of the young girl in Malibu and instead became nonjudgmental about it. The memory evaporated. His hunger faded a bit. The need became less urgent. He was in the car, in the moment with Jennifer again, her life and safety utterly dependent on him. *That was the whole idea from the start,* he thought. Faint ligature marks marred the skin on her wrists and Alex dipped two fingers into his mouth, wetting them with saliva. He massaged her wrists with the healing saliva and the marks faded as he did so. He did the same with her ankles.

"And so, Jennifer," he murmured, finishing up the hypnosis session. "You are free from the memory of tonight. Your subconscious, your dreaming mind, is releasing it in the healthiest possible way now, so you can be healthy and happy and go out with your friends and do whatever you want. The harder you try to remember tonight, the further away it will go. All you will remember is a long walk through your neighborhood earlier tonight. You can tell your girlfriends you changed your mind about going out. You'll remember the trees and houses and seeing a friendly gray cat and that's it. Because that's all that happened tonight. You are healed now in all ways, mentally, physically, emotionally and even spiritually. You are safe and free and happy from now on."

Alex kept her in trance until he had pulled up a few houses down from her house. He counted from one to three and, with a deep breath, she opened her eyes. They focused as she recognized her house a short distance away. Alex knew she was still a little suggestible after emerging from trance. "Go back home now, Jen. Did you see anything interesting on your nice long walk?"

She nodded. "I saw the cutest gray cat," she said. Then she exited the car, and he watched her for a moment as she walked down the sidewalk, pulling her keys from her clutch. The hunger still gnawed at him, but she was safe now and Alex relaxed a bit at last. He turned the car around and drove off into the night.

# 2

— · —

Alex awakened for the second time at noon. The first time had been at 7:45 a.m., to let his two dogs out and feed them. Once Dizzy, an energetic white Labrador Retriever, and Midnight, a more laid-back black Lab, had gobbled down their kibble, Alex had crawled back into bed and fallen asleep again, still exhausted after a couple of late-night feeds near a few rough-and-tumble bars in La Porte. He had pretended to carelessly flash some Franklins from his wallet as bait, and a few hapless would-be robbers had gotten more than they bargained for. The two partial feeds were enough to keep Alex going for two or three days.

A full feed would sustain a vampire for about a week, but then you might have another vampire on your hands. And that was a problem. In books like *Salem's Lot* and *They Thirst*, an out-of-control geometric progression of vampires could wipe out humanity in just a few years. Fortunately, in the real world, not every death from vampiric feeding produced another vampire. It varied, but anecdotal evidence suggested that about 1 in 25 people killed by a vampire bite became a vampire. Partial feeds eliminated the problem altogether, and that's what nearly all vampires did. Judicious use of silver could prevent another vampire from being created, even with a full feed. Most vampires carried a small silver item just in case. For Alex it was a coin-shaped troy ounce piece that was featureless and smooth: a blank disk in a flat leather case. He had to handle the silver piece with gloves, or it would burn the skin on his fingers. He'd had it specially made in 1922.

And then there was APES. The acronym stood for Anomalous Profound Exsanguination Syndrome, a term originally coined by a medical examiner in Bryn Mawr, Pennsylvania, and which had become commonly used by medical professionals to describe corpses that presented as drained of blood but with no signs of penetrative trauma. MEs were also confused about the burn marks that appeared on some APES victims, but those were from silver items carried by vampires to prevent vampirization after full feeds, of course.

Alex showered and shaved, then made a cup of coffee. He took it into his office, bright with sunlight from two large windows in front of his desk. He sat in front of his computer and sighed. There had been a lot of unhappy sighs recently and he longed for something to raise his spirits. He caught up on the news on the computer while Dizzy and Midnight sat on the floor underneath his desk. From the second-story window he noticed the mail carrier put the mail in the box outside the fence, then reach out and press a button next to the box.

A chime sounded and the dogs were up in an instant, barking and running downstairs, their claws skittering crazily on the sealed concrete floors. They clumped down the stairs and ran through the doggie door with a clatter and into the yard, still barking and yowling. Alex smiled and said, "Listen to them: the children of the day. What music they make."

Across town in Montrose, Bardru Valeska, a vampire who might appear to be in his sixties to the average observer but was closer to thrice that age, half-dozed in his bed, propped up on pillows. The only sound besides his slow breathing was the steady ticking of a large ebony grandfather clock in a corner. Numerous shelves held scholarly tomes, bound in leather and cloth, and tables were crowded with antiques, including a large, ornate gold cross on a stand with an expensive Rembrandt Bible open at its base. Dominating one wall facing the foot of the bed was a huge oil painting of Jesus, bleeding from the crown of thorns and from stigmata on his hands and feet. His face was serene, with eyes downcast. Carved into the gold-leafed frame was the inscription THY BLOOD WAS SPILT FOR EVERY ONE.

The clock chimed one p.m., and Bardru's gray eyes fluttered open. Open on his lap was a large, vellum-bound volume titled *Vampires of Antiquity*, and there, amid columns of handwritten Latin and Greek names on the tattered parchment pages Bardru's thin fingertips rested near a particular name: Titus Seneca "The Scornful."

In Atlanta, Georgia, Senior Investigative Agent Emelia Cord sat on a stool in the training lab at the national headquarters of the Combined Departments of Paranormal Research (officially abbreviated as CDPR but nicknamed "See Deeper" by staff). She drummed her nails on the wooden counter. It had been two months since she had been out on assignment.

"Gack!" said the sprite in the tank in front of her. Even with her trained eyes she could barely make out its outline against the gnarled natural cork bark that formed the back of the tank. It was a small humanoid figure with batlike wings, two arms, two legs and a coiled, pterosaur-like tail.

"Gack to you," she said, and sighed. The door opened and two trainees, Melanie Sanders and Bjorn Jonsson, came in. Emelia brightened. They were young, intelligent and easy on the eyes. Her boss, Mark Petrovsky, sure knew how to pick them. See Deeper studies had shown that physical attractiveness helped when dealing with the public out in the field.

"It's sprite day!" Melanie said gaily, her green eyes bright.

"It's got to be better than will-o'-the-wisp day," said Bjorn. They sat on stools near the table on which the tank rested.

"Well," Emelia said, donning leather gloves, "you won't have to feed any life energy to this little guy."

"Where is it?" Bjorn asked.

"I don't see it either," said Melanie. "Is there one in there?"

"He's there against the cork bark." Emelia said. "Look closer—look for six little shiny eyes about the size of sewing beads."

"I got nothing," Bjorn said.

"Me neither," Melanie said.

Emelia nodded. "Sprites have as close to perfect camouflage as it gets. Watch."

She took a pair of red plastic tongs with padded tips in one hand and a plastic cup with the other. Fishing a mealworm from the cup with the tongs, Emelia slid open a panel on the top of the tank. She lowered the wriggling mealworm and there was a blur of movement as the tiny head grabbed the worm and chomped on it. Both trainees uttered cries of surprise. The interior of its mouth was white.

"I was looking right at him!" Melanie said.

"I can't believe it." Bjorn was shaking his head in wonder. After gulping down the last of the mealworm, the sprite settled back against the cork and was still.

"Can you see the outline now?" Emelia asked. "Yes—barely," Bjorn said. Melanie nodded in agreement.

"It uses chromatophores like an octopus, but they are much more sophisticated. And their skin can physically mimic textures to match the background. Octopuses also do that to some degree, but sprites are way better at it. Sprites are surprisingly common out in the environment, our environment, but their camouflage makes them virtually impossible for lay people to see."

"Wow," said Bjorn. "How did they even get discovered?"

"Gack!" the sprite said, as if in answer.

Emelia laughed at their surprised faces. "Well, that's one way. They've also turned up in traps set for bats. They're nocturnal. Watch."

She reached back into the tank with the tongs and gripped the sprite's body. It *gacked* angrily as she lifted it off the cork bark and it suddenly went jet-black. Its wings flapped and its mouth bit repeatedly at the padded tips of the tongs. "Gack! Gack! Gack!"

"That's their normal coloration," she said. She released the sprite, and it dropped onto the soft moss covering the floor of the tank. In the blink of an eye, it just vanished.

The trainees laughed again.

"Nature and supernature," Emelia said, sliding the lid of the tank closed. "They intersect like a Venn diagram, and part of what we do here at See Deeper is study the relationship between the two to better understand supernature."

"Now that they've been discovered," Melanie ventured, "Aren't sprites just a peculiar part of the natural world?"

Emelia smiled. "That's an excellent observation. But when a sprite dies, the body sublimates. The flesh and bones convert to vapor and dissipate. That doesn't happen with any natural species. You can watch a short film in the video library and see it happen. That's part of your homework."

"*There are more things in heaven and Earth, Horatio, than are dreamt of in your philosophy,*" Bjorn said quietly.

Emelia nodded politely, despite having heard that quotation from nearly a dozen trainees in the past. The feeling of restlessness returned. Then she said, for the dozenth time, "That might as well be the official motto of the CDPR."

Alison Martin sat, resolute and resigned, as she waited for Linda to show up at Blue Fish, a trendy Houston restaurant. Linda wanted to have "a talk," which likely meant the end of their six-month relationship. Linda was having trouble dating an FBI Special Agent, and they had argued about it a few times. She didn't like the danger element and long hours alone when Alison was on assignment in another city. And there was that other reason.

Linda Ramirez came in through the glass door, a vision in tight black capri pants, a black tube top and expensive Alta pumps. *Already advertising for that next lucky girl*, Alison thought as Linda sauntered past empty tables (it was 3 p.m. on a Monday and slow) and sat down opposite her. Linda's lustrous black hair, pulled back in a ponytail, gave an artificially severe look to her impeccably made-up face. "Hey," she said quietly.

"Hey," Alison said. "No kiss hello?"

Linda sighed. "I'm kinda not comfortable with that here."

"You've kissed me here a dozen times," Alison noted. Linda tried to conceal a slight eye roll, but Alison, trained in body language and the facial tells of people, noticed it.

"Just not comfortable right this moment."

"So this is it?" Alison said.

"Are you going to stick with the Bureau?" Linda asked.

"You know the answer to that."

"But your boss is a fucking prick," Linda said. "You've told me that *ad nauseam*."

"Yeah, sorry to burden you with my feelings there."

Linda tried to soften her impatient expression without success. "Sorry. But it's true, right?"

"Lots of people have bosses who are pricks. And I'm a Special Agent. My work is important. I like my job, despite Crain being a prick." *A losing battle*, Alison thought. Linda had been raped by a police officer, who told her he wanted to "fuck the gay" out of her. Alison had wanted to put him behind bars, but Linda had refused to press charges after some anonymous threats. One more point of contention.

Linda sighed. "I'm really sorry. I thought this would work between us, but—" she trailed off and looked down at the table-cloth.

At that moment, a server approached the table and said, "What can I get you two ladies?" Alison waved her off, adding surreal embarrassment to the awkward moment.

Linda sighed. "Baby, you are an amazing woman. Don't do this to yourself."

A tear rolled down Alison's cheek. "Kinda feels like *you* are doing this to *me*."

"What I am trying to say is you're going to find someone else if you don't lose faith in how awesome you are."

"Not awesome enough to keep you, though."

Linda was silent. *Finality* was the unspoken word that echoed in Alison's mind. Suddenly she stood up to leave. Linda was a lost cause and she was torturing herself by even sitting here with her.

As she passed, Linda reached out and took Alison's left hand in both her hands. "Baby, I'm so sorry."

Alison gently extricated her hand from Linda's. Those soft, skillful hands had explored nearly every inch of her body, but they felt alien now. "I'm going. Goodbye, Linda."

Alison was halfway to the door when Linda called out, uttering an almost inaudible plea to her. But Alison just kept walking.

## 3

Alex stood in his spacious studio with his hands on his hips. The ceiling was 20 feet high, and the late-afternoon sunlight poured in from the skylights, augmented by fluorescent lights and tall windows on the east and west sides, casting a golden glow in the expansive room. The air was redolent of oil paint, varnishes and solvents. There were tables and 14 easels that held abstract expressionist paintings in various stages of completion. Four finished works hung on the windowless, white-painted north wall, along with some of his earlier pointillist paintings, done under his first alias, Max Ellis. Alex had studied fine arts at Brown University and had later earned his master's in fine arts at Syracuse University.

His pointillist paintings as Max Ellis had become sought after by collectors and some museums, and he had had a lucrative career in the '50s and '60s. His work evolved as he experimented with transitional paintings in 1965, with fields of painted dots merging into larger zones of paint comprising increasingly abstract forms. By 1972, he had transitioned fully into abstract expressionism, with bold, dramatic swatches of color competing for the viewer's attention. The art world had been lamenting the mysterious disappearance of the already reclusive Max Ellis for a few years by then (he had declined to market the transitional paintings through his intermediaries). Now he painted as Jackson Williams, and two of his more recent paintings were part of the Museum of Modern Art's collection. Three more were part of the Menil Collection here in Houston.

Alex sighed. He hadn't put brush to canvas in four months. He didn't want to admit it, but it felt like the spark had faded. Walking over to a large easel, he stood in front of a half-finished canvas with bold, deliberate splotches of reds, yellows, and greens that had the working title of *Senegal Summer*. Alex briefly considered renaming it *Painter's Block*. His cell phone rang, interrupting his reverie.

"I slept very late today," Bardru Valeska said on the other end. "I was reading much of the night. Shall I come over still?"

"Yes, Uncle. I could use some company."

"Still no painting?"

Alex sighed again. "Still no painting."

"Tsk," Bardru said. "I worry about you, Alexandru. In my dreams and my waking."

"I worry about me, too."

"Bah!" Bardru said. "We will have a nice walk in the sunset. I will regale you with stories of my time in the Buffalo Bill show. We will have some wine at a café and look at the skyline in the twilight."

Alex smiled. Bardru had indeed been a performer for *Buffalo Bill's Wild West* in the late 1800s. And a traveling circus performer in Russia before that. "That sounds good, Uncle," he said.

The two vampires sat across from each other on the faded wooden deck that served as the patio for the Cityscape Café. In the nearby trees, great-tailed grackles squawked noisily. Off to the left of the patio, the tall, gleaming skyscrapers of downtown

Houston shone reflected hues of violet, orange and pink in the dying sunset.

"It's beautiful, is it not?" Bardru said and sipped his wine. He was tall, with pomaded dark hair and perhaps more wrinkles than someone in their sixties (appearance-wise; Bardru had been born in 1846) ought to have. To Alex, he looked a little like Martin Landau made up as Bela Lugosi in that Ed Wood movie.

Alex surveyed the skyline and nodded. "It is."

"An inspiration for you, perhaps? To paint?"

"You're a wily old cat, Uncle. You know I'm saving it for a rainy day. One of these days, though."

"Are the days not rainy for you when it comes to painting now?"

"Well, they are, but I wouldn't be in a good head space to work on something so important as a piece like that. Houston deserves better from me."

"Ah, you are right. It does. I have been to many places, on this continent and others, but I love this city," Bardru said, waving a hand at the skyline. "Oh, there is traffic and pollution, certainly, but it is also green and lush and modern. And the alligators in the bayous to remind me of my time in New Orleans!"

Alex smiled. "I love it, too. Northerners think it's a cow-town, but it's every bit as cosmopolitan as New York or Chicago. Decent city for art. World-class opera."

"And plenty of crime for my vigilante nephew, eh?"

"Is that what I am?" Alex asked.

"It's what the Collective calls you." He was referring to the loose-knit coalition of vampires in Houston and the surrounding areas. Most major cities had an analogous organization.

"Well, I could probably come up with a couple of nicknames for the Collective myself," Alex said, frowning.

"That movie said it best," Bardru said, staring into the distance. "Maria Ouspenskaya, from my homeland—a fine actress—said the line in *The Wolf Man*."

"The way you walked was thorny, through no fault of your own," Alex recited.

"Yes, yes. You are different from those in the Collective. Your destiny is something different from theirs. And mine. When they feed it is just the blood. When I feed, it is the sacrament of Christ the Redeemer. When you feed on the wicked, it is...what?"

Alex stared out at the skyline for a moment. "Making things right. The full-feed deaths of the innocents in my wilder early days weigh on me. One in particular."

"Atonement," Bardru said. "It is a heavy cross to bear, if you will excuse my expression. But I have this question for you, dearest Nephew. When is it *enough*? When will the scales tip into balance? Will they ever do that to your satisfaction?"

Alex drew a deep breath and let it out, staring at the skyline. "That's a good question. I wish I could put my finger on the answer."

"When I found you after...*that woman* had left you to suffer and starve," Bardru muttered, "I decided to be your uncle. To guide you in the ways of a vampire. To introduce you to the Deepest Shadow and the other things you needed to learn. And of course, now you might as well be a real nephew to me, or perhaps even more. Certainly more. And thus, it pains me all the more to see you struggling."

Alex shifted in his chair as the memory emerged. "Silana. I vowed to kill her if I ever found her again," he said. "To feed her powdered silver and watch her as she choked to death. But you showed me kindness and understanding and restraint and my hatred for her has faded, in part thanks to you."

"Has it completely faded?" Bardru asked.

"I'd be lying if I said yes. But I don't think I would kill her if I saw her. My hypnosis mentor told me that 'resentment is a poison you take yourself, hoping someone else will die.'"

"Wisdom," Bardru said. "I never resented Strong Arms for making me a vampire. But the circumstances were different. He became an uncle to me immediately. He showed me kindness and compassion as I became what I am."

Alex nodded. Strong Arms was a Sioux who had worked with Bardru on the *Wild West* show. "Whatever happened to Strong Arms?" he asked.

"After he became my uncle, we fled the show and went east. He had had a Harvard education, you know, and he helped me acquire the same. He had connections at the university, and they treated me as a legacy. But the call of his people made him return to the West in 1915. The Indian Wars—imagine a vampire brave fighting the white invaders! I wanted to accompany him, but he forbade it. It was his personal odyssey. So I traveled south to New Orleans." Bardru sighed, staring out at the skyline. "I have long wondered if I will ever see him again."

"I hope you do, Uncle. From now on, I shall think of Strong Arms as my great uncle."

Bardru turned to him and smiled warmly. "He would consider that an honor. Let us drink to him on this fine evening."

They clinked their glasses, drank and sat in thoughtful silence amid the raucous serenade of the grackles, watching the last light fade from the sky over downtown.

## 4
— · —

T he horror came to Houston a few days later. An unusual summer fog shrouded parts of the city, including a
small traveling carnival set up in the expansive parking lot of a
Spring Branch strip center. It was Saturday night, and the carnival thronged with parents and kids from the nearby Hispanic neighborhoods. The fog amplified and fuzzed the whirling
colors of the rides, creating a surreal landscape punctuated by
laughter and screams from riders of El Diablo, a small roller
coaster. The dark ride was called The Haunty House, and its
façade was a panoply of ghosts, monsters, and a gothic-styled
house that looked like a face, with a broken door resembling
a toothy mouth and smashed windows for eyes. Luis Ramirez
pointed to it and asked his nine-year-old son Alberto if he wanted to ride it.

"Yes, Papi!" he shouted. "Can Mariana come too?" Luis
glanced toward his daughter as she clung to the slender leg of
his wife, Lina. The six-year-old surveyed the façade and shook
her head, her brown eyes wide. Lina laughed and said, "We'll
ride the Whirly Bird again, I think." Luis smiled. Beneath her
tank top, Lina's belly had a slight bulge where their third child
was growing. Later tonight, when the kids were happily asleep
in their room down the hall, Lina would climb astride him in
their bed, and they'd make love. That was the ride *he* was looking
forward to.

He leaned down to Alberto. "Let's go see the spooks, little man!" He waved at Lina as she turned and walked with Mariana toward the Whirly Bird ride. Then he took Alberto's hand and they ran noisily up the metal ramp to the entrance of The Haunty House. He handed two strings of tickets to the bored-looking ride operator, and he and Alberto climbed into the last car in the string of six. Parents, teenagers, and kids boarded the other cars, and after the operator gave safety instructions in English and Spanish, he pressed a button on the control panel and the string of cars clattered into motion.

Alberto leaned near and said in a timid voice, "What if I scream?" Luis smiled and squeezed his shoulder. "It's okay, little man." Alberto smiled back at him. The boy loved being called that.

The ride clanked along its rails and banged through twin doors painted to look like a ravening mouth bristling with teeth. Darkness enfolded them as the doors closed behind them, and a large grinning skull hung in the darkness over them, illuminated by a small spotlight. Its lower jaw moved in sync with a sinister-sounding recorded voice that said, "DO YOU DARE?"

The light blinked out and the cars took a curve. In the darkness, Luis heard a female voice in the car ahead say, "Stop it, Dale!"

Another spotlight blinked on, and a large dummy of Frankenstein's monster leaned out of the darkness, its recorded voice making an angry growl. Alberto leaned against Luis, who put his arm around the boy. The light blinked out again, and there was a female scream from the front car. Luis laughed, but the scream went on and on and the woman yelled, "My eyes! Oh god, *my eyes*!" And there was another scream, this time from a male, and it faded into a wet, ragged gargling sound. The cars weren't moving on the track anymore. Another scream pierced the darkness, this one a little closer. It was the high-pitched scream of a child.

"Papi!" Alberto whimpered, clinging tightly to Luis. He had discerned, like Luis had, that these weren't playful screams, but screams of fear and pain. Someone ahead shouted, "Don't! Please don't." Another gargling scream.

Luis yanked at the safety bar on his lap. It was designed to keep people from getting out of the cars and perhaps hurting themselves in the darkness. Or to prevent kids from messing with the props. But now it seemed like a trap, holding him in the car as whatever it was came closer. More screaming, and now sounds of weeping in the darkness. And a voice, a strange rasping, breathy voice, speaking in a foreign language. "*Accipe phallum meum!*" More screaming.

"Alberto!" Luis cried, "you have to get away!" There was a rattling sound, amid confused, urgent voices. Other people were shaking their safety bars, trying to escape. "Slide out on your side!" he said. "Follow the tracks back to the door!"

Alberto sobbed. "I can't see anything. It's dark!"

Luis grabbed his cellphone and punched in his code. Then he used the flashlight function and thrust it into Alberto's hand. In the glow from the light, he saw what looked like a skeletal old man—bald with a fringe of long, stringy white hair—in an ill-fitting black suit, standing next to the car ahead. He was leaning over a slumped male figure with his mouth latched onto a female teenager's neck. He held her as she jerked and twitched, a low whimper escaping her lips. He shuddered at the sound of the sickening gulping. And then the man glanced back at them, a wrinkled, demonic visage with his lips and chin smeared with blood.

"Go Alberto! Go now! Find your mother and sister!" He shoved Alberto hard, and the boy slid out from under the safety bar and tumbled to the ground. "Follow the tracks back to the door! GO!" He turned and saw the light bobbing as Alberto, sobbing, clambered back along the tracks.

Then he felt the creature's nearness, and its hot breath smelled of blood, a sickening charnel stench. A strong hand gripped his neck. Luis' bladder gave way as the strong fingers tightened on his throat. Then a lancing pain exploded in his left eye, and then in his right. Somewhere, mixed in with the awful pain, he heard the foreign words again: "*Accipe phallum meum!*" Something sharp slashed his throat and Luis' last thought was, *please God let my son escape.*

# 5
— · —

A lex stood in front of his large flat-screen television watching a news report of the carnival murders. His cell phone rang. It turned out to be Jonas Pemberton, currently the leader of the Collective.

"Have you seen the news?" he asked.

"Watching it now. The headline is lurid: 'Bizarre Murders at Kiddie Carnival.'"

"Our source in the Houston Police Department called. This is vampire related. Four people were drained. They're not releasing that information to reporters at the moment."

"A mass killing by a vampire? News says 11 people are dead. Three of them were kids."

"That's what it looks like. A nine-year-old boy survived. He told HPD an 'ugly, scary man' was kissing a woman's neck in the car ahead of him and his dad. She was an APES victim along with three other people in other cars. No word about the autopsies yet, but our source said four victims were drained with no marks on them. The rest had their eyes gouged out and either had stab wounds to the chest or slashed throats."

"Who would do such a thing? You don't think it's one of ours, do you?"

Jonas was silent for a moment. "I don't think so."

It was Alex's turn to be silent. Vampires worked to lay low and avoid attention, particularly when it came to law enforcement. Every vampire was taught this as a survival tactic. Too much attention would make people speculate, and someone might stumble upon the secret of killing vampires.

"Anyway," Jonas said, "I am calling for an emergency meeting a couple of days from now, at the Compound. As many of the Gulf Coast folks as we can get. I know you're not much of a meeting guy, but—"

"I'll be there. Has anyone called Bardru Valeska?"

"He's next on my list after you."

"I'll save you the trouble and call him right after this."

"This is going to bring the Feds down on us," Jonas said.

"Clearly. Did anyone see the suspect outside the ride?"

"No. It was dark inside, so I'm betting he shadowed in and then shadowed back out."

"Sure sounds like a vampire all right," Alex said. "Do you think whoever did this will do something again?"

"I sure hope not. We're going to discuss contingencies at the meeting. I'll text you the exact day and time for the meeting."

"All right."

"For the moment we're asking the Collective to feed out-of-town if possible. And only partial feeds. The Feds are going to be looking for APES victims after this. Tell Bardru."

"I will."

"I'll call if anything urgent comes up. Otherwise watch for a text for the meeting."

"Got it. One thing," Alex ventured.

"What?"

"What if our mass murderer is at the meeting?"

"We have a description from the kid, fortunately. It doesn't match anyone in the Collective."

"That's a stroke of luck."

"Watch for that text," Jonas said.

"I will."

They hung up and Alex stood with his arms crossed, watching the coverage. It showed a police spokesman saying, "Rest assured, we will get to the bottom of this and bring this killer to justice."

Alex doubted that. He lifted his phone and hit the button to call Bardru.

Emelia walked into Mark Petrovsky's office. He had a high-tech array of computer screens, keyboards, and two laptops on his desk. One wall had numerous photos on the wall, including what was purported to be the only authentic photo of a ghost ever taken. It was a blurry photo of a naked middle-aged woman in a dimly lit kitchen. It bore out the idea that when a person became a ghost, their clothing didn't go along for the ride.

Petrovsky emerged from behind the array of screens and greeted her. He was a tall man with handsome features, glasses that tended to slide down his nose, short-cropped, graying brown hair, and a small scar on his chin that he jokingly called his dueling scar.

"Is this about that thing in Houston?" Emelia asked.

Petrovsky nodded. "Yes, it is. I need you to saddle up."

"Over a mass killing?"

"It's a mass killing with four APES victims."

"I hadn't heard that."

"They're keeping that from the public for now," He picked up a slim bound report on his desk. "You wrote this a year ago. Your treatise on astral vampires?"

Emelia nodded. "Just a theory, but it's supported by Dr. Chavez and his team."

"Best theory we've got, then?"

She nodded again. "Best theory we've got. I did a ton of folkloric reading on vampirism, as well as modern cases—a minor hobby of mine. But nothing adequately explains APES."

He plopped the report on the desk. "What about the burns?"

"Best guess is that they are deliberate, but we don't yet understand what they are, or why some corpses present without them."

Petrovsky glanced at a screen and Emelia followed his gaze. It was a dossier on her. "You went through Behavioral Analysis at Quantico, right?"

"Yes. That, plus firearms, crime scene and mental toughness." She smiled. "Dunno how much of *the latter* I'll need." The CDPR and the FBI were uneasy allies, and several CDPR agents had gone through training at Quantico.

"So do you think this killer will strike again?"

"I'd be surprised if he didn't."

"P's and Q's," he replied, sliding his glasses up his nose. "What if the killer is a female?"

"It's just statistics," she said. "Most are male. It's not an assumption, however."

He smiled. "That's why we pay you the medium bucks. Besides, the description we got sounds like a male." He went to the printer and took a stack of printed material. He handed it to her. "Okay, you're on the case. The printout is what we know so far. I want you to take a partner. Do you want anyone from Chavez's team?"

"No. I can coordinate with them here if need be. I can overnight any samples he might need."

"Which of your trainees is most competent?"

"Melanie Sanders, for sure. She's way ahead of the other trainees: smart and observant. She's had the training at Quantico—she just finished that two months ago. She's a whiz with coding—she's worked with Rick Emerson in the lab."

"Sounds pretty good," he replied.

Emelia smiled. "Best of all, she won't be quoting *Hamlet* to me every five minutes."

Petrovsky grinned, his blue eyes sparkling. "Forsooth. Girl power it is. This'll be her first major field mission, so keep her under your wing. Get your gear together and if you need anything special, contact Gina Tompkins. FBI's got an agent from Houston assigned. Our FBI liaison in Houston is Vince Delgado, so check in with him when you get down there. They're in wait-and-see mode about a task force. Local cops may try to bulldoze you. Don't let them."

"I won't."

He reached out to shake her hand. "Make me proud."

She took his hand and smiled. "I will."

After the morning briefing for the Houston FBI Field Office adjourned, Jack Crain caught up with Alison in the hallway. "Half a minute?" he said, and pointed to a glass-walled huddle room connected to the hallway. Alison followed him in.

Crain had stern features, tousled black hair that seemed to defy combing, and a birth defect that made his upper lip thin and unusually wrinkled. He sat on the edge of the table and regarded Alison for a moment. "Well, as you heard at the meeting, you're our point agent for this mass killing," he said.

"Yes, sir."

He regarded her for a moment. "You okay?"

*A trap*, she thought. "Yes, sir."

"Looks like you've been crying."

She shrugged. "Allergies. Summer in Houston."

"I wonder," he ventured. "Trouble with Lipstick?"

It was his ugly nickname for Linda. Anger ignited in her chest. *Asshole.*

"Respectfully, sir, would it be any of your business if there were?" she asked, not quite as forcefully as she would have liked.

He watched her with his steely gray eyes. "Kinda. I need you to be on your A game for this. For a number of reasons, but mainly, as Hinrichs mentioned in the briefing, we think this killer is likely to strike again, and it'd be nice to nail his ass before that happens. It'd save us putting together a task force. It would look really good for you.

It was clear she was defending her ability to handle this case. "I lied to you a moment ago. I broke up with Linda eight days ago. I chose the Bureau over her."

He smiled, the first time she'd seen him do that, and it was an ugly little thing on those thin lips of his. "Really? Well, the Bureau appreciates that. Still grieving after eight days?"

It was the Bureau culture. Mental toughness *uber alles*. Emotions were for weaklings, whether they were male or female, but particularly the latter. It made sense, though. Emotions could cloud the mind at a crucial moment. But she had often thought Crain, and perhaps the Bureau overall, just wanted robots. Robots with guns.

"It's out of my system now," she said, straightening and squaring her shoulders.

"Good body language there," he replied. "I almost believe you."

She kept her anger tamped down, like coals that need to last the night to be rekindled in the morning. "I'm fine, sir."

He nodded. "I'll trust you on that. I need FBI Special Agent Martin out there, not mopey, heartbroken Alison. Can you give me what I need?"

She let just enough of the anger and hatred for him bubble up to power her voice. "24/7, sir," she asserted with just enough of an edge that he'd notice.

"That's all I can ask for," he said, standing. "You'll be working with HPD and, I regret to say, a couple of loonies from the CDPR in Atlanta. Play nice with everyone, if possible."

She nodded.

"One final thing—I *was* trying to get a rise out of you just now, but not for the reason you think. I wanted to show you what you are capable of under pressure."

Alison said, "I understand, sir." He held the glass door for her, and she walked out into the hallway. As she walked down the hall, clear of him, she heard Linda's voice in her mind. *He did all that because he's a fucking prick*. It was true, Alison thought. But I'll prove myself on this one.

# 6

It was called the Compound. It was a huge nondescript warehouse on US 290 about 15 miles outside the Beltway that encircled Houston. It had originally been a storage and shipping facility for Nodens Technologies, and the brick standalone sign next to the freeway feeder road still had the Nodens logo on it. A tall chain-link perimeter fence surrounded the warehouse and grounds. The site had been chosen because it was surrounded on three sides by woods. The large parking lot was situated at the rear of the building and was not visible from the freeway. Tonight, a few minutes before midnight, it was packed with hundreds of cars. Unlike any other warehouse, all the roll-up shipping doors at the truck docks on the west side of the building were welded shut. In fact, every exterior door had been welded shut from the inside. Windows and skylights had large steel plates welded over them from the inside. A half dozen empty 18-wheelers were parked in various truck docks. These were shuffled periodically, so from the air, it looked like business as usual for a warehouse.

In the rear, between the parking lot and the building exterior, ten pop-up single-person changing stalls of the type some beaches featured had been set up. The thick cloth exterior of each was jet-black. Alex and Bardru nodded at a uniformed vampire security guard standing at the edge of the parking lot and made their way to the stalls as the moon found a gap in the herringbone clouds above and shone brightly against the white-painted exterior of the Compound.

They unzipped the flap of one stall and stepped inside, zipping it shut behind them. It was a little cramped with the two of them, but they both turned toward the rear of the stall. The inky darkness there seemed more pervasive. It was somehow darker than dark, as though no light could penetrate it. The unmistakable aroma of cinnamon imperial candies enveloped them. They walked forward and vanished into the Deepest Shadow.

A moment later they emerged from the shadows at the back of a larger room. The interior had been painted black, except for the door, which was light gray. They passed through the door and were greeted by the muted, expansive swell of hundreds of voices in quiet conversation, echoing off the interior walls and ceiling of the warehouse.

A short, stoutly built, middle-aged woman hurried up to them. "Hello, Myra," Bardru said politely.

"Hello, hello," she said to each of them. Myra Blankenship, Treasurer for the Collective, always sounded breathless. Some quirk with her lungs, perhaps. "We've got seats reserved at the front for you," she said.

"Why?" Alex asked.

"Jonas requested it." She motioned for them to follow. As they walked down the wide center aisle, surrounded on either side by scores of vampires seated on folding chairs, Alex stared ahead, aware of hundreds of eyes on him. Someone whispered, "Our vigilante is here," undoubtedly aware that Alex's keen hearing would pick it up.

"Pay no mind," Bardru said as they walked. Alex said nothing in reply, but he frowned. *Like a bunch of small-town gossips*, he thought. Human nature was, alas, not lost when one became a vampire.

Myra showed them to their seats at the front, and Alex sat next to Bardru, endeavoring to keep his body language neutral. Half of the assembled company probably thought he was somehow trying to be better than they were. It wasn't true, but they thought so. Some mischievous part of his imagination quoted Popeye: *I yam what I yam*.

In front of them was a low platform resembling a stage with a lectern at the front. A row of nine chairs sat behind it, occupied by the leaders of the Collective. Myra hurried to her seat as Jonas Pemberton stood up. He was a robust, tall man, seeming to be in his forties, with a shaved head and a kind face. He walked to the lectern and looked out over the assemblage. There was no microphone on the lectern. Even those at the very back could easily hear his voice.

"Friends," he said. "We face a serious situation. One of our kind threatens our anonymity—that which we have sought to maintain above all else. As far as we can tell, this vampire is not one of the Collective, but some outsider. He is responsible for the mass killing you've all heard about. It happened at a small carnival in the Spring Branch neighborhood here in Houston. Four of the eleven killed were drained of blood with no external injury, so there is little doubt a vampire is at work. We don't understand the wantonness of the additional murders, three of whom were kids, but this mass murder has already made national headlines. We're lucky for now that the authorities have not made the nature of the drained bodies public. We learned this through our contacts with the Houston Police Department. Mark Clemmens has volunteered to watch the mortuary from the Deepest Shadow, just in case we get a new vampire out of this.

"I'm certain that the circumstances of those four bodies will be released in time, however. It will call attention to the APES phenomenon which has been a mystery thus far to medical examiners. But four APES bodies connected to the vicious knife-murders are going to intensify efforts by the medical community and the authorities to discover who is doing the killing, and how to stop him."

At that, a murmur rose from the Collective. Jonas raised his hands, and silence resumed. "Of course, humans have forgotten the old ways and will be skeptical and hesitant to employ them. And even then, our false mythology—the Stoker rules—created by our brethren in antiquity and given the weight of authority in countless books and movies, will protect us. At least for a while."

Again, the crowd murmured in agitation. Jonas silenced them with a gesture. "If this incident is isolated, we can trust that after all the excitement dies down, we can cease to worry. But if there are more killings like this, some inquisitive and creative human may stumble upon the actual method for killing us."

Compelled to quiet the crowd a third time, he went on, "Tessa, can you come up here?"

A well-dressed gray-haired woman in her fifties, at least by appearance, seated on the front row stood up and walked to the lectern, carrying a few sheets of paper. "Many of you know Tessa Cavatore." Jonas said. "She is a licensed clinical psychologist who is well-versed in forensic psychology. She has helped many of us have an easier time psychologically and emotionally with the initial transition and has coached many aunts and uncles who are present tonight. Tessa has prepared a statement at my request."

Jonas ceded his place at the lectern, and Tessa looked out at the Collective. "Hello everyone. It's good to see so many familiar faces. At Jonas' request I am working on a profile of the killer. I'm still gathering data but first let me clarify the differences between a serial killer and a mass killer. Serial killers often meticulously plan their murders and commit them singly, with a cooling-off period in between. The motivation is a psychological thrill or pleasure, sometimes with a sexual component, as with the Boston Strangler in the Sixties. Mass murderers, in contrast, kill several people at the same time, as happened at the carnival. These events usually end with the killer apprehended, committing suicide, or being killed on-site by authorities, as was the case with Charles Whitman, known as the 'Texas Tower Sniper.' Whitman was killed by Austin police after his mass-murder spree on the University of Texas campus on August 1, 1966. Whereas the psychology of serial killers is that of a psychopath, mass murderers tend to be dissatisfied people with few friends and poor social skills."

Tessa glanced down at her notes. "The motivation of mass killers is often less obvious than that of serial killers, although they may share some psychopathic tendencies. There is one aspect of this case, this vampire mass killer, that worries me. And that is that he *left the scene of the murders*. This is not typical for a mass killer, whose inclination is to hole up and kill as many people as possible at one time, and go out guns blazing, so to speak, when some intervention by authorities ends the killing spree and usually the life of the killer himself. This vampire could have killed many more victims outside the building, out on the carnival grounds, but he shadowed out after the eleven murders, we believe, before authorities were able to show up to the scene.

"In summary, Jonas asked me to predict whether this vampire mass killer will strike again, more like a serial killer would. I can't say conclusively, but my suspicion is that he will in fact make a similar attack in the future."

This created a hubbub among the assembly, and it took a few moments for Jonas to quiet everyone down as Tessa left the platform and took her seat.

"All right, settle down, please," Jonas said. "As Tessa noted, this isn't conclusive. We will have to wait and see. Tessa will continue to work on a profile as more evidence emerges. But if the killer strikes again, we will have to take action to stop him. Given that he is a vampire, it's almost certain he will know how to kill another vampire. With that knowledge, we must ask ourselves this question: Who will stop him?"

As Jonas asked, he looked directly at Alex.

"Fuck them!" Alex said as he drove Bardru home. "What do I owe those gossiping cowards?"

"Now, now," Bardru said, patting him lightly on the arm. "You needn't agree."

"Damn well right I needn't agree. There are at least four police officers in the goddamned Collective. Let them go after this psycho vampire. I don't know what the hell Jonas was even thinking. Special seats at the front so he could stare at me while asking who would be up for the job."

"It was less than subtle," Bardru agreed. "But there are reasons that make you ideal."

Alex frowned. Bardru was referring to his *reach*. It was an innate sense of where other vampires were. Alex's *reach* was phenomenal, measurable in miles instead of yards. And he had attained black belts in judo and jiu-jitsu before he was vampirized in 1932.

"You may not have to intervene," Bardru said. "It's not a sure thing that this killer will strike again."

"True," Alex replied, but he wasn't ready to let go of his anger just yet. "You know, it's pretty ironic to be talking about serial killers when all of us are serial killers."

"It is so," Bardru said quietly. "But our motivations are different. We must feed."

"I suppose. It still stinks of sanctimony to me."

"There is one thing that occurred to me," Bardru said, staring at the freeway ahead. "But I fear it may anger you if I say it."

"I'm already angry," Alex said. "How much worse could it be?" He glanced at Bardru and forced a smile. "Besides, how can I be angry with my uncle?"

"Very well. What if by setting you to this task, Jonas is, in his mind, trying to help you?"

"Help me?" Alex said, glancing at Bardru. "How's that?"

"Remember a few days ago, at the café? I asked you, regarding your vigilantism toward the wicked, your hesitance to kill the innocent—" Bardru trailed off for a moment.

"I remember," Alex said, his anger giving way to self-consciousness. "You asked me 'when is it enough?'"

"Yes, yes, and do you see?"

"Are you suggesting that Jonas wants me to face this killer as some sort of catharsis? Some kind of release from feeling the way I do?"

"He mentioned the wantonness of the killings. So many innocents slaughtered, even for a vampire."

That phrase, *so many innocents slaughtered*, caught Alex off guard. He stared silently at the road ahead, gripping the steering wheel tightly, his shoulders tense. "I don't particularly care to be psychoanalyzed, especially by Jonas."

"It is so," Bardru said softly, his face expressionless in the soft glow of the instrument panel. "And yet Jonas is the leader of the Collective for a reason. I have known him for many years. He is a wise and thoughtful man."

"Has he talked to you about this?"

"No. It is just my observation."

Alex exited onto the ramp for the 610 Loop, driving south toward US-59 and Montrose. "Well," Alex said with a sigh, "Maybe we'll luck out and this will be an isolated incident."

"I hope it is indeed that, for your sake, my Nephew."

# 7

Emelia and Melanie had checked into adjoining rooms at the Marriott, just walking distance from the FBI headquarters in northwest Houston. After a brief courtesy visit with Vince Delgado, CDPR liaison at the Bureau, who introduced them to Alison Martin—the Special Agent assigned to the case—they had taken their rental car to a nearby Mexican restaurant, Loco Tacos. They had ordered margaritas, which were half-price because it was Taco Tuesday.

"I'm glad we didn't sit on the patio," Melanie said over her margarita. "This is definitely a lot hotter than Atlanta."

Emelia sipped her frozen margarita through a straw and said, "It's a lot like New Orleans, climate-wise. Nearly the same latitude, in fact. Have you ever been there?"

"No, Atlanta is the farthest south I've been. I was born and raised in Georgetown."

"Home of the *Exorcist* stairs!" Emelia cried.

"Bingo. Before the movie was filmed, they were informally called the Hitchcock steps for Alfred Hitchcock. They're a half mile from the house I grew up in. My mom was superstitious and told us never to walk up or down them."

"So of course you did."

Melanie laughed. "Over and over again!"

Emelia smiled. "I'm a Portland girl, myself. But I did go on assignment in New Orleans after I joined See Deeper. That will-o'-the-wisp we have at headquarters? I helped capture it

in a swamp just south of Delacroix on the Mississippi Delta."
She laughed. "The goddamned mosquitoes bit worse than the
will-o'-the-wisp!"

"Sounds like fun," Melanie said. "Not."

"Definitely not. But it *was* an adventure. At a certain point
civilization just *stops* on the Delta. It's just you and the wild."

Melanie nodded and glanced out the window at the midday
traffic on the nearby freeway. "What can we expect here in the
wilds of Houston?"

Emelia sighed. "I'm not sure, really. Some field assignments
turn out to be a bust and I've got a feeling this might be one of
those. Keep your expectations low. But no matter what, we're
here to do the job. We're scheduled to view the APES victims
tomorrow morning. Have you seen a postmortem?"

"Yes."

"Good. I'm not sure when the ME is going to do the autopsies, but the FBI called ahead at our request and put them on
hold until we get a chance to examine the bodies."

Their food arrived and they chatted while they ate. Melanie
was married and she and her husband had two cats. Emelia was
more of a dog person, but she smiled as Melanie happily showed
pictures of the felines on her phone.

The waiter brought two fresh margaritas, and Emelia looked
at him in surprise. He nodded toward a blonde woman at the
bar. It was Alison, the FBI agent. She smiled and raised her glass.
Emelia waved her over.

They exchanged greetings. "The FBI is keeping tabs on us
already," Emelia said, laughing. "But you blew your cover."

Alison laughed and sat down at the table. "Hard to maintain
cover on Taco Tuesday. It was just luck. I tend to stop in here
because the food is good and it's close to the shop."

"Well," said Melanie, raising her glass. "Let's drink to inter-agency cooperation."

"Too formal," Emelia said. She and Alison had made eye contact, and neither seemed to want to break it. "To new friends."

They clinked their glasses.

An hour later, Emelia and Alison lay in the bed of Emelia's hotel room, savoring the afterglow of their lovemaking. Melanie had taken her leave to do a Zoom call with her husband, and the two of them had ended up here. It had just seemed natural.

Emelia stretched and smiled at Alison. She was cute; her nose was just a little too prominent for her face. Beautiful, soulful green eyes and a winning smile more than made up for it, however. As did her lustrous blonde hair.

"Inter-agency fraternization," Emelia said, still smiling, "is bad luck."

Alison smiled back, tracing a finger over Emelia's left nipple. "If this is bad I don't wanna be good."

"No one special here in Houston?" Emelia asked.

Alison's smile faded and there was a shift in her tone. "There was, but it's over."

"Sorry. Recent?"

Alison nodded. "What about you?"

"Nah," Emelia said. "A girl here, a boy there. It's a thing."

"Oh," Alison replied, her voice flattening.

Emelia decided to change the subject. "Work keeps me pretty busy, though."

"I was talking with Vince before you arrived. Are we really dealing with some kind of—vampire?"

"It's just a theory so far. Do you know what APES is?"

"Anomalous Profound Exsanguination Syndrome. I was briefed on it. Four cases of it in the carnival murders. I've read some case histories on it from other cities. What do you think the burns are in some of the other cases?"

"We're not sure. I read a prelim report after the bodies from the carnival were examined. No burns." Emelia sighed. "I sometimes despair that we will ever figure it out. It's been happening for decades, but no one has figured out the 'how' of it or who is doing it."

Then she laughed. "I'm one of the country's foremost experts on something that no one, including me, can figure out. I would love to be the person to solve the mystery."

"What got you interested in the supernatural?" Alison asked.

"An experience in Portland, when I was growing up. My little sister Annabel and I were playing hide and seek in the woods. She was hiding, and I stumbled on a loose rock and sprained my ankle so I could barely walk. It got dark, and I was calling for her and saying *Olly olly oxen free*, but she wouldn't come back. I hobbled over a ridge, and there she was! She was talking to a boy, or, more precisely, what looked like the ghost of a boy."

Alison had leaned up on an elbow. "A real ghost?'

"No. It looked like what we think a ghost would look like, but there was a niggle."

"A what?"

"An inconsistency. Ghosts are always depicted wearing clothing. Sometimes it's shrouds or what they were buried in, but they always have clothes."

"I never thought of that."

"Yeah, so the niggle is just that: is there really such a thing as *ghost clothing*? The departed spirits of jeans and T-shirts and sun dresses?"

Alison said in an amused tone, "Ghost sneakers. Ghost sports bras. Now that you mention it, that is a weird thing."

"Most people never think about it. My boss has an authentic photo of a ghost, and she's nude."

"Huh!" Alison cried in genuine surprise.

Emelia nodded. "So this ethereal figure of a little boy—with clothing on—was talking to my sister. I didn't think anything of the clothing at the time. But he looked like he'd been swimming. Or drowned maybe. His hair was wet and plastered to his forehead. He looked sad and lonely. His lips were moving but

I couldn't hear what he was saying. I screamed out her name, but Annabel didn't seem to notice. And then she walked off, hand-in-hand with the boy. Off into the woods and I couldn't follow because my ankle hurt so bad. My mom and dad found me an hour later. Search teams combed the woods but never found my sister. No one believed my story. They assumed it was a real boy or something I had hallucinated."

Alison stroked Emelia's arm. "I'm so sorry."

"My parents were devastated. They moved away from Oregon, but I stayed on with my Aunt Morgandy. It was unfinished business for me, and I refused to leave. My parents were so demolished by their grief, they let me stay there. I went out to those woods again and again, searching for her, but I never found anything. Then aunt Morgandy—she was an Earth mother type, into crystals and aromatherapy and all that—suggested I use a dowsing rod."

"The forked stick?"

"Yes, but by then it was two L-shaped rods that sat in tubes you held vertically in either hand, The horizontal top parts of the rods could move freely and were supposed to cross when you found water or metal or whatever you were trying to find. Some people used them to try to find bodies. Morgandy made me a pair and off I went to the woods. I searched for a couple of hours. It was starting to get dark, and I was tired and ready to give up, but then the rods moved a little toward each other. I kept going in that direction, deeper into the woods. The rods moved closer and closer and then crossed when I came upon a small pond in the woods.

"I was astonished to see something across the pond through the gloom. It was a big ethereal shape, hulking like a hunched-over bear or something. It had the little boy's face."

"Shit," Alison whispered.

"My reaction pretty much, too. But that wasn't the worst of it. I felt a presence. It was Annabel. It was really strong. I thought I could hear her singing. Then the big hulking thing transformed. *It changed into Annabel.*"

Emelia shuddered and Alison reached out and stroked her hair. Emelia saw that she had broken out into gooseflesh.

"She—it—was singing, *Swim, swim, swim with me! Swim little fishie, deep down with me.* In Annabel's voice. *Swim, swim, swim with me! Swim little fishie, deep down with me.* She looked drowned, like the little boy had, her hair matted and wet. And she was walking around the pond toward me. I'm not gonna lie: I had this overwhelming urge to go swimming with her. The water seemed so inviting, and I was so happy to see her again. I imagined us swimming deep in a watery shaft, our hair and clothing swirling in the moonlit water. Annabel's dead face was gleefully smiling at me.

Alison shivered. "That thing—it was affecting your mind!"

"Yes. I actually took a step toward her, reaching out to take her hand. I'm certain now that I would have walked into the water and drowned a few moments later."

"What happened?"

"I heard a gunshot. It was hunting season, and I'd heard a few, far off, while I was searching, but this was close enough to startle me—and I snapped out of whatever it was doing to me. I turned and ran and never looked back. I never went back into the woods after that."

Emelia closed her eyes and touched Alison's body, alive and warm and real against hers as they embraced in silence for a moment. Then Alison's mouth met hers, soft and inviting. It was succor, and the terrible memory swirled away as they made love again.

It was really, really cold. That was the first thing Bonnie Glaser noticed when she woke up. And dark, pitch-black. And silent.

She was lying on her back on a hard surface, and even with her eyes open, she couldn't see anything. She felt a gnawing ache like hunger in her gut. She didn't want to move at first—she wondered if this was a dream of some kind. Then she sniffed the cold air. It was fragrant, like—cinnamon candies! She couldn't remember whether she'd ever *smelled* anything in a dream. There was a soft cloth draped over her, and she began to move her hands beneath it. She discovered that aside from the cloth she was nude. Her hands ranged over her torso. Light stubble on her pudenda and thighs—hadn't she shaved before her date? Her hands moved up and she felt the smooth soft skin of her belly, her navel, her ribcage and her breasts. Dale had tried to reach under her shirt and touch them on that ride. *That ride!*

Suddenly a horrific flood of memory swept through her mind: the darkness, the screams, pulling desperately at the lap bar, Dale screaming next to her as *the bad man* hurt him, and then *the bad man*'s strong hands gripping her in the darkness. She shuddered as she remembered his foul breath and his mouth on her neck. He had *licked her neck*, like he was tasting her. And then she had felt the pain as he *bit her neck* and a sudden light from behind had illuminated his face. He had parted from her a moment to glance back at the light. Bonnie shuddered. That horrible, wrinkled face, the bald head with a fringe of withered white hair and those soulless red-rimmed gray eyes. And his wrinkled lips were *red and slicked with her blood*! Then he had latched back onto her neck like a suckerfish, and she heard the sickly sucking sounds as she grew faint and then—nothingness.

*But I lived*, she thought, as her hands went to her throat. There were no bite marks, just smooth, supple skin. I survived somehow, and they fixed my neck, and I'm in the—*hospital?* Then several things happened almost simultaneously: she noticed something tied to her left big toe, like an index card or something, and she reached up above herself in the darkness and felt a cold sheet of metal only a foot or two above her. Her hands explored the space around her. Her breathing sped up and her heart raced as she felt metal walls close by on either side. *Coffin*! I'm in a metal coffin! Buried alive!

She screamed and struggled crazily, beating and clawing at the metal enclosure. She reached over her head, expecting another metal wall, but there was nothing but empty space. Still panicked, she gripped the edges of the metal enclosure near her head and scrambled out, pulling herself forward, her nude body sliding awkwardly along the metal surface until she tumbled down into the open darkness. She came to rest on a spongy surface that felt like a thick layer of moss. The darkness of the space she was in seemed vast and she saw all manner of blurry gray shapes somehow imprinted on the darkness: some close and some seemingly distant in the expanse of darkness. Some were angular and geometric, and others were amorphous. The cinnamon candy smell was much stronger now, surrounding her with a crazy candy shop smell. And as she scrambled to her feet, gasping in fear, she saw a person moving toward her through the darkness off to her right. A young man hurried toward her.

"Stay where you are," he said as he approached. "Let me help you."

But something about the man reminded her of *the bad man*, and she ran wildly into the darkness. Something was flapping on her toe as she ran, and she realized it was a toe tag like they put on dead people. Disgusted, she tried to reach down and pluck it off as she ran and tumbled down, sprawling on the mossy ground, or whatever it was. She yanked the tag off and then, as she turned to get up, she saw a swirl of glowing blue ovals moving in the distance ahead of her. They undulated, trailing each other and she realized they were luminous markings on some kind of huge, black fishlike creature that for all the world looked like it was *swimming* through the darkness.

Then strong hands gripped her, and a hand clamped over her mouth. "Don't scream," the male voice said in a whisper. "You'll attract it to us. You're safe. My name is Mark and I'm a friend. I'm here to help you. Just stay calm and don't scream. Understand? Nod if you understand."

She nodded out of instinct more than anything else. *This is some crazy nightmare*, she thought dimly. "Stay still," Mark whispered into her ear The hand moved away from her mouth, and the luminescent blue markings of the dark thing ahead swirled as it seemed to turn away. It made a sound: *whup-whup-whup-whup-whup*. Then the blue ovals grew dimmer as the creature undulated into the distance and then disappeared.

"Good," said Mark. "You did good. What's your name?"

She turned to see a young man with wire-rimmed glasses and brown eyes, crouched next to her. He looked to be in his twenties. She saw he was wearing clothes and tried to cover her nakedness with her hands.

"You'll be okay," Mark said. "I've got a blanket back there. We can put it around you and then get some clothes for you. What's your name?"

"Bonnie. Bonnie Glaser. Where am I?'

"Hello, Bonnie. I know you're confused and scared," he replied. "This place is called the Deepest Shadow. We're going to get you back to the real world now, okay?"

As he helped her stand, she asked, "Am I dead?"

He led her by the hand, looking ahead and walking toward a cluster of gray shapes ahead. "You were for a little while," he said. "But you're not anymore."

# 8

Fletcher Jimson emerged from Garage Mart, a converted garage in a residential neighborhood in Houston's Fourth Ward, and began the short walk to his house. Garage Mart (it was a nickname, as the place didn't really have a name or sign) was a tribute to Houston's infamous lack of zoning in certain residential areas. Live in a residential area? Want to open a tiny convenience store in your garage? No problem! Fletcher smiled. It was within walking distance and good for grabbing some milk and snacks for the wife and kid. Plus, it was a good way to put some extra steps on his Fitbit.

A sound met his ears—a female scream. He set the small paper sack he was carrying down and looked in that direction. Fletcher was a security guard for the Bar-T Construction Company and sometimes moonlighted as a bouncer at the Tiki Bomb club downtown. His thoughts went to the ankle holster and the slim Sig P365 subcompact pistol he carried there. He was licensed for concealed carry. As much as he loved living in the Ward, it was not the safest place after dark.

He weighed whether he wanted to walk a bit in that direction. There was another scream, also female, but closer. This time the scream was followed by a man shouting. Then the man screamed and went silent. From the sound, it seemed only a block or two away. He jumped when Nick Willis, the owner of Garage Mart, slammed the roll-down steel door closed just around the corner.

"This is cop work," Fletcher muttered, but his feet were rooted to the spot and he craned his neck, looking down the street, which was dimly lit because of the shade from big oak trees on either side. How long would it take the cops to respond? A distant sound of anguished crying and wailing rose up.

*What the hell is happening in my Ward*? He realized that he hadn't heard any gunshots. Maybe it was some crazy person with a knife, just walking from block to block and stabbing people or something. In *his* Ward, where he had grown up and made friends and started a family. *A good guy with a gun could surely stop a bad guy with a knife.* He reached down, pulled up his loose-fitting pants leg, and got the firearm. He checked it and switched off the safety. Fletcher watched intently, listening. No shots and no sounds of a police siren yet. *Damn HPD*, he thought, but realized that he'd only heard the first scream maybe two minutes ago.

A dark figure emerged from the shadows of a large oak tree down at the corner, moving toward him. He saw a silvery glint in the figure's black gloved hand. It was some kind of weird dagger with two round gold orbs on either side of the blade where the quillons should have been. They looked for all the world like *testicles*.

"You better stop there!" Fletcher shouted, raising the pistol. "I've got a gun and I'll blow your goddamned ball-knife-carrying head off! Whatchoo hurting people in my Ward for?"

The figure picked up its stride. It was a skinny white man, really old and wrinkled and wearing a rumpled dark suit. He had a fringe of long white hair around his mostly bald head. His sunken gray eyes seemed mirthful.

"Just out for a stroll, like you," the man said in a thin, reedy voice. He came closer.

"I'm telling you: you better stop right there."

The old man stopped and smiled and his incisors were longer than the rest of his teeth. The tips were thin and pointed and suddenly the bloodless bodies from the carnival flashed through

Fletcher's mind. Everybody'd seen it on the news. He shook his head in disbelief. *It's my imagination.*

"Do you think your plaything, that toy in your hand, can stop me? Does it make you feel safe?"

"Damn right," Fletcher said. "I ain't never shot a man, but you'll be the first if you come any closer."

"*Fortissimi,*" the man said, still smiling. He raised his arms perpendicular to his body, as if inviting Fletcher to shoot, and took a step closer. The bizarre dagger gleamed, silver and gold in the harsh light of the streetlamp.

The sound of a distant siren became audible. *'Bout god-damned time*, Fletcher thought.

"That's the police. You just stay where you are."

"*Magistratus,* yes. I am sure I will meet them soon enough. It will matter little." He took another step closer. The canine teeth seemed even longer now.

"One more step and I'll fire! I'm fucking serious!"

The man leapt and Fletcher fired off shot after shot, the sound pummeling his eardrums. There was no way he could have missed, but the man was upon him nevertheless, seemingly uninjured. With his free hand, the man twisted Fletcher's right hand until the bones cracked like twigs, and he dropped the gun. Fletcher howled at the pain in his hand. "Couldn't miss—I hit you!" he shouted through the pain.

The man embraced Fletcher with immense strength, and his stinking breath—a smell of rot and decay—assailed Fletcher's nostrils. "*Non est nisi una via ut interficias me,*" he whispered, and a lancing pain stung Fletcher's neck. He was aware as his consciousness faded that the siren, though closer, still seemed very far away.

Jonas's tone was strident over the phone. "Well, where is he?"

Bardru said simply, "In California. Los Angeles, I think."

Jonas had told Bardru that Alex was not answering his phone, and that there was going to be another meeting at the Compound after the late news had reported five killings on West Climson Street in the Fourth Ward. Two bodies had been drained of blood. Three others had been stabbed in the eyes before they were killed.

"What is he doing in Los Angeles?" Jonas asked.

"I don't know," Bardru replied. "He texted me this morning. I think he was already at the airport."

Silence on the line. There was a note of frustration in his voice when Jonas spoke. "Is he coming back?"

"I assume so, yes. His dogs are here. His paintings are here. If I may ask, why is Alexandru the apparent chosen one for this task?"

"We can't pull our cops out of their HPD duties without arousing suspicion. It's important they remain undercover. Alex can act freely. He has better *reach* than anyone and his martial arts training may help."

"He has not practiced for at least a decade."

"Well, perhaps he can resume practicing now. It may give him an edge in a fight with this killer. Our cops in HPD will give him whatever clandestine support they can. We also have a witness from the first attack: she became a vampire, and Mark Clemmens brought her in from the Deepest Shadow. She has already given us a description."

"That is fortunate," Bardru said. "But Alexandru must do this alone, yes?"

There was a short silence. Then Jonas sighed, "I regret to say this has caused a lot of fear in our group. It's embarrassing to admit, Bardru. This vampire certainly must know how to kill other vampires. Our witness said he was old. Very old. Who knows how powerful he is? Everyone is afraid."

"That is most unfortunate. What if Alex is afraid as well?"

"I worry about that, especially since he fled the city. If that is the case, we may be fucked. You're his uncle—can you talk to him?"

"I will do what I can," Bardru said simply.

That night, Alex stood barefoot on the beach at Malibu Point, his hair blowing in the breeze. The sand felt cold around his feet. Clouds scudded overhead, and in the breaks between them the stars glittered in the night sky, timeless and watchful. This was the spot where he'd taken her. She had been a fourteen-year-old runaway, and her name was Jellybean. Well, that's what she had called herself. She had been turning tricks to make enough money to eat and had walked down here with Alex, perhaps thinking she'd do him and then get a hot meal somewhere. His charisma pheromone had made her smile, and she looked up at him, her gray-green eyes seeming to catch the starlight above. "You're the most beautiful man I've ever seen," she said, her voice soft and distant. "Do you want to kiss me?"

Somewhere in the distance, he had faintly heard a boom box with Meat Loaf singing about how he'd do anything for love. Alex nuzzled Jellybean's neck, and her perfume reminded him of magnolia blossoms back home. And then, even through the pain, she had murmured, "So beautiful." Then she had slumped in his arms, lifeless, and it was over.

Now, thirty years later, he looked out over the crashing surf of the Pacific and was not at peace. He thought of Jellybean, and of sixteen-year-old Miriam Wilkins, who had been drained by some maniac in the Fourth Ward attack last night.

"Who will stop him?" Jonas had asked at the Compound, creating what Alex's hypnosis mentor would have called the illusion of choice. Because he had been looking at Alex as he intoned the question.

Alex took a deep breath and looked up at the stars and the clouds. The chill wind ruffled his clothes. Then he turned and walked back to the stairway on the cliff and ascended to the rental car that would take him back to LAX.

# 9

— · —

"I'll do it," Alex said into his phone as he drove from the airport to his house in the EaDo district of Houston. The sun was just rising, and it cast an orange glow to the morning clouds over the city.

"I can't express how grateful I am," Jonas said. "We were a bit worried about you."

"I just had to sort it out, is all. Reflect on some stuff."

"Good. I'm setting up a meeting tonight at the Compound with some people who can help. We've got a vampirized witness who was a victim at the carnival attack, and Tessa Cavatore is working on a profile of the killer. Clint Nabors from HPD will be there. We're arranging for a forensic sketch artist. When was the last time you practiced judo or jiu-jitsu?"

"A long time. About fifteen years."

"We'll see about getting you a coach."

Alex smiled. He'd earned his black belts before becoming a vampire. He would need to be careful with a human coach, given his vampiric speed and strength. But Jonas was right. If he had to fight hand-to-hand with another vampire, martial arts training could be an edge. "Okay," he replied.

"I'll call you later with an update," Jonas said. "Glad you're back."

"Okay, talk to you then." Alex ended the call, then pulled into his driveway and saw his housekeeper's car parked at the curb. Apprehension mixed with his exhaustion, an unpleasant morning cocktail.

There was a strong disinfectant smell in the air of the tiled room. As Alison, Melanie, and Emelia stood by, the medical examiner pulled the sheet up over the black man's shaved head. He had been autopsied and bore the long, neatly stitched scars of the procedure, but the ME had also shown them multiple photographs taken of his body before the postmortem. The ME's careful inspection prior to the postmortem had found no evidence of physical trauma except for his crushed right hand.

"APES?" Emelia asked.

The Medical Examiner, Ronnie Gardaretto, nodded. "That's the official diagnosis. Only trace amounts of blood in him. Not even enough to cause livor mortis. Right hand and arm, along with face, as well as clothing, tested positive for primer gunshot residue. He was the shooter. He got five shots off before the killer mangled his hand. Our perp's gotta be one strong sono-fabitch." He blushed and said, "Er, pardon me, ladies."

"It's all right, Mr. Gardaretto," Alison said. "Anything else we need to know?"

"Well," he said, pushing his glasses up his nose with a blue-gloved hand, "Just an observation. I've been working for the city for thirty-two years come September, and I had only seen a couple of APES cases in all that time. Now, in just over a week, we've got six cases, and in one of them, the body's gone missing."

Alison glanced at her tablet. "That would be Bonnie Eliza-beth Glaser."

He nodded, and his glasses slipped down his nose a bit. "That's her. From the carnival attack last Saturday. Vanished into thin air. Damndest thing." He shook his head.

Emelia had read the police report, and that was essentially what seemed to have happened. The last person who had seen her was the mortuary resident who had placed her body into the refrigerated cabinet. When it was opened the next day for her postmortem, the body was gone. The investigation was ongoing.

"It's happened before," Alison noted. "According to our database, fourteen bodies that presented with APES in various locations have vanished under similar circumstances in the past eight years."

"Huh," said Gardaretto. "Any of those cases solved?"

"Not a one," Alison said. "So I wouldn't hold my breath on this one."

"There's one more thing," Gardaretto said. "Have you seen the mortuary box Bonnie Glaser was in?"

They shook their heads.

He went over to a counter and opened the drawer underneath it. He dug around and came up with a small LED flashlight. "Follow me."

He led them down a wide tiled hallway to an adjacent room containing the mortuary coolers. The door of one cooler had an X across it where police crime scene tape had been affixed to it. "Kinda silly," Gardaretto said, shaking his head. He reached up with his blue-gloved hand and gripped the handle. As he opened the door, cold air flowed from the box. He shined the flashlight into the box and the three women peered in. Toward the far end, the metal on the sides and top had shallow dents in it. "Damndest thing," Gardaretto said. "Like she woke up and freaked out and punched the sides and top, trying to get out. I did some boxing in college, and I doubt I could put a dent in that metal."

Alison consulted her tablet. "She was five feet one inch tall and weighed 127 pounds. Seems really unlikely she was that strong."

"Hysterical strength, it's called," Gardaretto said. "Not scientifically recognized, but there are numerous anecdotal examples of extreme strength exhibited by some people *in extremis*."

"We're forgetting one thing," Emelia said, still peering down into the box. "She was dead."

Yeah," said Gardaretto with a chuckle. "I guess it doesn't get more *in extremis* than that."

Later, the trio sat at a table drinking coffee at a cafe near the Medical Center. Emelia said, "Okay, I was totally unaware of that statistic about APES bodies vanishing."

Alison sipped her coffee. "I can send you what we've got on it, but it's not going to be very useful. Multiple investigations have come up with nothing. Someone wrote up a Minneapolis morgue attendant for leaving the mortuary door unlocked, but that's about it. There was nothing to connect him to the disappearance and he passed a polygraph."

Emelia sighed. "One more missing puzzle piece in a puzzle with mostly missing pieces."

Alison nodded. "In other awesome news, my boss is freaking. The second attack last night has him thinking about a task force. Looks like I might have to share my investigation."

Melanie looked at Emelia. "What about us?"

"I talked to Mark this morning. Still just you and me for now. Dr. Chavez is on call in case anything turns up."

"Our Behavioral Analysis Unit is working on a profile of the killer," Alison said. "It's unusual, though. We've got a mass killer acting like a serial killer. And those are two distinct *modus operandi*. I've never heard of something like this. As you've probably seen on the morning news, the media is hanging on the lurid details. They already have a nickname for the killer: the Vision Killer. The little boy who survived the first attack used words like 'vampire' and 'monster.' We need to not let the media distract us."

"I feel like we have so little to work with," said Melanie. "Is it normal to feel this frustrated?"

"I can't speak for See Deeper—that's your nickname for it, right?" Alison said, glancing at Emelia, who nodded. "I've solved a number of cases for the Bureau, but it does feel a bit frustrating right now. We need to remember that it's also early in the investigation. We only know just now that this guy is a serial murderer. With luck, more information will emerge with each attack."

"So you're expecting more?" Emelia asked.

Alison nodded. "Oh yeah. I think our killer is just getting started, unfortunately."

Melanie said, "I have an idea of what might be behind the disappearances of those APES bodies."

"We're all ears," Emelia said.

Melanie's face brightened. "Sublimation! Remember? With the sprites?"

"Of course," Emelia said. "That's good thinking." Seeing the confused look on Alison's face, she explained about the sublimation phenomenon that occurred when supernatural creatures died.

"That's intriguing," Alison said. "So why hasn't it happened with all the previous APES bodies?"

Melanie's face darkened a bit. "Yeah, not too sure about that."

"It could be," Emelia said, "that certain conditions might cause it to happen with some victims and not others. That's not conclusive, though."

"I think I'm feeling frustrated again," Melanie said.

Emelia and Alison laughed.

The sunset had given way to early evening, and the clouds had gone from orange to red to purple. Emelia, Melanie and Alison had had a few margaritas at Los Tacos. Melanie had excused herself to go back to the hotel for a Zoom call with her husband. Emelia shifted in her chair as Alison beamed at her across the table.

"Okay if I come up with you to your hotel room tonight? A little nightcap?"

"Would you think badly of me if I said no?" Emelia asked. "I'm pretty wiped."

"No, it's okay," Alison said. Disappointment flickered across her features. "I'm kinda wiped myself. I had another call from Jack Crain. He's still talking task force."

"Maybe you could think of it as extra resources," Emelia offered.

"It'll just be a bunch of goddamned male agents trying to horn in on my investigation."

Emelia nodded, trying to look supportive. "Any word from Behavioral Analysis?"

Alison shook her head. "Way too early. They're still analyzing what they've got, and that's not much."

Emelia sighed. "I guess we need to be patient. Hard to say that when more murders are looming ahead."

"Yeah. I hate that there's so little we can do at the moment. But that's part of this grim game we play." She was silent for a moment. "I guess I need to be patient with you, as well."

"Let's just take it slowly," Emelia said. "Is that okay?"

Alison nodded with a forced smile. "I know. I'm on the re-bound. I need to take everything slowly, I guess. Gotta put that mental toughness to work." She took a deep breath, and her smile became more relaxed and genuine. She reached out and took Emelia's hand. "Let me know?"

Emelia squeezed her hand. "I promise."

# 10

Even though he'd slept on the return flight from Los Angeles, Alex slept for another four hours after arriving home. He had greeted Norma Espinoza, his housekeeper, and waited for his dogs to settle down from their excitement at his return. When he awakened, Norma had already left, and fresh flowers in a vase adorned the kitchen counter on the second floor. "She's the best," Alex said, feeding Dizzy and Midnight their kibble. He made coffee and called Bardru.

"I am proud of you, my Nephew. I had hoped you would decide to do this thing."

Alex's shoulders sagged. "I'm not so sure it's the right decision, but since no one else is willing to do it—" he trailed off.

"Nevertheless, I am proud. Stopping this enemy will save many lives. I know Jonas and our allies in law enforcement will help to the extent that they can."

An hour later, Alex and Bardru sat in a conference room at the Compound with Jonas, Tessa, and Clint Nabors, one of the clandestine vampires working as a Houston Police officer. Clint was dressed in street clothes for this meeting. He positioned Alex against a wall and snapped a headshot photo of him. Then he said, "We'll have an undercover detective ID and badge for you tomorrow. Use it sparingly, if possible, and always in conjunction with your charisma pheromone. It should work like a charm under casual scrutiny, much more so than that piece of crap fake ID you've got now."

Alex nodded. He sat down across from Jonas. "What's next?"

Jonas slid a business card across the table. "We've lined up a martial arts instructor for you. His name is Zheng Sun, a master of Jeet Kune Do."

"Bruce Lee's martial art?"

"Yes. Way of the intercepting fist. He's the best in Texas—maybe the best in the country. He's trained CIA agents and special forces operatives. Said to be near Bruce Lee's skill level. He's quite a character, as you'll see. Private lessons at his dojo three days a week. Can you swing that?"

"Yes. I was a first dan black belt in aikido in the 30's and 40's. It'll be good to get back into it."

"Your first lesson is day after tomorrow. I'll email the schedule to you. Tessa?"

"We've interviewed the girl, Bonnie Glaser, who was vampirized at the carnival," she said. "I'm serving as her aunt; she's transitioning well enough. Clint has arranged for a freelance forensic artist to create a picture of the suspect from her description."

"We should have it in a couple of days," Clint said. "She also said the knife he used was unusual, so we're going to get a drawing of that as well." He shifted his thin frame in the chair and tugged at his mustache. "The FBI is in town for this, as well as a government organization devoted to investigating the supernatural. It's called the Combined Departments of Paranormal Research, or CDPR."

"First I've heard of that," Alex said.

Clint nodded. "First any of us have heard of it, I think. It's been hush-hush up until now, although the FBI knew about them." The others murmured in agreement. "Anyway," Clint went on, "I talked with Jonas, and we've got a plan to leak the forensic drawing to law enforcement once it's ready. The only witness they've got now is the little boy from the carnival killings and he didn't see the killer clearly. Once the drawing from our witness is leaked, we expect the media will pick it up as well—they're pretty much all over the story, especially now that the killer has struck again. The idea is that, even if the provenance of the drawing is questioned, the image will stick in people's minds and it might help if he's spotted out there."

"I worry that there may be a number of fake sightings," Tessa said.

Clint frowned. "He's pretty distinctive-looking. Bald with a fringe of long white hair. In the interest of completeness, they'll likely will show it to the boy, who may corroborate the likeness. That would be a big help."

"Thanks, Clint," Jonas said. He turned to Alex. "The final thing is for you to work on your reach. Since yours is more powerful than anyone else's as far as we can tell, we're hoping you can develop and sharpen it. It could make the difference in locating our bad guy."

Alex nodded. "Already planned. Bardru and some of the other vampires in the Collective will be helping me. We're mapping it out, but we should be ready to implement some training soon. Bardru also has a stronger-than-average reach, so I'm lucky in that respect." He glanced at Bardru, who was beaming. "Right Bardru?"

"Indeed!" Bardru shouted, and everyone laughed. For the first time in a good long while, Alex really did feel lucky.

Alex walked into the Zheng Tang dojo, carrying his new gi bundled neatly with a replica of his old 6th dan black belt. A short Chinese man wearing a loose-fitting business suit with white dress shirt and no tie, shoes or socks met him at the reception desk. "I'm Sun," he said with a slight bow. "Follow me."

They wound their way past glass-walled dojos where students were training. Most of them wore ordinary gym clothes. A few wore distinctive magenta jumpsuits. There wasn't a gi to be seen. They ended up in a small dojo with a lightly padded floor. A large photo of Bruce Lee in a combat pose hung on the wall. On the opposite wall a large yin-yang symbol had been painted. Finally, a smaller photo of Sun and Bruce shaking hands hung on the wall behind a lectern at the front of the space.

"May I?" Sun asked, reaching for Alex's gi with a knobby, callused hand. Alex handed it to him. Sun pointed at the six gold stripes on the belt that denoted his 6th dan status. "These are prison bars," he said with a look of disdain. "They impress limitation on your mind and spirit. 'Why are you not 7th dan?' they ask in a mocking tone. Or higher?"

He dropped the gi to the floor and faced Alex. "You will fight in what you wear. Loose clothing is best," he said, plucking at the lapel of his black jacket, "but when the fight comes, you may not be in the correct garb. Do you walk away to change your clothes?"

"No, *sensei*. I fight in what I wear."

"I am not *sensei* nor am I *shifu*. I am not master. I am just Sun. But yes, you fight in what you wear when the fight comes to you." He motioned to the mat. "Sit, please."

Alex sat cross-legged on the mat, and Sun sat facing him. Sun's bare feet were as knobby and callused as his hands. It looked like he could step on a thumbtack and not notice. "Most of my students train for a fight that may never come. Nearly all, in fact. It is so for most martial arts." He regarded Alex with shrewd, dark-brown eyes. "But that is not the case with you, correct?"

"Yes, Sun." Alex said.

"Your friends are paying me a pretty sum to train you for the storm you must endure at some point."

Alex nodded.

"Good. Then I will train you differently. Have you ever killed anyone?"

Taken aback by the blunt question, Alex hesitated. Then he gave a short nod.

Sun smiled. "I will not pry into the circumstances." The smile faded. "But it is useful for our purposes that you have. Death comes for us all at some point, but it seeks some people earlier than is their natural time. One way to prevent it is to deliver force in kind. It is the way of nature. Kill or be killed. Your task is to intercept death and turn it upon your foe."

Alex wondered if this small, taut man in his baggy business suit had killed anyone himself. "Yes," he replied.

Sun stood up and motioned for Alex to do the same. As he did, Sun kicked the gi away from them with a small grunt. He turned to Alex. "I will not kill you, and you will not kill me. It is counter to our purposes. But I would like to see what you are capable of. I urge you to, as the useful cliché suggests, to think outside the box. Exercise what creativity you can. You are not 6th dan. You are just Alex, but even so, you must prove more skillful, more resourceful, and more formidable than your opponent when his attack comes. Are you ready?"

Alex nodded and assumed a stance, open-handed. Sun nodded and assumed his own stance, fists at the ready. They sparred briefly, each looking for openings to attack. Sun swatted aside a few of Alex's blows. Then he stepped back and lowered his arms.

"You are very strong," he said. "But you are holding back, correct?"

"I am extremely strong," Alex said. "I can break bones. I don't want to hurt you."

Sun smiled again. "So and so." He motioned toward a wall-mounted vertical rack upon which several stout wooden staves hung. "Show me."

Alex walked over and punched one staff with his fist. The wood shattered and his fist continued into the sheetrock of the wall. A stray nail plunged between his knuckles, and he winced.

Sun let out a short laugh. "I thank you for not hurting me!" Then his face went serious again. He walked over and examined Alex's hand, which was coated with sheetrock dust. The hole between the knuckles had vanished. "The foe you must face," Sun said quietly. "He is as strong as you?"

Alex flexed his hand. "Maybe stronger."

"So and so," Sun said, releasing his hand. "I will train you, Alex. Sufficient skill can overcome an imbalance in strength. May I ask you one personal question? You may demur if you want."

"Ask."

Sun gazed at him for a long moment. "Your flesh is cold. You are exceptionally strong. Are you human?"

"Yes. And no."

Sun nodded, satisfied. He rubbed his knobby hands together. "Let us begin."

—·—

## 11

The call came from Clint three days later. "Multiple murders at 1296 Osage Boulevard," Clint said. "Sounds like our guy."

The address hit him like a punch. "What was that address again?" he asked.

"1296 Osage Boulevard. The owner is a Leonard Ortega."

"Lennie," Alex said, his voice barely a whisper.

"You know him?" Clint asked.

There was no answer. Alex had ended the call and was running downstairs to his car.

The thin light bar mounted on top of Alison's vehicle windshield flashed red and blue, splashing the white hood of her Chevy Tahoe with color as the car sped along surface roads toward the crime scene. Emelia had hitched a ride and her investigator's backpack sat in the footwell between her legs. Alison's FBI go-bag was in the back seat, next to Melanie.

Alison's face was a mask of professional concentration as she drove. Even though they were well above the speed limit, Alison handled the vehicle with precision when it came to turns, stop signs, and traffic lights. They blew through the latter two, of course, but not before Alison slowed a bit and darted her gaze left and right to make sure other cars were yielding. Emelia still felt jostled on some of the turns, but she resisted reaching up for the grab handle over the passenger-side door as a show of confidence in Alison. She glanced back at Melanie, who was hanging onto her grab handle with wide eyes. Emelia stifled a smile. "You okay back there?" she asked.

"Dealin' with it," Melanie replied.

"We're almost there," Alison said, eyes still on the road. Emelia turned and saw a dozen or so emergency vehicles parked in front of a large suburban house ahead. A police officer was stringing yellow crime scene tape across the road, but waved them past.

"Don't take offense if I ignore you while I'm working," Alison said, slowing the car as they approached the tape barrier around the house. "Not only do I need to make sure the local PD have done a decent job with the investigation so far, but I also have to make sure I fill in the gaps and get any evidence they may have missed. And there's navigating any inter-agency quirks and foibles (she glanced over and winked at Emelia) and dealing with male officers who may not see this as women's work."

"We'll stay out of your way," Emelia said. Then she poked a finger into Alison's arm and said, "Maybe."

Alex had arrived and weaseled his way past the HPD officers outside the house using the fake ID. Lennie lay sprawled in his living room among three other bodies. His eyes had been gouged out and his throat cut. The smell of blood was thick in the air. Alex resisted the urge to clench his fists in rage. Lennie had been one of his oldest friends in Houston and had given Alex, under his Jackson Williams pseudonym, his first break in the art scene, displaying his paintings in an exclusive show at the Nitro Gallery in Neartown. It had been a huge success.

Lennie had been hosting a small cocktail party; there were drinks, some upended and spilled, on the nearby coffee table and on side tables. Two of the still bodies looked untouched, and one woman had been killed in the same manner as Lennie. HPD officers huddled around two other bodies in the hallway past the adjacent kitchen. A voice drifted from an investigator, "—trying to escape."

Alex was breathing heavily, struggling to contain his rage at seeing his friend mutilated, and his hands were shaking. "Walk away, detective," a familiar voice said. He was surprised to see Clint in uniform nearby, his blue eyes sober. "Walk away and get some air if you need it. Maybe you know some of these people. No shame in it. You're no help here if you're this upset. Walk away." Clint was covering for him: a couple of other officers had begun to stare at Alex. He nodded and strode away to the fireplace, over which hung a large painting he had completed on a glorious late-summer afternoon many years ago.

He worked on being mindful, focusing on his breathing, immersing himself in the moment as he stared at the painting. He focused on dabs of color and marks left by his brush as he had worked. Mentally, he intoned the mindfulness mantra over and over: *it's not good, it's not bad—it's not important, it's not unimportant.* Control slowly came back, and rational thinking with it. Then he heard the woman's voice.

"Are you all right?" she asked. He turned and stared in shock. He'd seen eyes like that once before: that shade of greenish-gray like the ocean waters off Galveston after a storm. "Jellybean," he murmured, barely even aware of the word escaping his lips.

"Did you say jellybean?" she asked. He quickly replied, "It's nothing. One of the people by the couch over there is my good friend. This is his house."

She put her blue-gloved hand out and touched his arm. "I'm so sorry. I saw you here looking at the painting, and it—" she trailed off.

"What?" he asked. Those eyes held him captive.

She smiled. "In my training at Quantico, one of my instructors told me, 'When investigating a scene, look for the anomaly, either physical or behavioral, and ask yourself: what is behind its anomalous appearance?' Here was a room full of investigators busily looking for clues, and this guy, who, from his dress, looked to be an undercover cop, was just standing there staring at this Jackson Williams painting. It seemed out of place. I had no idea you knew one of the victims. I'm sorry."

"So you're FBI?" he asked.

"Actually, I'm with the CDPR. Combined Departments of Paranormal Research. We're working in tandem with the FBI on this rash of killings. I did do some crime scene, psychology, and weapons training at Quantico."

He was silent for a moment, processing that. She held out her hand. "Senior Investigative Agent Emelia Cord." Her face was pleasantly angular, the cheekbones and chin softened by a sensual mouth and those gray-green eyes. Her ebony hair was pulled back from her face and done up in a braided knot at the back of her head.

He took her hand. "Alex Stoica. HPD undercover." He suddenly felt like an idiot. *You just told her your real name!* Still not thinking clearly, he thought.

She glanced down at their clasped hands. "Your hand is so cold. Are you okay?"

He smiled. "I run a few degrees low." To change the subject he asked, "You knew this is a Jackson Williams painting?"

She nodded, still smiling. "Fine art buff in my spare time. He reportedly lives here in Houston, but he's super reclusive. Sells his art through intermediaries and doesn't do interviews. I think there's only one photo of him from back in 2012 or so." She turned back at the painting. "The title is *Sunlight on Boughs.*

I can't remember the date, but it's part of his Temporal Sight series."

His eyes widened in surprise. "Yes. It was completed on August 23, 1982."

"You must be an enthusiast as well," she said, her face brightening in that way when common ground is discovered in a stranger.

Alex smiled. "You could say that."

At that moment a slender woman with red hair tied back in a similar manner to Emelia's came up, holding a bulky electronic device in a leather case with a leather carrying strap. The device emitted a soft hum. "Emelia, I've got a genuine signal on the VPD. Three-point-two and steady." She looked up from the device and seeing Alex, she said, "Oh, sorry."

"Melanie, this is Alex," Emelia said. "HPD undercover. Alex, this is my trainee, Melanie." Alex shook her hand. Like Emelia, she glanced down at the handshake but didn't say anything.

VPD?" he said, glancing at the device.

"Void Particle Densitometer," she said. "I wish I had time to explain," she went on. She dug in her pocket and produced a slim silver case. She opened it and handed him a business card. "Talk later? About art?" She smiled an irresistible smile. "And VPDs."

Alex felt a spark of curiosity about her. He nodded and slid the card into his pocket. "Definitely."

"Condolences on your friend," she said, and then turned and followed Melanie, who was walking toward a hallway at the back of the room. Alex went over to where Clint was gently brushing fine black dust, colorfully known as dragon's blood, on a glass lying on its side on the carpet. He looked up and said, "Better?"

Alex ignored the impulse to glance over at Lennie's body. "A little. Thanks for reeling me back in" He glanced toward the back of the room and saw Emelia and Melanie as they disappeared down a hallway with the device held out in front of them. He glanced back at Clint. "I think I'm going to get out of here."

"Probably a good idea. We ought not to be seen talking." Then he turned back to dusting for prints. Alex glanced around and saw everyone in the room was occupied with the crime scene, so he turned and made his exit.

It was the morning of August 24. Alex walked into the Zheng Tang dojo dressed in what would become his normal attire: loose-fitting jeans, leather belt and a long-sleeved knit shirt. His footwear was soft leather loafers with crepe soles. Sun met him at reception, dressed in his baggy business suit. He glanced at Alex briefly and pointed at his jeans. "How high can you kick in those?" Alex quickly raised his arms into the _en garde_ stance Sun had taught him and snapped out a lightning-fast pendulum kick that would have easily struck an opponent in the forehead if one had been in front of him.

"Damn that was fast!" said a voice from behind him. Alex whirled to see a thin young man dressed in one of the signature magenta jumpsuits behind him. He had just walked into the dojo behind Alex. The left sleeve of his jumpsuit had been cut off and his left arm was in a plastic-and-metal brace from shoulder to wrist.

Sun let out a little laugh. "So and so," he said to the student. "Off to your lesson, now, Jordan. Work on your kicking speed today, so that one day you may do the same."

Jordan bowed slightly and jogged off toward the glass-walled practice rooms.

Sun turned toward Alex, still smiling. "Your first fan. But don't get a big head. Your pivot was only adequate. Along with speed, which seems a natural talent with you, we need precision and economy of movement."

They worked for two hours, sometimes sparring in a dizzying array of blows, parries, and kicks. Other times, Sun instructed him in specific moves for attack or defense. Finally, Sun bowed to him, signaling the end of the lesson. As Alex moved to return the bow, Sun lunged toward him. Alex pivoted and blocked Sun's right arm at the wrist. The knobby fist was an inch from his nose. "Good!" Sun said, easing out of his strike. "Sometimes it's like the scary movie. You think the monster is dead and *zap!*" He stamped his bare foot hard on the mat for emphasis. "The monster is still alive!"

*If only he knew*, Alex thought soberly.

"One more thing," Sun said. He motioned toward a lectern at the edge of the room. Once they were there, Sun picked up a tablet. He held it up and pressed play on a Youtube video. Alex recognized it right away: it was the famous scene from *Raiders of the Lost Ark*. After fighting off numerous black turbaned bad guys with fisticuffs and his whip, Indy faces down with a formidable opponent wielding a huge scimitar. As the assailant demonstrates his prowess with the scimitar, an exhausted Indy pulls out his pistol and shoots him dead.

"Now Alex," said Sun, turning off the video with a broad grin. "What is the lesson for us here?"

"Never bring a scimitar to a gunfight?" Alex ventured.

Another broad grin. Sun pointed to the large picture of Bruce Lee on the wall. "He was famed for his unarmed fighting, but he also fought with close-combat weapons like the nunchaku and the tabak-toyok. It's not commonly known but sometimes he carried a firearm. He once said, 'When you're talking about fighting, as it is, with no rules, well then, baby you'd better train every part of your body!'"

Sun winked at Alex and held up an open hand. He mimed holding a pistol and moved his index finger like he was pulling a trigger. "Click-click! The trigger finger is a part of your body. When I train government operatives, I make sure they are trained in firearms. Most are by the time they come to me. This enemy of yours—might he employ firearms?"

It was the first time Alex had even thought about it. "I'm not sure."

"Then it is imperative to assume he might. And you must consider your response. And your preparedness." Sun regarded him with his dark eyes. "You are a strange being, Alex: with your cool skin, your exceptional speed, and your destructive power in hand-to-hand combat. But I like you. I want you to stay alive after your encounter with the one you seek." He held up his hand and did the *click-click* thing again.

"I mean to survive, Sun. I will train every part of my body." He mimicked the *click-click* with his own hand. Sun grinned again and slapped him on the arm. "You may go."

It was mid-afternoon when Alex walked into the pub to meet Emelia. The place was called Desdemona: the name glowed in cursive blue neon over the mirrored bar. The smell of coffee and baked goods filled the air. Emelia waved to him from a booth situated in a cozy nook, and he strode over to meet her. They shook hands and she glanced at his hand briefly. "Cold hands, warm heart, I hope," she said with a hesitant smile. He smiled back, and, wanting to build rapport, he pointed at the dark beer in a pint glass in front of her. "Whatcha drinking there?"

"It's called The Devil's Hopyard," she replied. "Craft brew from Connecticut. You should try it. No wait staff here—you'll need to order from the bar."

He did just that, and when he returned, he slid into the booth opposite her.

"I'm playing hooky. Hiding from my protégé. It's embarrassing."

"If you're the boss, I'm sure she won't mind a little down time," he said.

She nodded, sipping her beer. "I am indeed the boss."

She stared at him with those haunting gray-green eyes. "So," he said a little too quickly, "Any findings from the crime scene yesterday?"

She brightened. "Actually, yes. Something strange. The Void Particle Densitometer led Melanie and me down the hall, and the reading, which had been erratic a little earlier, grew stronger. It led us to a closet, and we opened the door. Just a coat closet. We followed the trail and it dead-ended at the back wall of the closet."

The realization was sudden. *She can help me find him.*

"What is a Void Particle Densa—?" he trailed off, shrugging.

She smiled. "Densitometer." It picks up traces of particulate matter from something we at See Deeper refer to as 'the void.'"

"See Deeper?"

She laughed. It was sweet and melodic. "Our nickname for 'CDPR.'"

He nodded. "Got it. So the device picks up traces of supernatural creatures?"

"Well, more like residue *shed from* the creatures. See Deeper has studied supernatural creatures that have somehow bridged the gap between the void and our natural world. They usually, at least for a while, have traces of distinctive exotic molecules attached to them that can be measured."

"What kind of supernatural creatures?"

She leaned forward. "Are we doing shop talk?" she said. "I kinda thought we were going to talk about art."

Alex took a sip of his beer, trying to organize his thoughts. Though his taste leaned more toward wine, it was smoky and delicious. "In a bit," he replied. "But this is important. You may have stumbled—well, that's not the right term, but you may have discovered a way for us to track the guy responsible for these killings."

The surprise was plain on her face. "How would an HPD officer know that?"

"Bear with me," he said as he took another swig of beer. He realized that he was going to have to confide in her. But what would happen then? Somewhere at the back of his mind an urgent voice was saying *she...is...an...investigator...for...the...government*. "What kind of supernatural creatures?"

"Well," she said, "there are seven catalogued, but the most common is a small bat-like creature called a sprite. They have near-perfect camouflage, so regular people don't notice them. There are also will o'the wisps, floating spherical organisms found in remote forested areas. It falls off pretty steeply after that. We've only examined one specimen of a spinner, a strange bioluminescent critter that looks a little bit like a spiral DNA strand that corkscrews through the air. Big, though—about a foot long."

"Have you encountered any creature that could be described as humanoid?"

"Not so far. What are you getting at, Alex?"

"Do you have that VPD device with you?"

She nodded. "Out in the car. Why?"

"You're a scientist. Let's do an experiment. Go get the device."

Emelia returned with the VPD. She sat across from him. "What now?"

"Measure me," he said. "If you can."

She leaned back, incredulous. "What are you suggesting?"

"Just try it. Trust me, Emelia."

She shrugged and turned on the device. "I guess we could use you as a baseline for calibration or something," she said. "We won't get a reading, though."

Alex waved his hand past the receptor grille on the back of the instrument.

She glanced at the screen, her eyes wide in disbelief. "Shit."

## 12

The destination was the crime scene at Lennie's house. Alex drove as they conversed. The VPD sat in the footwell by Emelia's feet.

"This is big," she said. "We've never picked up void particles on a human being or other terrestrial creature before. But it also explains why Melanie and I were getting fluctuating readings when we were near you at the crime scene. It was confusing, so we figured it was some unknown interference. The signal stabilized again when we moved away. But what it means is that we were picking up *you*. How is that possible?"

*Past the point of no return*, he thought, but he just couldn't bring himself to say it. "It's better to show you."

A long silence followed. He glanced at her. Her gaze swept over him, taking in his face, his hands, his clothes. "You're not an HPD officer, are you?" she finally said. "No," she said, answering her own question. "You don't act like one, for starters. But the bigger question is: how does a human present with void residue?

"And I almost forgot," she said, reaching out. She stroked his cheek with the tips of her fingers. He instinctively flinched away.

"Cold skin," she said softly. "Do you have some kind of medical condition? My mom had hyperthyroidism, and it made her hands and feet cold."

He could have gone with that, but he didn't want to lie to her if possible. "It's not anything medical."

She leaned back, scrutinizing him again. "That leads me to ask a more difficult question: are you human?"

He let out a sharp, short laugh. "That's the second time I've been asked that recently."

"Well," she said. "What did you tell the other person?"

"Yes. And no."

Emelia blew out a breath. "Am I in danger, Alex?"

"No. Absolutely not. Let me ask you a question: how long have you been investigating the paranormal with CDPR?"

"Twelve years—professionally."

"What is the biggest discovery you've made?"

"Aside from today, you mean?"

He nodded, turning a corner. Lennie's house was just ahead, its Gothic Revival columns framing the porch. Crime scene tape still encircled the house.

"Actually, it was the discovery of void particle residue on our supernatural critters. They all have it to some degree. It degrades over time. Faster in sunlight, it turns out. Dr. Chavez—he's our chief scientist—speculated that it may be evidence of an alternate dimension. It's the reason our tech department created the VPDs."

"Have you found any other evidence of this alternate dimension?"

She shook her head. "No. Is there one?"

*Nothing if not direct*, he thought. She stared at him. "Is there?"

He pulled up and put the car in park. "Let's go find out."

They ducked under the tape and went to the front door. Emelia carried the VPD on a strap over her shoulder. Alex raised his keychain and selected a key.

"You have a key?" she asked.

"He was one of my best friends." He unlocked the door, and the metallic smell of dried blood met their nostrils. Turning on lights as they went, they made their way into the den. The bodies had been cleared, but bloodstains and signs of mayhem remained. Alex led her to the hallway off to the right. She raised the VPD and switched it on.

"I've got a signal, but it's fluctuating. I think it's your proximity."

He went back into the den and stood near *Sunlight on Boughs*.

"Yes, good. Same signal we had last night. Somewhat weaker but still reading."

He came back to her side. "Show me the closet."

She led him down the hallway. The door was closed.

He took her by the arms and turned her to face him. "Emelia, you remember when I asked you about your biggest discovery?"

She looked very vulnerable at that moment. "Yes."

"Beyond that door lies the biggest discovery you or anyone in See Deeper will ever make. But if I am to show it to you, it comes with a secret that must be kept. The secret is about me. Who I really am. What I really am. It must be kept secret, at least for now."

He felt her trembling in his grasp, and then she eased out of his hold on her and stepped backward down the hall. For a moment he thought she might flee. "I'm a scientist, Alex. I—I don't know if I can honestly promise that."

"Just for a while, until we catch this guy. We can solve this together. We can stop the killings, you and me. But for now, my secret must be kept."

She took a deep breath, her face clouded with uncertainty. "I'll try," she said.

He opened the door and stood by it, waiting.

She hesitated and then came forward. Alex stepped through the door, and she entered, standing beside him. The light was still on in the closet. Clothing hung on dowels to either side. He closed the door behind them. "That wall?" he asked, pointing toward the back of the closet.

She nodded. She had regained her composure, but her eyes were wide. "Take my hand," he said. She did.

Alex reached up to the chain pull with his free hand and snapped off the light.

# 13

—·—

T hey were plunged into darkness. Emelia gasped as a cinnamon-candy aroma swirled around them. "What is that?" she asked. "What's happening?"

"Don't let go of my hand," he said, and led her across the threshold and into the vastness of the Deepest Shadow.

Emelia's knees felt weak. The utter *strangeness* she saw was too reminiscent of her encounter with the thing in the forest so long ago. As she tried to regain her composure, she thought: *this is what you've searched for all your life.* She went silent for a moment, shutting out the emotion so she could observe more clearly.

Alex led her a few steps forward, and she turned to glance behind her. She saw a gray rectangle glowing behind them.

"Yes," Alex said. "That's the closet in Lennie's house. The other gray shapes around it are other ways into and out of the Deepest Shadow from his house and nearby houses. That's what this place is called. You may be the first non—" he caught himself, and corrected quickly, "the first human ever to see this."

She turned and looked at him, her investigator's mind still sharp amid the jaw-dropping wonder. "Your secret?"

"Part of it."

Emelia looked left and right, taking the strange sight in: to the left and right she saw a myriad of gray shapes, rectangles, squares, and angular and even blurry, indistinct gray shapes that curved off to the left and right and diminished in the distance.

To Emelia, it looked like a seashore, reminiscent of a circular bay at night seen from the vantage point of the shore. But there was no sky, just a very dark, almost black emptiness overhead—in the center distance, it was the same: there was no apparent horizon separating what served as ground and the bleak, empty darkness overhead. And yet she was aware of an ambient light of some kind surrounding her: in the dimness she could still see herself and the device in her hands. She assumed it was light thrown from the gray shapes behind her, including the rectangular "doorway" that she had come through. Her eyes continued to scan the darkness at the gulf's center, and she was surprised at how badly her mind craved a distinction between ground and sky. As she stared, her eyes picked out something else in the blackness ahead. It was very distant, and at first, she thought her eyes were playing tricks on her, but she blinked and saw, very far off, what looked like a cluster of tiny phosphorescent blue dots, like pinpricks of light against the darkness. They almost seemed to undulate like—

"Try the device," Alex said.

She had almost completely forgotten about the VPD. Alex had moved his gentle grip to her upper arm so she could hold the device with both hands. She held it up and looked at the screen. "Very strong reading, but nothing directional." She twisted dials below the readout screen, but it didn't seem to help. "Seems like a lot of void particle interference or overload."

"Let's move out a little farther," Alex said, and guided her forward into the darkness, away from the doorway. The ground underneath her feet felt spongy and soft, like walking on thick mounds of moss. She couldn't really make out any texture or shapes in the dimness. Once they were maybe fifty or a hundred yards away from the glowing shapes behind them, she said, "Yes, that's better." Moving slowly to allow Alex to stay in touch with her—apparently it would be bad if they broke contact—she scanned in a circle around them. "The doorway we came though is just a big fuzz of feedback or interference, but I am getting two linear signals now, both leading back to the closet. One is from you, Alex, and the other—"

She cried out as his grip tightened painfully on her arm.

The voice boomed in Alex's mind, powerful and malevolent. "So you would hunt me, eh? But then I was wondering when another of our kind would try to *intervene*. And here you are. You can tell the rest: *do not oppose me*. I am not just old. I am ancient: the *lamia*, the *striga*, who dined on emperors, priestesses, and kings. They knew me and called me Titus the Scornful when they dared whisper my name at all.

"My scorn has grown, too, centuries of it: a disdain for the crawling, groveling sheep whose sharp, inquisitive eyes fell upon me. And judged me for...*for that*. I forbid them now to see. I *scrape* that inquisitive jelly from their sockets. I care not who lives or who dies at my hand or by my teeth. *Moriantur omnes*!

Now it is their feeble struggles—their cries for mercy, that lush, gargling, *bubbling* sound as the *sescespita* slashes them: only these things have amusement for me anymore." There was a pause, and then the voice sounded very tired, like an echoing whisper. "Oppose me not in my task. Tell the others. Be warned." It was gone.

"*ALEX!*" Emelia shrieked and pounded on the hand gripping her arm with her free fist. "You're hurting me! Stop! Stop!" The grip was like a vice, and she fought against the urge to scream in pain. Then his free hand caught her fist in a gentle grip, and the painful grip on her arm was gone. She slumped, her vision swimming, and he gathered her in his arms, so gentle now, preventing her from falling. She felt an unsettling admixture of fear and—was it *safety?*—in his embrace. *That's crazy.* A shudder rattled through her.

"I'm *so sorry,*" he said, his face close to hers. "Emelia, are you all right?"

She went silent, focusing again, and took a deep breath. She reached up and massaged where he had gripped her. It was sore and throbbing, but it was such a relief to be free from the crushing pain. She flexed the fingers on her hurt arm. "I think so. What happened?"

He raised her up so she was standing facing him. She felt his hands softly touching her arms near her shoulders. She noticed the VPD on the dark spongy ground near them where she had dropped it.

"You didn't hear it?" Alex asked. "It was so loud—that horrible voice."

"No. Suddenly you went rigid, and you gripped my arm really tightly. It hurt so bad. I didn't know you were so strong. Are *you* okay?"

He sighed. "I'm so sorry I hurt you, Emelia. So sorry. It must have been in my mind. Some kind of trance."

"Telepathy," she said. "Was it him?" she asked, looking at Alex's face. His face was clouded, and he stared off into the emptiness. "Our bad guy?"

His gaze met hers. "Yes. And now I know his name."

Without losing his touch on her, Alex bent down and retrieved the VPD. He slid the strap over her shoulder. "Come on."

He led her back to the door shaped portal they had come through. As they neared it, Emelia heard a familiar sound not too far away: "Gack!" She managed a weak smile despite the aching in her arm and resisted the urge to call back to the sprite out there in the darkness. They crossed the threshold into Lennie's coat closet. Alex clicked the light on, and Emelia saw the closet looked normal again. The cinnamon candy odor faded, giving way to the mundane smell of clothing hanging in the closet.

She rubbed her arm. She expected one hell of a bruise tomorrow. "Unbelievable," she said, glancing around. "It seemed so unreal."

"It's real," Alex said, leading her out of the closet and into the hall. "A bit much to take in the first time."

"Understatement of the year. What now?"

"Pen and paper. I want to transcribe as much of what I heard as possible."

They went to the kitchen and found a notepad and an ink marker. Then they sat in the dining room and Alex scribbled on the notepad. He scrutinized what he had written and then looked across the table at Emelia. "Some of it's missing already. I'm going to do a little self-hypnosis thing to jog my memory," he said.

"You're a hypnotist?" she replied, her eyes wide.

"You could say that, but not professionally ."

He closed his eyes and took a few deep breaths. He murmured something about *perfect memory* and then uttered, "queen of diamonds." His body slumped, his head dipping down toward his chest. Emelia noticed a change in his breathing: it was slower and shallower. He was still for what seemed like a few minutes, then opened his eyes and started writing on the pad again. He looked up at her and smiled. "I think I got most of it." He slid the pad across the table, and she read it. It was chilling and it got her imagination racing.

"It's a villain speech," she said.

He looked at her, confused.

"A villain speech, like in the movies when the villain pauses to make a speech. I'm surprised he didn't say 'we're a lot alike, you and I.'"

"I think I've spent too much time in the studio."

She glanced at the note again. "Alex, he talks about being centuries old. How can that be?"

He looked down at the table. "It has to do with my secret."

She reached across the table and touched his hand. "Alex, you have to come clean with me. We're in this together now. You said it yourself: we can catch him together. But I badly need to know."

He was silent for several seconds. Then, "Okay, but not here. Lennie—" he fell silent and glanced toward the den. Emelia noticed the stale blood smell hanging in the air. *Of course*, she thought.

"I understand," she said. "Maybe back to the bar?"

He looked up and nodded. "The bar."

# 14

They said little during the drive. Emelia checked her phone, listening to her messages and reading texts. Both Melanie and Alison were worried about her. *What the hell am I going to say?* Conflict tore at her. The existence of the Shadow dimension and simple proof that the strange creatures See Deeper had studied had originated from there was *huge*. But Alex was terrified that some larger secret of his would be revealed, and she had agreed not to reveal it, whatever it was. *Speaking of that mystery, what the hell was he?*

He had a supernatural signature like all the critters from the Shadow dimension, and apparently so did the bad guy. He was unusually strong, and his skin always felt cold. Words flitted through her mind. *Demon? Astral entity? Monster?* After what she had seen today, *anything* might be possible. Her thoughts wandered back to the shapeshifting thing that had taken her sister so long ago. It had taken on the semblance of a boy, and later her sister. *Was he something like that?*

A detail snapped into her mind. The bad guy had said *another of our kind*. Alex wasn't unique. It suggested that there were more of—*whatever* he was!

Her phone vibrated, and she checked the screen. Alison. *Worried about you—pls check in soonest*. Her shoulders slumped. *What had she said to Alison about inter-agency fraternization?* It had been a half-joke then, but not anymore. *Dammit.*

Her attention turned to his car stereo. It was tuned to the Forties station on satellite radio. A singer named Mel Waiters was singing a lively song called *Friday Night Fish Fry*.

"Big band fan?" she asked. He smiled, still watching the road. "More like the music of the decade," he said. "I just find it soothing. I like a lot of other music, but I find I keep coming back to the Forties."

Back at Desdemona, they found a secluded booth at the back of the bar. Alex got a tumbler of red wine, and she got another Devil's Hopyard and a pint glass to pour it into.

Alex's gaze met hers. "A while back, you wanted to talk about art."

"Well, that was before you took me on a tour of an alternate dimension. I've got about fifty thousand questions about that, for starters." She paused. "And a few about you—WAIT! Something you said back at the house. 'I spent too much time in the studio.'"

"Good memory," he said, smiling.

Emelia smiled back. "Comes with the territory. I suppose you're going to tell me something crazy like you were friends with Jackson Williams."

"Something like that. But I need to know that if I confide in you, you'll keep my secret."

She let out a sigh. "You're making it hard on me, to be honest. I mean, this is my job. It really is the biggest discovery—" she trailed off, shaking her head slightly.

"What if I sweetened the deal and offered to give you a painting?"

"You're a painter, too? You're full of surprises, Alex. Interdimensional traveler, hypnotist, painter, friend of Jackson Williams—"

"No. I *am* Jackson Williams."

For a moment, Emelia felt like all the oxygen in the room had vanished. She took a long swig of her beer and set the glass back down. The room seemed to spin.

He reached out and touched her arm with that too-cold hand. "Breathe, Emelia. Breathe."

She gulped a couple of breaths and took another swig of her beer. "You're not lying, are you? Why would you be?"

"No reason to, at least not now. Not to you."

"There's a book called *The Oil Heresies*. Written by an art critic named Cooper—"

"Yes. Jamison Cooper. Written in 1989. You read his essay about me?"

*About me*, Emelia thought. *He really isn't lying.* Finally, she said, "Yes. Cooper theorized that Jackson Williams and the reclusive pointillist Max Ellis were—" She gasped.

Alex nodded. "—The same person. Cooper was right. I was Max Ellis, too."

She took another gulp of beer. "Now wait a minute. Ellis did a lot of work in the 50's and 60's. The High Museum in Atlanta—that's where See Deeper is based—has a big painting of his called *Sequoias,* painted in 1955, I think."

"It was 1956," he replied. "I wore out a dozen brushes painting that."

"How can that be? You look like you're in your late twenties or early thirties."

"Babyface," he said, smiling at her.

"Don't bullshit me, Alex. Please. How old are you?"

"I'm 119. 120 this coming September."

She drained her beer. "I'd say it can't be, but with what I've seen today, I guess maybe it can be." She paused for a moment. "That splendid painting at Lennie's: *Sunlight on Boughs.* You painted that?"

"Yes. Plus two others in that room. *The Canasta Game* and *Willows at Lake's Edge*. Lennie loved my work. He got me started in the art scene here in Houston. A great ally."

"And he knew you were *that old*?"

"No. He didn't know about the Max Ellis connection. He never read Cooper's essay like some really smart art buff did." He winked at her.

She stood. "I am going to get another beer and take several more deep breaths and hope my brain doesn't explode from all this."

While she was at the bar, Alex shook out the tension in his arms. The cat-and-mouse game had been fun, but he knew what was coming. She was in shock for now, but the biggest revelation was yet to come. And revealing that could be—likely *would be* the biggest mistake of his entire life. He'd only known her for a day. Somewhere at the back of his mind, he couldn't shut out a small voice saying *you're making a gigantic mistake. You'll undo all the secrecy we've kept for so long. And you're undoing it to someone allied to the FBI.*

He had an ace in the hole, though: his charisma pheromone. One whiff and she would be more than willing to keep the secret, at least for a while. But he didn't want to do that. Not to Emelia. Her knowledge of art was considerable—good grief, she knew about *Sequoias*! And her childlike wonder at making the discoveries of a lifetime was endearing. For better or worse, Alex was reminded of just how long it had been since he'd been attracted to a woman. Decades. He frowned. Silana had done him up good so long ago, that bitch. *Risking it all for a stupid crush*, the voice said, mocking. *Real smart, Stoica.*

Emelia sat down with her beer and poured it into the glass. Her gaze met his. "Chips are down," she said. "I don't want to do any more guesswork, Alex. Please, please tell me what or who you really are."

Alex nodded. "You deserve to hear it after all this. My actual name is Alexandru Stoica, and I was born in Romania in 1906. I was human, then. Until 1932."

"Romania? Is this going where I think it's going?"

He nodded. "The easiest thing now is to just say it: I am a vampire."

# 15

—·—

Words failed her. "A—a vampire? They really—" she trailed off. It seemed almost too much after this day.

Alex nodded. "They really exist."

Emelia looked toward the front of the bar. The late-afternoon sunlight was orange, and it shone brightly through the plate-glass windows.

"It's daytime!" she cried. "And you've been with me out in the sun today!"

"Stoker rules," he said. "That's what we call them. Bram Stoker did us a big favor with his vampire rules. Most of them don't apply to us."

Her eyes widened. "Crosses? Garlic? The sacred Host? Coffins?"

"None of those apply. I sleep in a king-size Sealy Posturepedic with my two dogs who take up way too much space. My uncle Bardru is a Catholic and takes the holy wafer regularly."

She leaned back. "But you do drink... blood."

"That, I'm afraid, is true."

Emelia was almost unaware that her hand went instinctively to her throat, because he said, "No need to fear, Emelia. I will not feed on you. That I promise."

"Holy shit," she said, still gobsmacked. "Do you have...I mean—"

He smiled, revealing his fangs.

She let out a surprised cry so loud the bartender looked over at them. "Sorry! Sorry!" she said. Alex had closed his mouth and when he opened it again, his canines were normal again.

Alex laughed. "You've been through a lot today. It's okay."

"You have a vampire uncle? How many vampires are there?"

"I'm showing off again, but a Bible quote suffices: *I am legion, for we are many*."

"Wait. I just thought of this: the bloodless bodies. APES. Anomalous Profound Exsanguination Syndrome."

"Yes. Our saliva has a powerful healing property. The wounds heal almost immediately after a bite."

"Yes!" she cried again, almost too loud. "That would explain it perfectly. What an amazing adaptation!"

"It's pretty handy. Now remember, Emelia, you cannot mention this to anyone, at least not for a while."

"Oh god, Alex, you don't know what you're asking," she said, overwhelmed. "Today is the culmination of everything I've been looking for my entire adult life."

"You saw *Sunlight on Boughs*," he replied. "Do you know how much it's worth?"

She shook her head, confused.

"That one painting is worth $750,000. I've got paintings in my studio worth that much or more. Keep my secrets, and I'll let you pick your favorite. To keep. It's bribery, I know, but it would be an ample reward if you help me find and get rid of Titus."

Suddenly it came crashing through the tapestry of wonder she'd felt in the past hours. That name. *Titus*. The bad guy. A vampire committing mass murders. The one who had killed one of Alex's dearest friends. Suddenly she felt sober despite the beers.

She gazed thoughtfully at him. "You've risked a great deal confiding in me today, haven't you?"

He reached out and touched her hand. Now she knew why his touch was cold. "More than you know," he murmured.

"I accept," she said.

Night had fallen as they conversed. Alex had told her more about vampirism and the vampires of Houston. She had been particularly interested in the idea of partial feeds to avoid a runaway vampire population. He had answered numerous questions about the Deepest Shadow to the best of his knowledge, sharing that the further you went into the blackness, away from the fringe of gray shapes, the more likely you were to run afoul of some dangerous creatures. He had mentioned taking martial arts training in order to confront Titus. Then the question he feared came up.

"So if you vampires are virtually indestructible," she said, "how can you kill Titus? You've said all the Stoker stuff—crosses, holy water, stakes, decapitation, etc. doesn't work."

"That secret I am going to hold on to for a while," he said.

"We've come this far," she said. "In for a penny, in for a pound."

"I just can't. Of all our secrets, that one is the most closely guarded. I would be hunted just like Titus if I told you."

"Well, today has been quite an educational day for me," she said. "It's getting late. I've got to figure out something to tell Melanie and Alison."

"The FBI agent?" he replied. "Is See Deeper that beholden to the FBI?"

She sighed. "It's, um, a bit more personal. That's a secret I'll keep as well. I'd be hunted by the FBI if I told you."

"You're teasing me."

She smiled. "I am."

"Well, it's late for me as well. I'm supposed to meet Bardru and work on my reach."

"Reach?"

"Yes. It's awareness of other vampires at a distance. It's a little like a muscle. The more you work on it, the farther you can reach. Mine is pretty good to start with and we are trying to maximize it. It may help me locate Titus if he's not too far away."

"Remarkable. This, plus the martial arts training—you're working very hard to stop Titus, aren't you?"

"Yes. He's a constant threat to our secrecy. We have to stop him."

She studied him. "But that's not the only reason you're after him."

He looked into those beautiful gray-green eyes and thought of the stormy Pacific surf of Malibu. And Jellybean.

"It's not," he said. "But that's a story for another time. I'm really sorry about that." He pointed at her arm. An ugly bruise was forming: purple and black on her pale skin. Finger marks were clearly visible. "I can make the bruise go away," he said.

"I'll be okay," she said a little too quickly, glancing at her arm. "Long-sleeved shirts for a couple of days," she said, smiling. "One last thing: I'm going to do some calibration of the data on the VPD. I think I can get a distinct signature for Titus. Easier to track him that way."

Alex nodded. "Meeting you has been the best thing that's happened to me recently."

She blushed at that. "Meeting you has been the most mind-blowing thing that's happened to me in, well, maybe ever." She laughed. "I don't think I've used 'mind-blowing' in a sentence in a long time."

He smiled as he stood. "I'll pick up your tab at the bar," he said. "Meet again in a few days?"

"Maybe sooner if necessary."

"Okay."

She disappeared through the door as Alex paid the bar tab. The little voice was back. *What the fuck have you done?*

As Emelia drove, she called Melanie. "Where have you *been*?" the latter said.

"Are you alone?" She hoped Alison wasn't hovering near, waiting for news.

"At the hotel. Yes. It's been quiet."

"I've been information gathering," Emelia said.

"Anything useful?"

"Still collating." *Lying to my protégé. Not a good look.*

"What are you, Ash from *Alien*?" Melanie said, laughing.

"I promise not to try and choke you to death with a magazine," she replied. They shared a laugh this time.

"I also had a little bit of a scare with my mom. She had a medical emergency. I've been on the phone off and on for hours. She had to go to the emergency room, but she's been discharged. She'll be okay."

"That's a relief," Melanie said. "Do you want to get some dinner?"

"No, I'm kind of emotionally exhausted. Just a snack from room service and I'm going to call it a night. Fresh start in the morning."

That seemed to satisfy Melanie, and they ended the call.

*Now for the call you really don't want to make*, Emelia thought. She dialed Alison's number.

When Alison answered, she said, "You had us worried there. Are you all right?"

Emelia was surprised at how professional she sounded. *Well, good.*

"Okay. Medical emergency with my mom."

"What kind of emergency?" Alison asked.

"Is this a personal or professional conversation?" Emelia asked.

"It's an innocent question," Alison said. "I just—never mind. Glad you are okay."

"Yes. My mom is okay, too."

"Good. This got off to an awkward start. Sorry. This is a personal question, just so we are clear: mind if I drop by your room tonight? Girl talk and raid the mini-fridge for drinks?"

"Not tonight. I'm exhausted."

There was a momentary silence. Then, "No worries. Rain check?"

Emelia suppressed a sigh. *All this plus a girl crush.* "Maybe," was all she could manage.

"Okay. Get some rest. Sweet dreams."

*Ay yi yi*, Emelia thought. *No more hotel trysts, like ever.* "Thanks," she said. "Talk soon."

"Yes," Alison said, and they ended the call with goodbyes.

As she parked in the hotel garage, Emelia decided that raiding the mini-fridge was a damned good idea.

Stars glittered overhead in the new moon darkness. Alex pulled into a gravel parking lot next to Bardru's old Mercedes. There was a single sodium vapor lamp on a pole nearby, casting a baleful orange glow on the lot. Beyond lay an overgrown baseball field surrounded by chain-link fencing and wooden bleachers gone gray with disuse. Beyond lay dark outlines of pine forest.

Bardru exited his car. He tapped his bare wrist as though there was a watch there. Alex found the gesture endearing—Bardru hadn't worn a watch in a decade. "You're late," he said quietly.

"I'm sorry, Uncle. It's been a crazy day."

The older man nodded. "One of many to come, I think."

Alex gently gripped Bardru's arms. "Uncle, I heard his voice in my mind today. In the Deepest Shadow. He told me his name."

"The one we seek? What is his name?"

Alex pulled the note from his pocket and read it.

Bardru gasped at the mention of the name. When Alex finished reciting the note, Bardru said, "I know that name! It is in one of my books. I will have to look it up, but he is Roman: from the Roman Empire!" He paused. "So old! He spoke to your mind?"

"Yes. A loud, booming voice. I went into a kind of trance."

"This is not a vampire power I am aware of. I must do some reading."

Bardru's phone rang, and he answered it. "Yes. Sorry to make you wait. He is here now. Stay there and we will begin." He ended the call.

"Shit," Alex said. "Who is it?"

Bardru smiled. "Who indeed! That is for you to determine."

Alex nodded. He walked out to the center of the lot. He took a deep breath and closed his eyes. As he slowly let the breath out, he stretched out that mysterious sense that vampires called *reach*. It felt like an invisible web, expanding from his person slowly at first and then faster. It definitely felt two dimensional—a flat plane of awareness—at first, but then a portion of it took on a vaguely human shape several yards away. He focused on it for a moment, and the shape gained definition and, somehow, *meaning*. He almost heard a familiar, accented voice from long ago—*let me help you, my ailing one. call me uncle—you are safe now.*

"Bardru," he whispered. He stretched his *reach* further now, expanding past the baseball field, and through the pine forest. He was surprised to find something strange in the forest: *interference*? Not human. No. More like a globe the size of a beach ball floating between the tree trunks. He sensed mindless *hunger* and *confusion* and *fear* almost simultaneously, and then it fled, trailing *electricity*? He knew now what it was. Because Emelia had told him. "Will-o'-the-wisp," he whispered, delighted.

"Concentrate," a quiet, familiar voice in his web of awareness said. *Yes*, Alex thought. *Yes*. He stretched farther and farther, past forest, past freeway, past dwellings, past lakes and streams, past shell-gravel roads and all the time the web feeling more and more *attenuated*. And as it wavered at the edges, so fragile, so thin, there: a shape. Vaguely human: *sitting*. *Waiting*. *Impatient*. But who? It seemed familiar, but *who* of the many he knew? He searched for some aspect that might confer *meaning*. Barely there. Maybe not. Wait. Two. Words. *Loose* and *cannon*.

"Jonas?" he guessed, still unsure. He raised his arm, pointing in the direction that felt. That. Felt. *Right*.

"Yes!" Bardru said. The awareness snapped away like the release of a stretched rubber band, and Alex opened his eyes. His mouth was dry. He was still pointing. He noticed moths fluttering around the light.

"Four miles, northwest," Bardru said as he hurried to Alex's side. "The farthest yet, yes?"

Alex nodded, exhausted. "Jonas?"

Bardru laughed. "Yes, your old friend!"

"He's a goddamned prick—that's why he was so easy to find."

Bardru laughed again.

# 16

— • —

F our restless nights in four different rooms ensued.

Alex lay in bed, staring at the ceiling in the darkness. Dizzy and Midnight snoozed on their half of the king-size bed next to him. Dogs lived the most mindful existence of any intelligent creature. Always living in the moment, never concerned with past or future (for the most part). It's why you weren't supposed to punish them when you got home to find they'd chewed your favorite pair of shoes. Once that moment was hours gone, the dog didn't know why you were punishing it. He'd read that somewhere. Punishing them afterward made them neurotic. As they had several times already tonight, images of Lennie flooded back: lying on the floor, his face red with blood, ragged, empty eye sockets staring up, two halves of his ribbed trachea visible in the open gash on his throat.

He almost heard that silly movie-preview voice saying, "This time it's *personal*." And it was, of course, more so than any of the deaths caused by this Titus so far. Why did Titus feed on some and kill others in this gruesome fashion? He'd have to talk to Tessa about it. What had he said? Something about them not seeing—what?

Clint had been right. Seeing Lennie like that had affected his thinking, his reasoning mind. He had been struggling to regain some semblance of emotional control with mindfulness when Emelia had spoken to him, and it had evaporated like spit on a griddle. Emelia, with those gray-green eyes so like Jellybean's, a beautiful smile, and a strange *je ne sais quoi* that had appealed to him on some primal level. She had talked knowledgeably about his art and for a moment he had been transported out of that charnel-house room and into a place he didn't realize he longed to be.

He had talked about his art to Bardru many times, of course, but as much as he loved the older man, he would always just say, "It is good in its way, in the colors and shapes, and it is good for you and so I like it." Hardly sophisticated art conversation. But Emelia the art buff was also a paranormal investigator, and Alex had not only revealed the Deepest Shadow to her, but admitted he was a vampire! And told her about the existence of the Collective! Only now did it seem clear to him how successfully the vampires in America and elsewhere had hidden themselves from the general populace, and here he was admitting their existence to an investigator linked to the FBI. If the Collective found out, he'd jeopardized this carefully cultivated secrecy, he might indeed be hunted more vigorously than Titus.

He almost laughed. *By whom?* He himself was the one hunting Titus. The only one. No one else was brave enough, (or perhaps stupid enough) to do it. *I'll just have to manage it,* he thought. He rolled over on his side and began to mentally intone his mindfulness mantra until sleep reluctantly came.

He dreamed of Emelia.

Melanie Sanders wiped tears from her eyes with a corner of the bed sheet. This was supposed to be her big break with See Deeper: a chance to show what she was capable of in the field. Her chance to leave the title of Agent Trainee behind and become an Investigative Agent instead. The disappointment clung to her. Something was going on between Emelia and Alison: the interpersonal chemistry there was weird. She suspected they'd slept together, and Alison had seemed more than just professionally concerned with Emelia's whereabouts. *Ugh*.

Melanie sighed. The rotten cherry on top had been the Zoom call with her husband David a little while ago. Like her, he was from Georgetown: they'd met at Georgetown University and got married after graduating. It had seemed like a major stroke of luck when they both landed jobs in Atlanta at nearly the same time after graduation. But David had told her that Tekton was downsizing and his job as an IT integrations specialist was under the ax. He also missed Georgetown and was eager to move back to D.C. and perhaps get on with a government firm there. But Melanie liked Atlanta, and until very recently had been happy with her prospects with See Deeper. They had argued a bit about the situation and then signed off.

Melanie yawned. The melatonin she'd taken earlier was finally kicking in, and she surrendered to sleep.

She dreamed of her cats Toffee and SecondCat.

Alison stared at the ceiling, restless and frustrated.

"A girl here, a boy there," she muttered into the darkness, parroting what Emelia had said to her. Alison had known she was on the rebound when she'd slept with Emelia. So did Emelia, unfortunately. Now she was showing signs of discomfort and maybe, *probably* regret that they had slept together. Alison had hoped against hope that an emotional bond might form after Emelia shared that story about her sister. But no. Emelia seemed ready to move on to that next girl or—*ugh*—that next boy. Alison grimaced, thinking that the dirty cop who had raped Linda had fucked up two lives for the price of one. God-damned men. Always fucking shit up. She sighed—she didn't want to be thought of as a stereotype and so she needed to not stereotype others. Alison had worked with a lot of capable, good men at the Bureau. And some of the Houston Police officers investigating the killings had been good guys.

She rolled over and thought about Jack Crain. She'd had another call with him. He was still making noise about a task force, but for now, he was going to call for a weekly briefing at HQ.

She knew the pressure to solve the mass killings was on, and she was nowhere near figuring out anything about who the perp was behind it all. Crain had said he'd try to get a best-guess profile from the Behavioral Analysis Unit in a day or two, but what good would it be? *We conclude he's a psycho fuck who appears out of the ether and kills a bunch of people and then vanishes without a trace. Good luck catching him!*

There was a glimmer of good news, though. At least he wasn't calling her into the field office to demoralize her even more. She doubted he'd be like that in a briefing with others present. And for the moment, she still owned the investigation. That was something. She fumbled on the bedside table and found a mini bottle of vodka. She put it to her lips and felt the last few drops burn her lips and tongue.

She yawned and was grateful sleep was finally arriving. She dreamed of Emelia.

Sleep came last and least to Emelia: it was the *last* thing she wanted. She sat at the modest desk in her hotel room with her laptop open. Her mind raced, but she was trying to slow it down enough to write a list of questions to ask Alex. She smiled to herself. She had spoken to Rick Emerson in Atlanta, who had promised to create some new code for the Void Particle Densitometer in a day or two. She also spoke briefly with Dr. Chavez, and he had mentioned her theory about astral vampires. It seemed suddenly quaint, even if the real ones did use some kind of alternate dimension to get around. It had been *really* difficult not to say anything to Dr. Chavez about what she had experienced today. And she hadn't talked with Mark Petrovsky. The boss knew about the problematic rhythms of paranormal investigations and had never been a micromanager.

Alex drifted into her thoughts. The real-and-for-true vampire who also happened to be the most beautiful man she had encountered for some time. Rugged features, long hair that seemed out of style but somehow timeless as well. Clean-shaven, which was just a preference. *He'd probably look great with a beard*, she thought. A thought crashed through her reverie: *Goddammit, Emelia!* She mentally intoned the words again: *He is a killer. He. Kills. Human. Beings.*

She sighed. Well, he was a killer who was utterly fascinating. She mused about those women who wrote letters to serial killers in prison. *A strange mystique*, she supposed.

At one point in their conversation, Alex had said, "I've seen cowboys and flappers." Astonishing. She couldn't imagine living long enough to see that much history. And he'd made a small fortune, having become not one, but two esteemed painters with works in national galleries. That was something she needed to keep at the forefront of her mind, situated right next to *he's a killer*. The offer of a painting *was* a bribe. He'd said so himself. He also knew she'd never be able to afford one of his paintings on her modest government salary.

But what a bribe! She imagined something like *Sequoias* or *Sunlight on Boughs* hanging over the fireplace in her humble Atlanta living room. *Delight!*

Her mind wandered. Alex was a killer on a mission to kill a vampire who was a mass killer. *Set a thief to catch a thief.* She wondered about the provenance of that statement. A quick browser search revealed it had roots tracing back to ancient Greek writings, specifically attributed to the poet Callimachus, who wrote about recognizing a thief's tracks due to being a thief oneself. And Titus, the bad guy, was apparently an ancient Roman. He and Callimachus could have been contemporaries. She paused and yawned deeply. Every cell in her body craved sleep, but her mind refused to cooperate, running like a coked-up gerbil on an exercise wheel. She had a couple of Ambien tabs in her go-bag but opted for a few Benadryl instead. It was 4:45 a.m. when sleep finally came. She dreamed of Alex.

# 17

—·—

T he next morning was a bleak, rainy Wednesday. In a meeting room at the Compound, Alex sat at a table across from Jonas and a muscular man with a crew cut, serious features, and, of all things, a prominent beer belly. He wore a blue T-shirt and his arms bore smudged, faded tattoos done in ink that some tattoo artists called "military black."

"Alex Stoica, meet Maxwell Bright," Jonas said.

"Maxie, if you please," the man said, reaching across the table. A smile played across his face and then fled. They shook hands.

"Marines?" Alex asked.

Maxie shook his head. "Nah, nah, man. A jarhead? Don't make me spit on Jonas' nice table." He pointed at fuzzy crossed cannons wreathed with olive branches on his right arm. "Naval artillery. Gunner's Mate. Pistol expert. Shoot the fin offa shark with a .45. Even outta the service, never got the gunpowder outta my blood. My wife, Myrna, God rest her soul, always said, 'Maxie and his guns.' I had a big collection in the basement. Hardly a day went by she didn't say that." The smile returned and decided to linger a bit. "Fine woman. Died before I got bit, God rest her soul."

Alex smiled and Maxie smiled back. "Helluva woman."

"Maxie is here to help us in the firearm department," Jonas said.

Alex nodded.

"You got a vampire you want dead?" Maxie asked. "Don't want to tussle 'cause he's old and strong—Jonas told me early this morning. Anyways, you want him dead, and him being a vampire, one of us, and I bet you thought silver bullets right off."

"Yes," Alex replied. "That's what I thought."

The smile returned and fled again. "See, silver and firearms are tricky. All morning I been watching Youtube videos and reading threads on Reddit. You'd be surprised how many gun guys are interested in silver bullets. That and a buncha other stuff. The popular thing right now is sabot rounds for shotguns. Russian guys make 'em and send them to American guys to test."

"Sabot?" Alex said.

"Discarding sabot. It's a finned dart made of metal. It's fitted with a segmented plastic sabot that breaks into three pieces once the round leaves the barrel. The sabot falls away and the dart is on its way. They're used successfully in tanks for armor-piercing rounds. Cool-looking as all hell, but a bad choice when ya scale down to shotgun rounds. As the sabot peels away, it affects the flight characteristics of the dart, and it tends to veer or tumble.

"Then there are flechette rounds. Fancy fancy. Shotgun shells filled with a bunch of tiny metal darts instead of shot. They also tend to tumble, and in the videos I saw penetration was piss-poor. So we're back to silver bullets in a rifle. Classic, right?"

Alex shrugged, but even though he wasn't a "gun guy," this Maxie was fascinating. Even Jonas seemed captivated.

Maxie went on. "Anyways, it's what I thought. Rifle's good for range, but for our needs we need something with a lower velocity. You don't want that high-velocity round zipping right through your guy and then going on about its business elsewhere. *Through-and-through wound* is the tech term. You want the silver to stay *in* the target, right?"

"Right," Alex said. *Maxie and his guns*, he thought. *I'm going to enjoy training with this guy.*

"So I'm a pistol guy from way back. Shorter range and usually lower velocity in the smaller calibers. I kinda veered too far in that direction when I thought about varmint loads."

"Varmint loads?" Jonas said.

Maxie nodded. "Pistol rounds filled with fine shot to kill rats or snakes on the farm. Like mini shotgun rounds. But those are *too* slow and you gotta be fairly close to the target. So I'm gonna suggest .22-caliber silver pistol rounds with custom cartridge loads tuned to get the velocity just right to penetrate but not zip through at about 40 feet or so. .22's already pretty good for that. See?"

Alex nodded, still smiling.

"Maxie is going to make those custom rounds for us. He's also going to give you some pistol training."

"I got just the thing for you, Alex," Maxie said. He reached down into a bag and brought up what looked a little like a military .45 but much more compact. He quickly checked it to ensure it was unloaded. "First rule of firearms," he said, and then slid the pistol across the table to Alex.

"Sweet little piece," Maxie said as Alex picked it up. "Keltec P17. Fires .22LR and has a 16-round magazine. One in the chamber makes 17 shots. Ambidextrous grip. Easily conceal-able, too. You can mount a compact laser sight under the barrel there, but you don't wanna depend on that. Better to be a good shot, and a little training and some range time will take care of that."

"Shoot the fin offa shark," Alex ventured.

Maxie laughed. "Yeah, man! That's the spirit! But this ain't no .45. You'll get the shark's attention, though. And if he's a vampire shark, well, that silver slug is gonna ruin his day!"

Maxie's expression went serious, and he regarded Alex and Jonas for a moment. Then he said, "Just one thing to worry about now, fellas."

Neither spoke. Maxie tapped his temple with one finger. "C'mon, guys, you gotta think this stuff through. What if this guy you're hunting has a gun with silver bullets too?"

Alex arrived thirty minutes late for his lunch appointment with Emelia, only to see her entering the restaurant as he got out of his car. The rain had slowed down to a desultory drizzle. He trotted over and caught up with her at the host stand. She turned and her shoulders slumped. "I know," she said. "I look terrible. I barely slept and I was running late, so makeup was an afterthought."

She had dark circles under her eyes, which were a little blood-shot. "It's not so bad," he said. "Yesterday was an eventful day."

"An understatement, to be sure."

The hostess got menus and led them to what might have been, on a sunnier day, a cheery table at a big window at the front of the restaurant. Once seated, Emelia glanced at the menu. "All day breakfast! This is just what I want." She glanced at Alex's hands resting on his menu. "Not hungry?"

Alex was still coasting from his partial feed on a particularly violent drug dealer in Sugar Land the night before. "No. I might have some wine."

"I'm listening to the audiobook of Dracula," she said. "'*You will, I trust, excuse me if I do not join you. But, I have already dined, and I never drink wine.*'"

Alex smiled. "First part's spot-on. The wine part? Stoker rules."

"Can you eat regular food?"

"I can if I absolutely must, but I can't keep it down more than a few hours. It's kinda yucky for lunchtime conversation. Wine and beer I can drink, although the effects are somewhat muted."

The server arrived. Emelia ordered eggs, bacon, and coffee, and Alex ordered wine.

Her gaze met his once the server left. "I had a ton of questions, but I forgot my laptop at the hotel." She sighed. "It's a slow day at work. Which is actually bad."

"How so?"

"Because we're waiting for the bad guy—Titus, that's his name, right—to strike again. Which means more people are going to die."

"When that happens, we can track him," Alex said. "You and me."

She leaned toward him, her hands on the table, staring with those bloodshot gray-green eyes. "And what happens when we find him?"

Alex took a deep breath and let it out. "Well, I'm working on that." He told her about training with Sun but omitted any mention of Maxie.

"Do you think you can actually defeat him? Is kung fu going to be enough?" she asked.

"That I don't know. I'm going to do my best to stop him."

"Alex, will you forgive me if I ask you a really tough question?"

He squared his shoulders. "Ask."

"Don't you kill people? I mean, how are you really different from Titus?'

He was silent for a long moment. "I'm sorry for—" she began.

"No no. It's a valid question. I'm not going to lie. I have killed people. But mostly what I do is partial feeds. It's what nearly all of us do. But I will, if I may, quote my uncle Bardru: 'He only kills the wicked.'"

He went on to tell her how he rescued the young woman named Jennifer from the bad guy with the van.

"I see," she said, thoughtfully. "That was a good thing you did. Titus is certainly wicked, from what we've seen so far."

The food and drink arrived. She tucked into her breakfast with gusto. He was grateful for the break in answering tough questions. *With just enough lies,* he thought. He enjoyed watching her eat. She paused, sipped coffee and smiled at him. Her smile seemed to reveal a warmth that transformed her entire face. The clouds parted for a moment and the sunlight streaming through the window cast a soft glow across her well-proportioned features and highlighted the rich ebony of her shoulder-length hair, which was still a little wet from the rain. Disheveled, but still beautiful.

"You don't know what you're missing here," she said, holding up a yellow forkful of scrambled eggs. "Wait. When was the last time you actually ate breakfast: like this I mean?"

"The summer of 1932. June. Biscuits and sausage gravy. Coffee and orange juice. I was vampirized later that day, and that was the end of breakfasts for me."

She sipped her coffee, her expression more serious now. "Who vampirized you?"

"Her name was Silana. No surname. Burlesque dancer at a club in downtown Houston. I was a plaything for her. She drained me and left. Left me to suffer. I didn't know what had happened to me. I was cowering in a tiny room above the club where she danced. I was starving, weak, and miserable. I couldn't even stand up. Bardru saved me a few days later. He became my adoptive uncle. That's what we call our vampiric mentors: aunts and uncles."

"I'm so sorry," she said. She put her knife and fork down on the plate and pushed it aside. "I seem to be asking all the hard questions today," she said. "Has there been, um, a woman since then?"

"Not really," he said. "I guess I was afraid I'd meet someone like Silana again."

"So many decades," she said with concern in her voice. Then she met his gaze. "Alex, listen to me: there are better people in the world than her. Many better people." Alex stared into the distance, lost in the memory of Silana laughing and slamming the door as she had left him to starve.

The server appeared with red wine in a stemmed glass. His reverie broken, he lifted the glass. "To slow work days."

She nodded and tapped her coffee mug against the glass. "I talked to a colleague in Atlanta—don't look at me like that—your secrets are still safe. He works in our tech department, and he's going to write some new code for the Void Particle Densitometer. It should help to distinguish between those particle trails we found. We want to build a signature for Titus specifically."

Alex nodded. "Last night when I worked on my reach, I picked up one of your critters—the globe-shaped one—in a stand of forest."

Her face brightened. "A will-o'-the-wisp?"

"Yes, that was it. It fled and it seemed like it left static electricity in its wake."

She smiled. "They are electrically charged. We have a specimen in Atlanta. I collected it in Louisiana, and it kept stinging the hell out of me with little electrical sparks. Harmless, but *ouch*!"

He nodded. "Speaking of ouch, how is your arm?"

She held up her arm, clad in the long sleeve of her white cotton blouse. "You don't want to look beneath this sleeve, is all I am saying. Yellow, purple, and green, oh my!"

"Ugh. I'm so sorry about that."

She reached across and touched his hand. "I know. It wasn't your fault. Are all vampires as strong as you?"

He nodded. "Most of us. When I'm doing martial arts training with Sun we have to be careful, so I don't hurt him."

"Did you tell him what you are?"

Alex smiled. "He was the other person besides you that asked if I was human. And I said, 'Yes and no.' He seemed satisfied with just that."

She took a sip of coffee. "Clearly not a scientist. Every time I learn something new about you, I feel like I want to ask fifty more questions."

"Well, you *are* a scientist," he said.

"That I am. But as of yesterday, I feel like Galileo must have felt when he first looked through his homemade telescope and saw moons spinning around Jupiter."

"A beautiful thought," he said. *Even with dark circles under her eyes, she's beautiful*, he thought. "Hey. Since it's a slow work-day, what if I showed you some of my paintings at my studio?"

She leaned forward with a playful smile. "Are you inviting me to come up and look at your etchings?"

He laughed at the joke. "I will be on my best behavior. My dogs will see to that. You're okay around dogs, right?"

"Dogs and I get along just fine. I wish I was home enough in Atlanta to have one of my own."

"Well, then you'll love my big, slobbery goofballs."

She smiled that glorious smile again. "Okay, Mr. Alex Stoica. You won me over, but only because of the dogs. One more sip of coffee and we can be on our way."

As they stood and prepared to leave the restaurant, neither Alex nor Emelia was aware of a plain white Chevy Tahoe parked across the street at a parking meter. Inside, with her hands gripping the top of the steering wheel, and her head pressed against her hands, Alison Martin wept.

Emelia was glad the downpour had broken. As they drove, sunlight glinted off the towers of stone and glass that comprised the Houston skyline, reflecting white, pink, green and gray. It loomed about a mile away, dominating the flat landscape. Atlanta was hilly, situated as it was near the verdant green mountains of Appalachia, but Houston occupied a great flat coastal plain, and the only things that had any elevation in this urban landscape were structures.

She was still getting used to riding in a Miata: the compact two-seater was, well, *intimate*. It rode low to the ground, and its engine purred. Of *course* it was sporty red. A vampire *would* drive a red car, she guessed. Was Alex even aware of the term *chick magnet*? Not in the last several decades, she mused. Her mind raced, wondering if it would be too intrusive to ask Alex about vampire sexuality. Could they even have sex? More questions to add to the 500 Questions of Bartholomew Cubbins. She suppressed a sigh.

"This area is called EaDo, for East Downtown," Alex noted. "It was a hub for Cantonese immigrants back in the 30s, and then for Vietnamese immigrants in the 70s. For a long time, it was the closest thing Houston had to a Chinatown. But now it's becoming trendy and more gentrified, though it still has issues with a significant homeless population. I don't mind, though. It's a dynamic area and still evolving. Houston has always been a melting pot. Lots of cultural diversity."

He turned a corner and said, "There it is, my humble abode. Used to be a shipping warehouse in the '60s but heavily remodeled by another local artist before I bought it."

The stalwart three-story building occupied a corner lot, and the pressure-washed antique brick exterior had a nice retro appearance to it. Large arched windows had been installed on the two upper floors. It was surrounded by a tall redwood fence that obscured the bottom floor. Alex thumbed a remote and a large gate opened, revealing a gray gravel driveway bordered on either side by green grass. As he drove in, Emelia saw that there were fewer windows on the ground floor, and they were narrower. "Are those the original windows?" she asked.

"Yeah," he said, as the gate closed behind them. The artist I bought it from was a stone sculptor, and he wanted to preserve some of the original façade of the warehouse. I agreed to honor that when I bought the place. In fact, I did better than that."

They exited the vehicle and walked across the manicured lawn. Off to the right was a rectangular swimming pool with green water choked by algae.

"Yeah, I don't swim much," Alex said, laughing. "But the damn dogs love it."

He led her around to a large, corrugated steel roll-up door on the side of the building. There was an old-fashioned metal sign next to it that said, *IN CASE OF FIRE THIS DOOR WILL OPEN.*

He punched a code into a keypad next to it, and with a metallic groan, the door rattled up. Beneath that, Emelia heard dogs barking. A welcome gush of cool air surrounded her as she followed him in. He closed the metal door with a wall-mounted button. The ground floor was dimly lit by a few bare bulbs hanging from the ceiling, augmented by light from the narrow windows. It was dusty and cluttered with blocks of marble and granite, and some half-finished stone sculptures here and there. A few others seemed to be finished. There were old wooden tables with tarnished chisels, files, rasps, and hammers. There was a definite smell of dust, old stone, and wood.

On one side, there was a concrete loading ramp that went up to the second floor. At the top, restrained by what must have been the longest baby gate ever constructed, Alex's two dogs, one black and one white, barked incessantly. He raised his voice and said, "Settle down, you mutts!"

They *did* settle, their barking giving way to impatient grunts and whines.

"I'm impressed," she said. "You have vampiric power over the beasts?"

"Stoker rule," he said. "More like $700 in dog training."

Emelia laughed and began to explore what must have been the stone sculptor's workshop.

"His name was Janos Horvath," Alex said. "Hungarian. He was retiring, so I preserved his studio when I bought the place. He took a few pieces with him at the time, but I bought them from his estate sale after he died. Brought 'em back here. I've never put a chisel to stone or made anything three-dimensional, so this place holds unattainable mystery for me."

"So he wasn't a vampire?" Emelia asked, inspecting a carved marble panel.

"No. He died in 2001. Buried here in Houston. He sculpted his own tombstone before he died! Remarkable guy. He's got some sculptural installations around town. Let me show you the *pièce de resistance* down here." He led her to the back of the shop. Mounted on a pillar was a white marble bust of a woman wearing a Greek helmet. Perched on her shoulder was a stuffed raven, its black feathers and bill gray with dust.

"Pallas Athena!" she said, smiling. "Quoth the Raven!"

"Janos was a Poe fan, sure enough," Alex said. "Come look at this." He led her to a gilded frame that held, beneath glass, a carved wooden panel with a large bas-relief scarab beetle. The beetle's carapace was skull-shaped, and it glimmered golden in the natural light from a nearby window.

"It's the Gold Bug, after Poe's short story of the same name," Alex noted. "It's one of only two wood carvings he did. A collector bought the other one, but I don't know anything else about it.

"Gold leaf?" Emelia asked, pointing to the finish on the bug.

Alex nodded. "I think so. Somewhere in a drawer in here is a little booklet of gold leaves and some soft brushes for burnishing. Pretty sure that's what he used."

She turned to him. "Thank you for sharing Janos' work with me. But I must admit: I am dying to see some work by another particular artist." She poked her index finger into his chest.

"Then the time has come to brave the four-legged beasts," he said. "Up we go!"

## 18

—·—

Emelia followed Alex as he ascended the concrete ramp. At the top, his dogs shivered and shimmied. The white lab spun around a few times. "That's Dizzy, of course, and Midnight is the black one." Emelia let them sniff her hands, and she petted them as best she could. Glad she had worn jeans today, she stepped over the top of the baby gate one leg at a time, and the dogs ran around her, wagging their tails. The dogs were good-sized and could easily have leaped over the baby gate at any time. *$700 well spent.*

Alex led her to a door in the wall ahead, fitted with a large dog door in its lower half. They passed through the door, with the canines following close behind. They were in a kitchen that, though it was clean, looked disused. There was a range with four burners, but they looked brand new, as if they had just been installed. There was a coffeemaker on the counter, along with bagged coffee and some filters. She couldn't resist opening a cabinet or two, only to discover that they were devoid of dishes or anything except for a row of wine glasses, a few coffee mugs, and some tumblers. Alex stood by as she opened drawers, finding no utensils or cookware of any kind. Meanwhile, the two dogs sniffed around the kitchen and nudged their stainless-steel dog bowls at the opposite end.

"I tell my housekeeper I eat all my meals out," he said.

Emelia shut an empty drawer and said, "I guess that's accurate. Doesn't she suspect?"

"She is very well-paid and convinced that her boss is a rich eccentric. I sometimes bring home empty takeout containers and put them in the trash to convince her she's right." He waved a hand and said, "There's wine and beer in the fridge, and dog food in the pantry. That's about it."

"I confess I never expected—" she trailed off. "But then why would I?"

"Fair enough."

He led her down a short hallway and commenced to give her a tour of the second-floor living quarters, with the two dogs following. The overall aesthetic was that of a modern gallery: white walls along with stained and finished concrete floors with terrazzo accents. The high ceilings had bleached wooden arched trusses. The ceiling echoed the *tip-tip-tip* of the dogs' claws on the floor. A few of his paintings adorned the walls down here, including a Max Ellis pointillist work called *Dogs in the Park* and a small Jackson Williams abstract called *Experiment in Reds*. But much of the artwork on this floor was done by other local artists. "Houston's got a vibrant art scene, and artists love to collect art by colleagues," Alex noted as they paused in front of a large abstract painting called *Topsy Turvy IV*.

The living room had a gigantic television opposite the couch, with bookshelves on either side packed with hardcovers and paperbacks. There it was, tucked between the art books. "Hey!" she cried as she pulled out a slim green hardback. It was *The Oil Heresies* by Jamison Cooper.

Alex laughed. "Cue the *You're So Vain* song."

Emelia replaced the book and turned to see that the dogs were sitting on the couch, tongues lolling from their mouths. "They kinda own all padded horizontal surfaces," Alex noted.

But Emelia's attention had been drawn to the arched window off to the left. Next to it, its white marble glowing in the sunlight, was a full figure statue of Edgar Allan Poe, pen in hand, glancing sadly down at a sheet of paper at his feet.

"Janos?" she asked, admiring it.

"Yes. One of the finished works I bought from his estate. It's called *Poe's Lament*."

"Okay, I love this," Emelia said. "That likeness!"

"He captured him, all right," Alex said.

In the opposite corner was an ornate black metal spiral staircase leading up to the third floor. Emelia pointed at it. "Is that where the magic happens?"

"Well," Alex said with a sigh, "There hasn't been as much magic as I'd like of late, but that's the studio floor. C'mon."

As they approached the staircase, she stopped. "I think I've seen that staircase before. It looks really familiar."

"My turn to quote literature: *No live organism can continue for long to exist sanely under conditions of absolute reality; even larks and katydids are supposed, by some, to dream.*"

She gasped. "Shirley Jackson. *The Haunting of Hill House*. But this is from the movie, right?"

"Yes. *The Haunting*, directed by Robert Wise. My favorite book and my favorite movie, personified," he said.

"I'm more partial to *We Have Always Lived in the Castle*, truth be told."

"Merricat, Merricat, come out and play," Alex said.

She laughed. "Not quite, but close enough for government work!"

They were at the staircase now. Emelia reached out and tested the black metal rail with her hand. "Is this thing gonna go all wonky like in the movie?"

"It's perfectly safe. This isn't the actual one that was in the movie. Just a reproduction I had built. After you."

*This man*, she thought as she started up the staircase toward the third floor, which already offered a tantalizing partial view of what was likely one of his Jackson Williams canvases. *This amazing man. What the actual hell?*

Emelia emerged into a windowless foyer or antechamber of sorts on the third floor, greeted by the large canvas she had seen before. It was much larger: a finished version of *Experiment in Reds*, occupying nearly the entire wall with long swatches of various darker shades of red against a background of muted grays and blacks. It was the only piece in the room. There was a subtle smell of oil paints and solvents in the air.

His footsteps sounded behind her.

"Not gonna lie," she said, "It looks like rivers of blood."

"The artist working through some stuff," Alex said softly. "You are the first person to see this. Same for everything on this floor. He nodded toward the painting. "It's a reminder of—" He was silent for a moment. "Let's just say it's a reminder."

She turned and hugged herself. A shiver passed through her. "Not a fan of this one."

He nodded. "It's okay. This is a very personal work."

He led her through an arched doorway. The studio was a vast open space with metal trusses supporting the ceiling. Skylights added light to the banks of fluorescent tubes in reflectors suspended by chains. There was a riot of tables and easels with paintings in various stages of completion. The oil-and-solvent smell was much stronger and dried spills of paint marred the concrete floor. There were dozens of cans of brushes and palette knives, as well as innumerable tubes and bottles of paints. Gallon cans of solvents and varnishes were here and there. Paint-stained metal sinks lined one windowless wall. The opposite wall had three of the arched windows, closely spaced, offering a spectacular triptych view of the Houston skyline. Emelia shivered. Her voice echoed in the space as she said softly, "Wow."

"Frankenstein's workshop," he said jovially. "Only with canvas and paint."

Emelia walked over to view the completed works on the north wall. "Works by Max Ellis and Jackson Williams hanging side by side," she said. "Your life in microcosm."

She wandered around the rest of the studio for several long minutes, surveying the various works, feeling like a kid in a candy shop. *This is where Max Ellis used to work and where Jackson Williams works now—it really is.* As she walked around, she noticed that a disproportionate number of the pieces were only partially completed. She called out to him. "Is there such a thing as painter's block?"

He sighed and said nothing. She came over to where he stood and looked at him. "I'll take that as a yes. What's going on, Alex?"

He shrugged. "The muse seems to have fled in recent months. I've completed and sold a few pieces over the past eight months—two of those Jackson paintings on the north wall are spoken for—but a lot of these pieces just don't jazz me after I get to a certain point. So I start something new. Rinse and repeat, unfortunately."

"Something to do with Titus?" she asked.

"No. He only appeared recently, as you know."

His dismayed expression tugged at her heart. She wanted to take things slow, but her attraction to him had grown steadily since arriving here. *Emelia, what the hell?*

Her natural bluntness pushed her to say it: "I know this sounds kinda crazy given how long we've known each other," she said, stepping a little closer, invading his space. "But I really badly want to kiss you."

He closed the space between them, and there was a delicious frisson of anticipation at his nearness. "I've been wanting that too," he said, his voice almost a whisper. Their gazes met: his eyes dark green and hers limpid gray-green. And then it happened.

At first, it was disconcerting enough for her to open her eyes in surprise. His lips and tongue were cool, and his mouth had a slight, odd taste to it. *You've kissed people who smoke. Deal with it.*

She was surprised that, after a moment, his mouth absorbed the warmth from hers. She closed her eyes and, enclosed in his strong arms, leaned into his embrace. It became very good.

After a long moment, they gently parted with that peculiar sound that can only signal the end of a kiss. Emelia, still in his embrace, looked into his eyes and smiled. "I really wanted that," she said, her voice a little breathless.

He smiled back. "Me too."

"Seconds?" she asked.

He leaned in and kissed her again. This time, it was very good from the start.

# 19

<br>

A short while later they descended to the second-floor kitchen (much to the excitement of Dizzy and Midnight) and Alex poured a beer for Emelia and decanted a tumbler of an excellent Chilean Cabernet Sauvignon for himself. The dogs capered and whined, and Alex said, "Feeding time!"

He scooped kibble for them and added fresh water to their water bowl. Emelia beamed at him.

He returned and they clinked glasses. "Is everyone happy?" he asked, glancing over at the dogs noisily crunching their kibble. Emelia laughed. She looked up at him and said impishly, "Don't think I don't know that this is, um, the *bedroom* floor."

Alex sipped his wine. His stomach fluttered a bit. He'd been wondering what happened next. "It's the everything floor," he stammered. "Except for workshop and gallery spaces."

"Let's go join Edgar Allan for now," Emelia said. Relieved, Alex followed her into the living room. They sat down on the couch. Emelia placed her drink on the glass end table and said, "Alex, don't think for a moment that I don't want you. I do, more than I care to admit."

Alex remained silent, as she clearly had something important to say.

"But I'd like to take things slow for a bit, if that's okay."

"It's perfectly okay. It's been a whirlwind!"

"Yes: a new thing for us both, and, well, I've got questions."

He nodded. "I understand. You *are* Question Girl, after all."

She smiled at him and leaned in to give him a quick peck on the lips. "I'm making you nervous. I don't mean to."

He took a deep breath. "Not gonna lie," he said, mimicking her statement from a while back. "I am definitely nervous."

"Me too. More reason for us to take this slow."

"Sure."

She laughed. "I feel like I'm sitting with my aunt back in Oregon and she's trying to explain the birds and the bees." She laughed again.

Alex couldn't think of anything to say. Listening seemed better at this point.

"Poor baby," she said. "Your expression! Put your drink down for a minute."

He set his glass on the end table, leaning across her to do so. She grabbed him by the lapels with both hands and kissed him passionately. Her mouth had a delicious smoky taste from the beer. As far as Alex was concerned, they could have continued for hours. He lifted his arm to hold her, and it brushed against her breast. She moaned but broke the kiss. "Ay yi yi," she said.

"Sorry about that."

"Don't be. Feel a little less nervous now?"

He smiled. "A little."

"Okay. Question Girl time: have you ever made love to a, well, a non-vampire woman since Silana?"

"No. It's a little embarrassing, but there's been no one, human or vampire, since her."

"I aim to change that—" she said simply. "After some information gathering. First things first: can humans and vampires have sex?"

"Yes. But they can't have children."

"Check. Can vampires have sex with other vampires?"

"Yes," he said. "I know of several couples, including married couples. But again, no children."

"Okay. All the mechanics pretty much the same, including, um, the Big O?"

*Direct as ever*, he thought. "I'm assuming so."

he glanced up at the ceiling and took a deep breath before returning her gaze to him. "You haven't had an orgasm with a woman for *nine decades*?"

Alex couldn't find any words. She came close to him again, her eyes bright and guileless. "Alex, I'm so sorry I said that. It wasn't a judgment. It's just my scientist's mind being blunt. Please please forgive me." She kissed him again, pressing her body against him. His erection pressed against his jeans. His only thought was *well, that still works*. Emelia must have noticed too, because she drew back. Glancing down at his jeans, she said, "So that's some good news."

It caught him off guard and he laughed in spite of himself. "Whew!" he said. She laughed again.

"This is, I'm betting, the most bizarre conversation I think either of us has ever had," she said.

"By far. Listen, Emelia. I know we've only known each other for a few days, but I really like you. It seems like it happened so fast."

She nuzzled up against him. "Research indicates that adrenaline and/or shared danger or discovery can accelerate feelings of closeness. Who are we to argue with science?"

He gently squeezed her. She felt so good in his arms.

The two dogs came bounding in and leaped up onto the couch, tails wagging. Midnight licked Emelia on the cheek. "There goes our romantic moment," she said cheerfully.

"Damned mutts," he said, smiling.

"Don't say that! Midnight loves me already." She patted the dog's head.

Alex laughed. Tension leached out of his body. Eager for a change in subject, he said, "While you were touring the workshop, did any of the paintings jump out at you? As something you'd want for our trade? I thought if you saw something you liked, I could finish it for you. Or maybe one of the finished works?"

She put her hands on her heart and frowned. "Would you be terribly upset if I said no? I don't know why, but—"

"No, it's okay. Because I have a much better idea."

She looked relieved. "I'm all ears."

"Brace yourself, Emelia Cord. I'm going to give you *Sunlight on Boughs*."

She gasped and went silent for a moment. "But it belongs—it belonged to Lenny."

"I know, but as they say in the old detective movies, I got an angle."

She fell against him, hugging him. "Oh, Alex!" He held her in silence for a long time after that.

Donnie Borowicz looked up from his phone as the electronic door chime sounded. As the compact man in an impeccable black business suit approached, Donnie said, "Welcome to AmmoRite."

The man had olive skin, dark hair, and was well-muscled with thick, knobby hands. *A goombah if I ever saw one*, Donnie thought. He smiled and said, "We carry a full line of guns, but specialty ammo is, well, our specialty."

"It is well, then," the man said. Donnie couldn't place the accent. *Can't keep track of all the goddamn greaser dialects.*

The man went on. "I require a special type of buckshot loaded into shotgun shells."

"This for home defense, sir?" Donnie asked.

"It is so. I must explain. I work for an eccentric man who has a morbid fear, a phobia if you will, of being devoured by werewolves."

Donnie just stared. *A crazy goombah.*

The man nodded and smiled. "Indeed, it sounds insane to me as well. But he is my employer, and I am—" he cleared his throat. "*Well-paid* to indulge his flights of fancy."

"Werewolves?"

Another nod. "It is so. *Canis lycanthropus*. Seen in many movies. Very violent creatures. My employer saw perhaps too many of those movies as a child and his morbid fear took root. It has grown over the years as a phobia is wont to do."

"So silver buckshot is what you're looking for?"

The man produced a small notebook and opened it. Glancing down at the page, he said, "Specifically, my employer wants 12-gauge, eight-pellet, double A buckshot in standard shotgun shells." He paused and pulled a gleaming metallic bar from his pocket. It was about the size of a matchbox, and he laid it on the counter. Donnie's eyes widened. "Bullion?" he asked.

"It is so. This particular bar is worth about $360 on the market. Purity is important to my employer. Can you convert this to 12-gauge pellets?"

"Yes, sir!" Donnie said, his eyes bright. "We'll have to use steel molds, but yeah, we can do that."

"How many shells would a bar like this provide?"

Donnie pulled out a small electronic scale. He weighed the bar and scribbled a calculation on some scratch paper with a pen. "This one here, at about 283 grams'll get you a standard load of about 8 shells. Perfect load for a tactical home defense shotgun.

The man nodded. "We will require fifteen of these, as you call them, perfect loads. So 120 shells in total, according to your calculations."

"Whew," Donnie said. "You got that much silver laying around?"

"We will procure the requisite amount of silver bars and provide them to you, yes."

Donnie paused, doing some math in his head. The amount of silver needed would sell for about $5400. He remembered his late mom, who had a diamond ring appraised by a crooked jeweler who had "taken it in the back" to appraise it and returned her ring with an inferior diamond he had quickly mounted in place of the original diamond. The shit diamond looked the same to the naked eye. Donnie started to hatch a plan.

"How," the man said, "would one check for authentic silver pellets?"

"Oh, that's easy," Donnie said. "A simple magnet will work. Silver is a non-ferrous metal, so a magnet won't stick to it. Here, lemme show you." He reached under the case and brought up a disk-shaped magnet mounted with a plastic handle and a single shotgun shell.

"This has steel buckshot in it." He demonstrated how the magnet clicked up against the plastic shell casing but did not stick to the silver bar.

"Ah," said the man. His dark little eyes surveyed Donnie's face for a moment. *I'm a poker player, bro*, Donnie thought. *No tells here.*

Finally, the man smiled and nodded. "A very simple method. It is good."

"You provide the silver bars, and I'll do up the shells for, say, $8000."

"Very good," the man said.

"You need any shotguns for these?"

"Thank you, no," the man replied. "We have the weapons on hand." He retrieved the silver bar. "How long will it take?"

"Well," Donnie said, "I got the molds on hand. Coupla days once we have the silver."

"That is acceptable. A man will deliver the silver before 5 p.m. today. We will make payment upon delivery of the shells."

Donnie nodded and smiled. "Sounds good. Your boss won't have to worry about werewolves at all."

"I'm sure he will be glad to feel safe. Good day." He turned to leave.

"See you in a few days," Donnie called out as the man left.

Once he was gone, Donnie said, "*Easy money, easy money*," as he dialed his phone. He held it to his ear and after a few rings, a voice said, "What?"

"Spider, Donnie. I'm going to need about 75 pounds of tin, ready to be melted down and poured into molds. It's a rush job."

# 20

—·—

The late-afternoon sun shone golden through the arched windows. They were on their third drink, and Alex had called out to order pizza since there was nothing in the house. As they sat next to each other on the couch, he said, "A while back Lennie told me that if anything ever happened to him, he wanted those paintings to go back to me. But it depends on whether he amended his will to reflect that. We won't know until after probate."

"And if they didn't make it into the will?" she asked.

"Then it's plan B: the Janos solution. I'll buy it back from the estate."

"Well, I hope it's plan A," she said. "Okay, I'm a little tipsy, and it always interferes with me remembering things that I want to ask you, so I need to ask before I forget: tell me more about that pheromone thing."

"We call it a charisma pheromone," he said. "In scientific terms, it aids in the hunt. The pheromone retards inhibitions and creates a sense of trust and friendliness in the, um—"

"Prey," she said. Without missing a beat, she said, "Another amazing adaptation."

He nodded. "It's useful in many situations other than feeding. Lasts for about a half hour. Kind of an ace in the hole."

She set her glass down on the end table and nodded. "Okay."

He looked at her, eyebrows raised. "Okay, what?"

She leaned toward him, smiling. "I'm ready to experience it. The charisma pheromone. For science."

He sighed. *I wish that pizza would arrive.*

"No, Emelia," he pleaded. "Since I met you, I promised myself I wouldn't use it on you. I wanted you to like me organically. Like me for me."

"I do, Alex," she said, stroking his cheek with her hand. "I already find you intensely charismatic. For you. How much more could there be?"

He smiled at her. "Maybe another time. Will you trust me on this one? Please?"

She nodded, frowning. "Science delayed is science denied."

He laughed. "I think you're thinking of justice."

She belched and her hand went to her mouth. "Oops!" she said and giggled.

The doorbell rang. "Saved by the bell," he said over the cacophony of dogs barking.

He went down to the first floor at the front of the house, via a narrow set of stairs. In the small foyer, he shooed the dogs back from the doggie door, which was locked. Edging out of the door, he went across the lawn, unlocked the front gate and paid for the pizzas. "Thank you, sir!" the delivery guy said when he saw the generous tip. "De nada," he said.

Alex ran the gauntlet of pizza-hungry dogs and made his way back to the second floor. He parked the pizzas out of canine reach on the counter and went to the living room. She was gone. He called her name and heard her voice from upstairs. He started up the spiral staircase, but she appeared and came down, her shoes echoing on the metal steps.

"Two things," she said, following him toward the kitchen.
"Yes?"

"I still don't like that painting at the top of the stairs."
"Noted. And?"

"And that workshop is amazing, except for one thing."
"I'm all ears."

"I'm the in-house OSHA liaison at See Deeper. All those cans of solvents and varnishes? Not a fire extinguisher to be seen. You're in big trouble with Emelia, mister." She smiled and kissed him. He leaned into the kiss, but the dogs started barking from the kitchen.

"It's the pizza alarm!"

"I'm starved!" she said. "Let's go."

After Emelia ate dinner at the counter—a necessary thing because the dogs were begging for pizza—she and Alex snuggled on the couch with beer and wine and watched *Duck Soup*. As the Marx Brothers caromed from one silly set piece to another, Midnight lay nestled against Emelia and Dizzy had settled next to Alex. As Chico Marx called out "Pea-NUTS," Emelia said, "This is cozy."

"It is," he agreed. After a pause, he said, "I was wondering if I could be Question Guy for a second."

"Ask."

"Do you have anyone in your recent history? Romantically, I mean."

"Well, you definitely deserve to know. It's been a bit of a dry spell for me until very recently."

"Oh?"

She nodded. "I had a one-night stand when I first got to Houston. It was nice enough for one night, but she was on the rebound."

"I regret to say," she continued, "that sparks did not fly. No, wait, I don't regret that. Because I was saving my sparks for you." She poked him and made a *zzzzt* sound.

He poked her back and made the same *zzzzt* sound. She laughed and they shared a languorous kiss. It became more passionate, and she climbed astride him, kissing him deeply and running her fingers through his hair. Alex's erection returned and she broke the kiss. Glancing down, she said. "Oh no, look what I did!"

He laughed.

"I've had a bit too much to drink," she said, climbing off him. "I think I'd better get a rain check for the rest of the movie. Drive me back to my car before I get carried away?"

"Okay."

"Thank you. It's just a little too soon, is all."

"Even with sparks flying?" he said as they stood.

She smiled at him. "Precisely because sparks are flying. I kinda want to savor it. Does that make sense?"

"Yes."

Midnight whined. Emelia bent down and kissed her snout. "Don't worry, Midnight. I'll be back soon, okay?" She went over to Dizzy, who was panting happily. She scratched him behind the ears. "I'll see you soon, too Dizzy."

Emelia dozed as Alex drove her back. He glanced at the illuminated clock on the console. It was 10:22 p.m. In the soft light of streetlights and traffic lights, he stole moments to watch her as she slept. She looked serene. *How did I suddenly get so lucky?*

She woke and stretched as they pulled up next to her car at the restaurant. "How was dreamland?" Alex asked.

She yawned. "This whole day has been dreamlike." She patted him on the thigh. "Thank you, Alex."

"You are most welcome, Emelia."

She reached for the door handle and then stopped. "Now I don't want to go back to the hotel."

"The power of Midnight compels you!"

She laughed and play-punched him. "I already *love* our dogs—I mean *your* dogs! Paging Dr. Freud!"

They both laughed.

She got out of the car and came around to his window. He rolled it down. Somewhere out in the darkness, a mockingbird sang. Emelia leaned in, close to his ear, and whispered, "*Journeys end in lovers meeting.*" It was from *The Haunting of Hill House.* Then she kissed him softly and went to her car.

As Alex watched her drive off, he listened to the mockingbird's asymmetric song and let himself get lost in that dreamy moment of profound connection.

## 21

The next morning, Emelia and Melanie sat facing each
other on the double beds in Melanie's hotel room. "I'm
sorry," Melanie said, dabbing at her eyes and nose with tissues.
"It's unprofessional to cry."

"If anyone needs to apologize, it's me," Emelia replied. She
was a little hung over from her amazing day with Alex, but
business was business. "I've been a shitty boss, and I apologize
for being distracted over the past couple of days."

"Well, you can't help it if your mom was sick," Melanie said,
dabbing at her nose.

*Now I really feel like a shitty boss*, Emelia thought. *Ugh.*

"Listen, Melanie. This business is a little like filmmaking.
Have you done any acting?"

"A little. Just some plays in college."

"I was an extra for two nights while they were shooting *Stars
in Her Eyes* in Atlanta before I started working for See Deeper."

"I saw that movie!" Melanie said. "You're in that?"

"For about six seconds over two different scenes. Filmmaking
is mostly hurry up and wait. They have to set up the cameras
and lighting and sound equipment and it takes *for-ev-er*!"

Melanie nodded. She had stopped crying. Emelia felt a little
better.

"And then you do a couple of takes and the director says 'cut'
and all the cameras and junk have to be reset to new angles or
whatever. I spent all night sitting on my ass on a stone bench

downtown between takes. I could barely walk at the end of the night."

"Working for See Deeper can be like that," she went on. "Long stretches of nothingburger and maybe you come away with a pet will-o'-the-wisp after being electro-stung fifty times. Fucking thing stung me in the nipples!"

Melanie sighed. The humor seemed lost on her. "I had a fight with David during my downtime," she said, on the verge of tears again. "He wants to move back to Georgetown."

"I'm sorry about that, but I might have a solution as well. You did some programming in the tech department, right?"

"Yeah. With Rick Emerson. He and I wrote some code for the VPDs."

Emelia came and sat next to her on the bed. "What would David say if he were married to a full-fledged Investigative Agent for See Deeper?"

"Really?" she cried. Her eyes were wide.

"You're about the tenth trainee I've worked with, and you are utterly the sharpest, smartest one of the bunch."

Melanie smiled, speechless.

"Now listen to me. I've got some stuff going on at the moment that is a giant distraction for me. Might involve a guy. Might not. I can't really talk about it at the moment. But here's the deal: In a day or two, Dr. Chavez is going to send us some new code for the VPDs. Rick's working on it now, back at the shop. I want you to integrate it into our two VPDs. You can Zoom with Rick if you need to. But if the new code works like I hope it does, and, well, even if it doesn't, I'm going to immediately request you be promoted to Investigative Agent with Mark Petrovsky. You've already had your supplementary training at Quantico."

Melanie's eyes brimmed with tears again. "You'd do that for me?"

Emelia put her arm around Melanie. "Damn straight I will. But be ready for the ups and downs of the job. And most of all,

I ask that you be patient with me if I'm not around as much as you might like during this investigation. I want you to pick up the slack, if necessary. I'll back you up if need be. That's all I ask."

The tears came freely, and Emelia held her while she cried. "Mark is a great boss. When I chose you to come with me, he said, 'girl power.' So, girl power, okay?" She held up a fist.

Melanie smiled through her tears and fist-bumped Emelia. "Girl power," she said.

"Good. I'm glad we had this talk, Investigative Agent Sanders."

Melanie hugged her. Emelia hugged her back.

A few hours later, Emelia carried a VPD as she navigated the hallways at the Houston FBI field office and found the conference room. She showed her temporary badge to the agent standing near the door and he checked a tablet he was holding. He nodded to her. "Go ahead in, Agent Cord."

"Thank you, Agent Grant," she said and entered the room. It looked to be a small meeting. She spotted Alison and a few men who looked from their dress to be FBI, a couple of HPD lieutenants, and, at the head of the table, a thin man with stern features and unkempt-looking tousled black hair. She sat across from Alison and met her gaze. "Hey," she said with a smile, using the familiar greeting of southerners.

"Agent Cord," Alison said. Her face had a deliberate, neutral set to it: no spark of friendliness or familiarity could be seen. *Uh-oh*, Emelia thought.

The man at the head of the table spoke. "I think that's everyone, so we're going to start. I'm Jack Crain, Special Agent in Charge of this field office." He gestured toward Alison's side of the table. "This is my second in command, Assistant Special

Agent in Charge Joe Plackett, Special Agent Danny Mix from Behavior Analysis in Quantico, Special Agent Alison Martin, our point agent in charge of this investigation, and that is Senior Investigative Agent Emelia Cord with the CPDR—"

"CDPR, sir," Emelia corrected him. "Combined Departments of Paranormal Research."

Crain frowned. "Yes, thank you Agent Cord." He went on, "Next to Agent Cord is Lieutenant Minh Nguyen and Lieutenant Martin Genner of HPD."

Crain cleared his throat. "Circumstances have not permitted a meeting like this until now, so apologies for that. As most of you know, political and public pressure to resolve this investigation is mounting. Local media is calling this guy "The Vision Killer" and national media is following suit. The appellation comes from the victims whose eyes are gouged out. I regret to say that the word 'vampire' is being bandied about because of the bloodless bodies. Therefore, we are partnering with the CPDR in this investigation." Emelia decided not to correct him a second time. *Is he really doing this deliberately?*

Crain looked at her. "Agent Cord, I believe the acronym regarding these bloodless corpses is APES, correct?

"Yes, sir," Emelia said. *Well, he got that one right.* "It stands for Anomalous Profound Exsanguination Syndrome. It's been seen in many cases in the states, but there are a disproportionate number of cases in these recent killings. The bodies are essentially drained of blood but there are no unusual wounds, penetrative or otherwise, that would suggest a mechanism for the blood being absent."

Crain nodded. "This has been an area of ongoing study at CPDR, correct?"

*Wow*, Emelia thought, certain now that he was doing it on purpose. "Yes, sir," she replied. "Our agents have examined APES corpses in nearly every state for several years."

Crain nodded. "And your findings?"

"Inconclusive, sir. We've published classified papers on this. They incorporate relevant in-depth studies by medical examiners and other professionals. I sent you those files before I was dispatched here."

"Yes," he said a little too quickly. "For the edification of those present can you give us the overview?"

Emelia nodded. "Honestly, sir, we've been at a loss to explain the phenomenon. We were hoping our involvement in this investigation might shed more light on it."

"I spoke briefly with your boss Mark Petrovsky a few days ago and he mentioned a theory of yours. Some kind of mysterious vampire-like beings?"

"Yes, sir, but it's only speculation, given the lack of evidence suggesting otherwise."

"Can you elucidate for us?"

*He's really putting me on the spot.* "Astral vampires, sir. Possibly extra-dimensional beings that somehow remove the blood from the victims using some heretofore unknown mechanism."

"Indeed," he said, his features tight with disdain. He turned to Agent Mix. "Danny, what have we got profile-wise from Behavioral Analysis on this killer?

The heavyset man looked uncomfortable. "Well, sir, we are still working on compiling a workable profile and modus operandi for the killer. A few things are clear. A disproportionate number of his victims seem to be minorities, so a racist element may be at work. He leaves some bodies in that, um, APES condition, but the others are mutilated: eyes gouged out and throats cut or stabbed in the chest with a sharp, non-serrated blade. Gouging out the eyes seems to be a symbolic act, a ritual of some sort. But he doesn't do that to the APES bodies.

"We have a physical description," he went on, "From a single 11-year old male Hispanic witness at the first incident at the carnival. Thin old man, black suit, bald but fringe of long white hair. The boy said he was kissing one of the victims on the neck. We think that it was the APES victim that disappeared from the morgue. He glanced at a tablet in front of him. "Caucasian female, 20 years old. Her name was Bonnie Glaser. Initial examination of her neck showed bloodstains but no penetrative marks at all. Just normal healthy skin. No penetrative marks elsewhere on her body. She vanished before a postmortem could be scheduled."

"Can we expect this perp to strike again?" Crain asked.

"Yes sir. We feel that is inevitable."

"Any pattern-based evidence for when we might expect for that to happen?"

"No sir," Mix said. "We're operating off statistical serial killer modi operandi for the moment."

Crain looked around the table and sighed. "We're gonna have to do better than space aliens stealing blood and bodies," he said. He turned to Alison. "Agent Martin, anything substantive to add?"

"Not at this time, sir," she said, refraining from making eye contact with him.

"Excuse me, sir," Emelia said. She tapped the VPD. "But at the last killing, we—"

"Thank you, Agent Cord. We are going to let you continue to chase phantoms and space vampires, and we will offer what help we can, but I need information grounded in actual facts. I'm going to adjourn the meeting now. Needless to say, people: we need to do better. Go forth and do that."

Emelia glanced across the table at Alison. She indicated Crain with her eyes and then shook her head slightly. *Don't* seemed to be the message. Emelia nodded and filed out with the others.

Emelia was just about to pull out of her parking space when Alison ran across the grassy esplanade to the parking lot and her car. Emelia rolled the window down, wondering *what now*?

Alison said a little breathlessly, "Sorry about what happened in there."

"Your boss is a piece of work," Emelia said.

"If by that you mean he's a prick, then yes."

Emelia nodded. "Kind of a chilly reception from you at the beginning."

"I apologize for that. I kinda got the feeling that it's not going any further with us and I felt hurt. I wanted there to be more, is all."

Emelia was silent for a moment. She didn't want to respond with platitudes. "Alison, you're a kickass Special Agent, and I want to remember our night together fondly. But—"

"I know," Alison said. "It's okay. I'll try to remember it fondly as well." She held out her hand. "Friends and colleagues?"

Emelia took her hand and squeezed it. "Friends and colleagues," she said with a smile.

"Jack Crain may not respect See Deeper, but I do. I want you to know that. An attitude like his can actually hurt an investigation."

"I'm certainly disinclined to interact with him on any meaningful level."

"I know. Hey, I could stand around and make this uncomfortable, but I'm gonna go. Thank you for a wonderful night and I'll see you at work."

"I look forward to that."

Alison nodded with a sad smile. Then she turned and walked away.

Emelia felt a bittersweet twinge as she watched Alison retreat. "I wish you love and success, Alison Martin," she said quietly.

Just after noon on the same day, Alex watched Emelia enter Desdemona from the booth they had sat at just the day before.

She was dressed in a black skirt and another long-sleeved white cotton blouse with a tie. She saw him and smiled and came over. "Same table?" she said as she approached. "I'm going to start thinking of it as *our* table if you're not careful."

He laughed. "Then I don't want to be careful." She leaned down and kissed him on the lips. She was wearing perfume today and the floral aroma swirled in his nostrils.

Sliding into the seat opposite him, Emelia saw the menu open in front of her. She said, "Very thoughtful of you, sir. I see you have some wine going there."

He lifted the glass and smiled. "Day drinking for the win."

She smiled and then pored over the menu. "Chicken-fried steak sounds good, but it's invariably really good or really bad," she said. Then she looked up at him. "I've been so anxious to see you I could barely concentrate on work this morning. The FBI director at the field office is a real jerk."

"Unfortunately, this may be the only chance we have to see each other today," he said. "I have kung fu with Sun, and then firearms practice, and then—"

"Wait," she said. "Firearms practice? You didn't mention that before. What kind of firearm would hurt an indestructible vampire?"

*Idiot*, Alex thought. It had just rolled out and now he was on the spot. He suddenly faced the dilemma of lying to this marvelous woman or telling the truth again.

"That's the secret, right?" she said. "I can see the wheels turning in your mind."

He nodded; pretty sure he had that guilty dog look that he saw in Midnight and Dizzy when he admonished them.

She leaned across the table, those gray-green eyes pleading. "Alex, please don't start our relationship with lies. Please."

It did not escape his attention that she had just used the R-word.

"It's silver," he said, whispering as though there was a listening device attached to the underside of the table. "Silver is toxic to vampires." *Now you've given it all away.*

"Silver?" she said thoughtfully. "Isn't that for werewolves?"

"Misdirection," he said. "Vampires spread that folklore in antiquity so that people would associate silver with werewolves and not vampires."

"Are there really werewolves?" she asked.

"No," he said. "But the average superstitious peasant didn't know that."

"Anything else toxic to vampires?"

"Silver is pretty much it. It's our most closely guarded secret."

"And they'd hunt you like you are hunting Titus if it got out. You said that."

He sighed. "I suppose. But they're a bunch of cowards. That's the real truth. It feels like they could barely even get me to pursue Titus. I didn't even want to do that at first."

"What changed your mind?"

Alex felt like going for broke. He was deep in unknown territory with Emelia. It felt crazy but *fuck it.* "A teenaged prostitute named Jellybean. I did a full feed on her in Malibu many years ago. She died in my arms."

Her eyes went wide. "You uttered that when you first saw me. Jellybean."

For a moment, as he teetered on the edge of tears, his admiration for her glowed. She was so sharp.

"Your eyes," he said, suddenly overcome by a huge swell of emotion. Tears streamed down his cheeks. "Her eyes."

She slid out of her seat and hurried to embrace him. "Alex, Alex, baby." She held him tightly as he wept, and it felt so good. Her perfume filled his nostrils. He let himself be held. He hadn't realized how badly he needed it.

She whispered in his ear, "I pledge to you that I will never, ever tell anyone."

Again, whispering to him. "That's all of it, isn't it? Jellybean. That's where it started."

He nodded, tears streaming against her chest. "Oh, sweet Alex," she said, "how can I comfort you? Please tell me how."

He said nothing and, eyes closed, let her hold him until his quiet tears subsided.

# 22

— • —

A little while later Alex watched Emelia as she ate. She attacked the chicken-fried steak with cream gravy and mashed potatoes.

"I'm guessing that's the good iteration of the dish!" he said, laughing.

She smiled between bites. "That it is!"

"I've never wanted to be with you more than today," he said. "But it's a full day for me. Kung fu, firearms practice with Maxie Bright, reach practice with Bardru, and some damned vampire party I got invited to. I am, in a word, booked."

She looked at him while cutting the steak. "Bardru is your uncle, right?"

"He's a lot more like a father. He rescued me when Silana left me to starve."

"Can vampires starve to death?" she asked.

"Yes. It's a long and torturous process. Awful."

"That's why you need aunts and uncles, right?"

He nodded. "Newly made vampires have to be taught—it's not instinctive. That's another Stoker rule."

"it fascinating," she said, "But I interrupted you. Bardru rescued you when Silana left you to starve?"

"Yes. He became my uncle."

"Tell me more about him," she asked.

"He's an old-school vampire with an incredible history. Born in 1846 in Russia. He was a horse trainer and horse wrangler for the Buffalo Bill Wild West show. He has a Master's in Classics from Harvard."

"Okay, I want to meet this Bardru for sure," she said.

"He's a real character. Full of stories."

"Well, that seals it. Now tell me what happens at a vampire party."

He shrugged. "This is the first one I've been invited to. Set up by some rich guy in the Collective. Invitation only. They want to trot me out because I agreed to hunt down Titus."

"Dog and pony show," she observed.

"Yeah. I don't really socialize with a lot of other vampires."

"Any way you can wriggle out of it?" she asked, smiling. "I want to do some socializing with the only vampire I know."

"Nothing would please me more, but some of the fat cats in attendance are financing my training. And Jonas, the leader of the Collective, has been bugging the hell out of me to attend."

"Still slow at work for me, annoying FBI briefings aside," she said. "Tomorrow maybe?"

He nodded. "What if we took tomorrow off and drove down to Galveston? Let the dogs run on the beach and drink margaritas and I could watch you eat a romantic dinner at sunset."

She laughed. "It is a little odd that we can't share a meal like other couples. But I would like that very much. How are the hotels in Galveston?"

He paused and looked at her. "Are you suggesting what I think you are?"

"That I am. I think I'm ready."

"Well, I'll get us a room at the Hotel Galvez. It's right on the Seawall. Very historic. We can drink excellent coffee and watch the sun come up over the Gulf of Mexico."

"I'd like that very much," she replied, sipping her Dr Pepper.

"I'll see to it," he said. He glanced at his phone. "Tempus fugit," he said.

"Let me pay for this real quick," she said about her half-eaten meal. "Sounds silly but I want to make out with you in your car before you leave. I've been dying to kiss you again."

"Who am I to argue with that?" he said, smiling.

Several minutes later they were kissing passionately in his car. Emelia took his hand and moved it to her breast. "Preview of coming attractions," she said and kissed him again. As he ran his hands over her, she moaned and ran her hands over his chest and torso, brushing lightly on his erection a few times. When they broke, she said, "I know you have to go."

"I've never wanted to go less!" he cried.

She laughed and opened the car door. "Go to work, Alex." Then she leaned close to him. "Thank you for confiding in me. We're getting new code for the VPDs tonight. We'll catch him together. You and me."

"Yes," he said.

She climbed out of the car and leaned down. "And make that hotel reservation."

"You got it."

Nighttime had fallen and it was the occasion of what had become informally known among the vampires of Houston as "Gordon's Party," an invitation-only birthday event held yearly at the mansion of Gordon Kliegman, who had made a fortune in the 1970s in oil and gas. Alex and Bardru had been invited for the first time, and they rode in Alex's Miata, navigating the private road through tall pines. The crescent moon was rising over the break in the trees.

"You should think of it as an honor," Bardru said.

"I'm thinking of it as anything but," Alex said. He imagined Emelia in a sundress with the sound of the ocean behind her.

"You are in a bad mood."

"No, there's just someplace I'd really rather be."

"Where?"

"I've been meaning to talk to you about that, but it's an ironclad secret, Uncle. Can you keep it?"

"Have I ever disappointed you in all these decades?" Bardru replied.

Alex turned and smiled at him. "Never."

"Then tell me."

"Very well. There is a woman."

"Splendid!" Bardru cried. He clapped Alex on the shoulder. "After so long!"

"It's been a long time, all right."

"I will tell you: I suspected as much!"

"What?" Alex cried. "How?"

Bardru laughed. He reached out and ran his index finger across the console and then held the fingertip to his nose. "Perfume! She has been in your car, has she not?"

Alex smiled. "You are indeed a wily old cat, Uncle."

Bardru chuckled. "Is she beautiful? Never mind! My nephew would not settle for anything less!"

Alex couldn't help but laugh. "I'm glad to see you so happy, Uncle."

"And why not? Love has long eluded you. It is an occasion for much happiness!"

"That's where I'd rather be tonight. But since I've agreed to do the dirty work for the Collective, I'm a cause célèbre. I certainly never got an invitation to this popularity contest before."

"Nor did I," Bardru said. "I am riding your tails."

"Coattails, Uncle."

"Yes. Are you going to be able to be civil?"

Alex was silent for a few moments. "I guess I can try. Jonas, in his so-called wisdom, has asked me to. He thinks it's important."

"Some of these people are funding your training, yes?"

"Yes, but I can afford that myself, if it comes down to it. I may not have Gordon's money, but I'm not hurting, either."

"It's been a while since you sold a painting," Bardru said.

Alex sighed. "That's true. But there is this thing called a savings account."

Bardru rubbed his hands together. It struck Alex as a very old-world gesture.

"I would be lying if I told you that I am not a little excited about this party, especially in light of your news. But if you decide to leave at any time, I will leave with you."

"I appreciate your resolve, Uncle. Particularly since I am your ride."

Bardru chuckled and poked two fingers into his arm. "Well, yes!"

The car rounded a bend, and the mansion came into sight. It seemed small for a mansion and was done in Georgian style with modest brick and white stone. There was a tall stone wall surrounding it with security cameras placed at intervals. Alex pulled up to a guard shack at the well-lit entrance gate. The guard stepped up holding a tablet in his white-gloved hands.

"Alex Stoica and Bardru Valeska," Alex told him.

The guard glanced at his tablet. "Very well, sir." The guard went back into the shack and pressed a button. The gate swung open.

They parked in the parking area. Alex counted maybe 20 or 30 cars. There was room for maybe twice that.

An attendant opened one of the double doors and they went inside. The mansion was opulent, with marble floors, rich carved and polished wood, and marble columns framing the arched doorways. Jonas was standing near one column and came over. He shook hands with them. "Didn't know if you were going to make it," he said.

"That makes two of us," Alex said.

Jonas nodded. "I know this isn't your kind of thing, but they wanted you here."

The best Alex could manage was a sigh. "Here I am."

Jonas touched him on the shoulder. "I'm sorry to hear about Lennie. Condolences."

"Thank you for saying that. As humans go, he was one of the best."

"Most everyone here has seen a transcript of what Titus said to you. People are jittery, of course. Even more so now. This is a way for them to say thank you for—" he trailed off.

"I know what you mean. Is Tessa here?"

Jonas shook his head. "Not invited. She's home working on a profile of Titus."

"There has been a development that might help me get my hands on an actual FBI profile." Alex said. "Several ifs involved at the moment."

Jonas' blue eyes were bright. "That'd be great. Can you keep me posted?"

"I will."

"Alex!" a voice called out. Gordon Kliegman hurried over. He appeared to be in his sixties and was tall and stately. His much younger wife hung on his arm, slim, beautiful, and silent. She wore a revealing black dress, and her nails and lips were the color of fresh blood.

"Thank you for being here," Gordon said enthusiastically as he shook Alex's hand and turned to Bardru. "You must be Bardu."

"It's BarDRU," Alex said.

"Of course!" Gordon said, shaking Bardru's hand and bowing slightly. "So sorry! Bardru, then! This is my wife, Rita."

The woman remained silent but took Alex's hand and her red lips parted in a smile. Her fangs were evident, as were a smaller but still sharp second pair of fangs where her bicuspids would have been. Alex had heard of a few cases of a deformity called *quadridentalia protrudens*, but this was the first time he'd seen it.

"Rita doesn't talk much," Gordon said as the woman took Bardru's hand, smiling that feral smile again. "Vive la différence, eh?"

Gordon led them down a short hallway and into the ball-room. It had a vast, domed roof from which hung a massive crystal chandelier. Dark blue paint covered the spaces between the arches, and the chandelier's reflections resembled glittering stars.

There were perhaps 30 people there. Some held what looked like stainless steel shot glasses, occasionally sipping from them. Red stains on their lips gave away the contents of the shot glasses.

"Friends!" Gordon called out. "May I introduce our own Alex Stoica, who is working to eradicate the threat to our safety and security."

There was a smattering of quiet applause as might have been heard at a golf match, and a few raised their blood-filled shot glasses in response.

Alex nodded toward the crowd.

Gordon turned to Alex. "Feel free to mingle and get to know the other guests. Help yourself to refreshments. You too, Bardu." Bardru frowned, but Alex led him away.

"To hell with him," Bardru muttered. "Him and his Vampira wife. Such a cliché."

Alex laughed. "And I thought you'd have to be calming me down."

"Bah," Bardru said.

A female attendant clad in white robes and turban came up with a thick black tray. A blue LED light glowed on the edge of the tray. Several of the blood-filled shot glasses sat on it. The attendant held it up to them and Alex sensed warmth from the tray and its contents. Bardru took one of the shot glasses and Alex shook his head at the attendant as she turned to him. "Do you mind, Nephew?" Bardru asked quietly.

"No, Uncle."

The older vampire bowed his head and quietly intoned over the shot glass. "I thank you Christ for this gift and sacrament from one of thy lambs. May it bring me sustenance in thy sight and mercy." He drank, licked his lips and said, "Amen."

A few people came up and introduced themselves and Alex did his best to be polite. He saw Jonas across the room and their eyes met. Jonas nodded. Alex returned the nod.

The attendant walked by with an empty tray and Alex excused himself as Bardru conversed happily with a couple of guests who didn't seem to have trouble with his name.

The attendant went down a hallway and, glancing around, Alex saw that no one happened to be watching her or him, so he elected to follow her. She threaded her way through opulent hallways and down marble steps to a dimly lit room in which ten gurneys had been set up. There were naked humans, male and female, on the gurneys, covered with towels like you might see at a massage parlor. Their eyes were closed but Alex discerned sluggish, sedated breathing from all but three of them. Two more female attendants were draining blood from an intravenous port on a fourth. One of the heated trays sat on a stool next to the body. The three dead bodies had folded cloths over their faces. *This is a pretty picture*, Alex thought with disgust.

He heard a sound behind him and turned to see Rita moving quietly into the room. She walked past him to the attendant Alex had followed, who was placing the heated tray on a stool on the opposite side of the person being drained. Rita, moving as stealthily as a panther, came up behind her. The woman turned, gasped, and her eyes grew wide, but then she relaxed and smiled at Rita. *Charisma pheromone*, Alex thought.

Rita leaned toward the attendant and kissed her on the lips. The attendant smiled as Rita's red lips, trailing lipstick, slid across her cheek and ventured toward her throat. At the far end of the room, the other two attendants were huddled, holding each other. *This is what I'm fighting for?* he thought.

"That's enough now, Rita!" Alex said sternly. She whirled around and silently snarled at him. She had not yet bitten the attendant in her embrace. Rita, her fangs still bared, glanced at the attendant, still smiling happily, and back at Alex. He shook his head and pointed back at the arched entrance. She let go of the attendant and took a step toward Alex, her fingers held out like claws, fangs still bared. Alex assumed the Jeet Kune Do *en garde* stance Sun had taught him, protecting his centerline, and waited for her. Seeing that, her expression changed, mouth closed but eyes wide and staring. With a scowl at the terrified attendants, she walked past Alex and left the room.

Alex followed her back to the ballroom. She never turned back. Spotting them, Gordon hurried up to them. "There you two are," he stammered. "Everything okay?"

"Peachy," Alex said, as he signaled Bardru with a wave. "I'm going to take my leave from this little exercise in genteel barbarity, if it's all the same to you."

As Gordon muttered a few words about *ungrateful upstarts*, Alex strode over and took Bardru by the elbow and the two walked toward the front door. Jonas came up, intent on saying something but Alex shook a finger at him, silencing him. They passed through the open door and into the warm night air.

# 23

The next day was August 27. It was 10:22 a.m. Alex and Bardru sat on one side of the table in a room in the Compound. Jonas and Tessa sat on the other.

Jonas sighed. "Well, that could have gone better."

"Those were *human* servers, or whatever the hell they were," Alex said. "I'm busting my ass to keep our secrets, and Gordon's got humans at his damned party. You think they went back to their day jobs the next day and didn't talk about it to someone?"

Another sigh from Jonas. "Don't be naïve. They never left the party."

"So they were little sweetmeats for dessert," Alex said with disdain. "Awake and ambulatory. And slinky snaggletooth lady was having one a little early." He thought of Rita sneaking back after he left.

Jonas took a deep breath. "You didn't make a very good impression with the people funding your training."

Alex stabbed a finger at Jonas. "I'm not going to dance like a hurdy-gurdy monkey for your creepy friends! They can kiss my ass."

Jonas sighed. "They're not my friends. That was my first time at one of those parties, as well. But the fact is they are part of our community, and they are assisting us when it comes to stopping Titus. My job is to coordinate *everyone* who is helping."

"It's my ass that's on the line," Alex said. "My job is to do the actual goddamn work while they clutch their pearls in their mansions."

Tessa tapped her fingernails on the table. "Let's calm down and talk this out," she said.

"Anyway," Jonas said, his voice measured. "I talked them down from withholding any funding."

"Did you get a little white-turbaned snack for your peace-making?"

Bardru grabbed Alex's arm. "Nephew! That is not helping."

"Emotions are running high," Tessa said. "Let's not escalate."

Alex took a deep breath. "Sorry about that crack."

"No problem," Jonas said. "Tessa, have you got the profile?"

"I do," she said. "Worked all night with that new information Alex gave us."

She slid a piece of paper over to Alex, who, along with Bardru, pored over it.

**Psychological Profile of Titus Seneca by Tessa Cavatore**

His core personality traits include grandiose narcissism, evident in his self-identification as ancient and powerful, demanding recognition of his status. He also exhibits profound misanthropy, seeing humans as "sheep" and demonstrating complete disregard for human life. Sadism is another prominent trait, evidenced by the pleasure he takes in "feeble struggles" and "cries for mercy."

His personality seems to be anchored in ancient Roman culture and status.

As for motivational analysis, his utterance of "And judged me...for *that*" suggests a past trauma or transgression that serves as a primary motivation.

His specific targeting of some victim's eyes suggests a symbolic punishment for those who, in his mind, saw his flaw and were perceived as judging him.

The disproportionate selection of brown and black victims (thus far) suggests either a racial prejudice connected to his ancient Roman worldview, or perhaps a symbolic association between these victims and whatever historical judgment he e xperienced.Titus' behavioral patterns, to this observer, suggest a need for ritualistic killing with consistent use of the sacrificial knife that Titus called a *sescespita*. His dramatic communication style suggests he views his killings as performances or demonstrations of power. That said, his statement that "only these things have amusement for me anymore" indicates escalation potential as he seeks greater stimulation.Assessing the threat: it's important to note that despite his apparent rage, his actions show planning and symbolic purpose. His warning to "not oppose me in my task" indicates he views Houston as his territorial killing ground.His centuries-old pattern suggests deeply ingrained behavior unlikely to stop voluntarily.How do we deal with this? He appears responsive to recognition from "his kind" (we vampires). This may be manipulated through acknowledgment of his status. The evident fatigue in his final words suggests potential psychological exhaustion that could be exploited in some way. Finally, uncovering the specific historical trauma, event or judgment that motivates him could provide leverage or offer some level of predictability.

"Wow, Tessa," Alex said as he finished reading it. "This is impressive."

She nodded. "I didn't put it into the report, but this *sescespita* is similar to something the British call a 'bollock dagger.'"

She handed him a picture of a dagger with elongated spherical crossguards reminiscent of testicles.

"So the dagger is likely a symbolic penis, and it may be a clue to whatever he doesn't want his victims to see. Maybe a sexual deformity or inadequacy of some kind."

"Excellent work," said Jonas. Alex nodded.

Tessa nodded. "In the eyewitness accounts and descriptions this guy appears to be very old, even for a vampire. Wrinkled and emaciated with a fringe of long white hair. He told Alex he is really old: centuries. We have discovered that older vampires in our population often become despondent and depressed as they age. The years pile on, and unless there is something to fill the emptiness of decades, like Alex's art or my writing or Bardru's scholarship, what is left?

"Normally what we see in older vampires who seem to have nothing left is suicide. The best-known case of that is Gerhardt and Nona Diletto, who were both 700 years old. They took capsules of powdered silver with their tea in 1947."

"I heard about them," Bardru said. "Sad."

Tessa nodded. "I was talking with my husband Martin about this, and he said, 'What if this guy is really old *and* mentally disturbed? What if he just craves some kind of stimulation, any kind of stimulation. I mean, for him, what if it's a case of *what does it take to get you out of bed in the morning*?'"

"Seems a little far-fetched," Jonas said.

"No, it tracks with the weariness in the voice, according to Alex," Tessa said. "He's tired of the compulsion, but being a compulsion it won't let him stop. It serves some purpose, some need, along with the symbolic elements like the *sescespita*."

"This is excellent." Alex said. "I may have a line on getting an actual FBI profile, but I can't say more about that at the moment. It's iffy."

Tessa nodded. "An actual Behavioral Analysis profile would help."

"See if you can get hold of one without attracting attention, Alex."

"I will. It's still up in the air, but this gives us something to go on," he said, tapping the paper. "Thank you for your hard work on this, Tessa."

She nodded. "Happy to help."

Alex turned to Bardru, who had several pages of notes in front of him. "Go ahead, Uncle."

Bardru nodded. "Since this began, I have studied many ancient texts and writings, looking for mentions of this Titus Seneca," he said, shuffling the papers. "What I found paints a different picture from his boastful claims."

"Go on, Bardru," said Jonas.

Bardru nodded. "The earliest mention I could discover appears in a fragmentary papyrus from Alexandria, circa 180 of the Common Era—a shipping manifest that lists one 'Titus Seneca' as a minor grain merchant. Very humble beginnings, to be certain.

"More telling is a graffito I found in Mommsen's *Corpus Inscriptionum Latinarum*—scratched into a tavern wall in Pompeii before the great eruption: 'Titus Seneca cheats at dice and waters his wine.' The hand appears to be that of a common soldier. Then there is a legal document from the year 190 which mentions a 'Titus Seneca' accused of selling spoiled fish in the Forum Boarium—the cattle market, you understand, not the Forum Romanum where the senators would gather. The case was dismissed when the accused failed to appear for his trial."

"Could this be our Titus?" Jonas asked. "Could those instances have been written about a different Titus Seneca?"

Bardru inclined his head thoughtfully. "I found myself pondering this very question. But here is what troubles me: if he truly fed upon emperors and high priestesses, *someone* would most certainly have written about it. The Romans—they are famous for documenting everything: murders, scandals, mysterious deaths, even the smallest gossip of the streets. Yet I find

no mention of him whatsoever in the writings of Tacitus, Sue-
tonius, Cassius Dio, or any of the major historians."

The old vampire drew a measured breath. "What I *did* discover are fragments suggesting he was made vampire sometime in the late second century, possibly by misfortune or as
punishment for some transgression. A Christian apologetic text
from Carthage mentions 'the demon Titus, who was cast out
from among the faithful for his blasphemies and unclean ritu-
als'—this has the ring of truth about it.

"The title 'Scornful' appears first in a fourth-century Byzan-
tine manuscript, but the context suggests it referred to his bitter
attitude toward his social superiors, not any grand philosophic
al... what is the word... stance. A petty, dishonest merchant who
became an envious monster. He has nursed centuries of bitter-
ness for never achieving the status he believed he deserved."

"This is amazing," Tessa said. "He's had two millennia to
invent a fictitious, grandiose, narcissistic personal mythology.
And he's done it for so long that now he believes it himself."

"Just so," said Bardru, nodding gravely. "But this is of great
importance: I could find no records of any vampire aside from
him who has ever lived to such an age. He has demonstrated
at least one power I have never encountered in my books or
heard spoken of by any other source: the mind-speaking which
Alexandru experienced."

"Telepathy," Alex said.

"Yes, yes—thank you, my nephew. I fear greatly that he may
possess other unseen powers, or at the very least, immense
strength and what you might call... presence. Even at my modest
age," Bardru held up his weathered hand, "I can crush a brick
to powder with these fingers. However humble his beginnings,
Titus is now a most dangerous adversary, both in his physical
form and in the workings of his ancient mind."

"May I borrow your notes?" Tessa asked. "I'd like to add them
to my profile."

Bardru smiled warmly and slid the papers across to her. "But of course, my dear. I must apologize for my handwriting."

At that moment the door crashed open and Myra Blankenship, the treasurer, burst in. "It's on the news! He struck again."

Alex's Miata tore down 290, its engine roaring. Bardru held the grab handle over the door but didn't complain. Alex was just about to dial Emelia on his phone when she rang through.

"Hey," he said. "Heading into town."

"I'm almost there," she said. "Listen, Alex, there is something important I need to tell you."

"Okay."

"This is just an intuition, but I don't know if it's good for you to be on the scene."

"What do you mean? I keep my fake ID in the glove box."

"It's not that. Well, it's related. You know that female FBI agent in charge of the investigation? Blond woman?"

"Vaguely."

"Special Agent Alison Martin. There's no easy way to say this: she was my one-night-stand when I got to Houston."

"Ay yi yi," he said.

"Hey, that's my line! But yeah. My intuition is this: I think she may have spied on me and seen us together. We were in plain view at that window at the restaurant the day before yesterday. I thought I saw a familiar car across the street, but I blew it off.

"Then I got a *really* chilly reception from her the next morning at the FBI meeting."

"So you think she saw us?" he asked.

"Yeah, I do. She kept hinting she wanted an, uhm, *rematch* under the covers but I wasn't feeling it."

He was silent for a moment. "Saving your sparks for me."

"Yes. And then when she saw me with you, well, I guess she got jealous. I would classify it as a serious complication. Sorry."

"But Emelia, this is a golden chance to track Titus through the Deepest Shadow."

"It *would* be—" she was silent.

"Tell me." Alex had slowed the car to the speed limit and Bardru nodded toward him, releasing his grip on the grab handle.

"The VPDs are both down. Melanie worked half the night on a Zoom call with a programmer back at HQ in Atlanta, but the code is acting up." She sighed audibly. "I'm so sorry."

"Our luck has been kinda funky," he said. "But it's not your fault."

"How was your vampire party?"

"It sucked," he said.

She laughed.

"I got into it with the rich guys. Wish I could have spent the night with a scientist instead."

"I wish that, too." She sighed. "And now our Galveston plans are shot, too."

"Yeah," he said. "Okay, as I understand it, I need to not be there at the scene."

"Yes. Sorry. Melanie is still at the hotel working on the VPDs. I think she had like two hours of sleep last night."

"Then I'll drop Bardru off and head home I guess."

"If I can get away by late afternoon or evening, can I come see you?"

"Absolutely. I have a little project I'm working on. Maybe it will be ready by then."

"Ooo," she said. "Is it what I think it is?"

"You'll have to come see."

"I'm at the scene," she said. "Gotta go. I will get away as soon as I can. I might have a little surprise for you, too."

"That would be nice. Did you see the message he left?"

She was silent for a moment. "It was on the news. Some news guy snuck in and got a pic of it. Gotta go. I'll see you later today."

The call ended.

"Your lady?" Bardru asked.

"Yes," he said. "I'm gonna take you home."

"Good. I could do with a nap."

Alex was silent. It had been on the morning news. A message left at the scene where the Vision Killer murdered six people. Written in blood on a whitewashed wall:

*SEX NUNC*

*DC PRIMUM*

It was Latin. Translated, it said, *Six now, six hundred soon*.

# 24

E melia gripped the steering wheel and sighed as she pulled up to Alex's house in the late afternoon. The discovery of another gruesome murder scene this morning had blown her Galveston plans with Alex and, despite Melanie's feverish best efforts, the VPDs might not be ready for another day or two. And the news had already broadcast the warning from Titus, written in blood at the scene. *Six now, six hundred soon.* The time pressure was ominous. Emelia sighed again. She turned into the driveway, dialed Alex, and said, "I'm here."

"Okay," he said. "Come on up."

The redwood gate swung open, and she parked behind his Miata. She exited her car and saw the gate swing shut. She walked across the lawn to the front door and found it open. There was a familiar cacophony of barking from the top of the narrow stairs. She smiled. "Doggies!" she said as she walked up the stairs. At the top, Dizzy and Midnight waited behind the baby gate, their tails wagging. They were damp, apparently from an earlier dip in the algae-choked pool, and the wet-dog smell filled her nostrils. Dizzy's white fur was, for the moment, pale green.

"Hey, you two!" she laughed, petting them until they settled down a bit. She navigated past the baby gate with a little difficulty since she was wearing a short, black leather skirt and high heels—civilian wear for a change. Once past the gate, she dug in her clutch for the dog treats she had brought. As she dispensed the treats, the dogs excitedly ran into the kitchen and crunched on them. Emelia glanced down, surveying the chipped polish on her nails and wished she had been able to get them done today. She took a step toward the living room, which was brightly lit with natural light. She shivered in anticipation at seeing him again. And at him seeing her like this.

"Alex?" she called.

She heard him call back from a distance. He was up in the studio. She went to the living room and saw golden light streaming through the window, illuminating *Poe's Lament*. She gave the statue a nod as she walked toward the staircase. "Mr. Poe," she murmured.

She went up the Hill House staircase and hurried past *Experiment in Reds*. She stepped through the arched doorway and gasped. Almost all the half-finished paintings had been stacked in a corner and an open space had been cleared in front of the triptych of windows. Yellow light streamed through them, illuminating a huge, prepared canvas supported by specially modified easels. It was six feet by eight feet, at least. A few cans of paint and a can of brushes sat on the floor in front of it, and there was a wooden barstool about five feet from it.

Alex stepped around from behind it, and his eyes widened when he saw her. "Look at *you*!" he said, grinning.

She smiled. *Mission accomplished.* Then she ran over, heels clicking on the concrete floor, and kissed him. When they parted, she regarded the canvas. "You've been busy," she said. "Starting something new?"

"Yep." He pointed at the stool. "Please sit, Ms. Cord."

She did, and he bent down to the can of brushes and selected what she knew was commonly called a flat. Her pulse quickened. *Jackson Williams wants me to see him at work.*

Smiling at her, he reached over to one of the cans of paint and opened the lid, which was just resting on top of the can. "Our Galveston plans are shot, but maybe this is the next best thing."

Speechless, she watched him as he leaned down and charged the brush with paint, a vivid orange, and then confidently made the first few strokes. The paint was rich and opaque, and he painted a zone of irregular orange at the left side of the canvas. Silence enfolded the room, and she heard the brush as it whispered across the canvas, shivering at the sound.

Alex paused, turned to her, and motioned for her to approach. She shook her head. "No, I—I couldn't. What if I mess it up?"

"Don't be silly," he said. He came over and took her hand. She resisted for a moment and then let herself be led to the expanse of canvas. He recharged the brush with paint and handed it to her. She could smell the rich, oily paint on the canvas and the brush.

She held it for a moment, looking from him to the canvas and back again. "I don't know what to do," she said.

He stepped behind her and gently took her brush hand. "Start here," he said, positioning her hand over a spot on the right side of the canvas.

"Let the brush go where it wants, Emelia," he whispered in her ear, gently guiding her hand until the bristles met the canvas. "You can't make a mistake at this stage."

She painted a few stiff, jerky strokes, and then he asserted a little gentle control, guiding her in creating another irregular zone of the rich orange paint. "Easy," he said softly. "That's it. Look at you being an artist." Those words set off a blossom of heat inside her. She shifted from foot to foot.

He took her shoulders in his gentle but firm grip and guided her a few steps back so she could take in the expanse of canvas with the two orange splotches.

He pointed at the canvas. "This is the beginning of a new Jackson Williams painting called *Conflagration*. On the left is my contribution. On the right is yours. I won't ever paint over that, so you will be able to see it even when the painting is done. I will always think of you as I work on this piece. Always."

She turned to him and kissed him deeply. Her heart raced, and she felt heat between her legs. The forgotten brush clattered to the floor as she embraced him. Arching against him she reached down and pulled her blouse out of the waistband of her skirt. She took a step back, feeling feverish. "It's time," she said quietly as she began to unbutton her blouse.

To her surprise, he bent and grabbed the brush again. He smiled at her, his dark green eyes flashed mischievously.

She stopped in mid-unbuttoning, puzzled. She watched, intrigued, as he charged the brush with the fiery paint again. He took a few steps away from her, still smiling.

He stood, brush in hand, and said, "Please continue."

"Order me to do it," she said simply.

"Take off your blouse, Emelia," he said.

His words lit her up inside as her desire churned. Her fingers moved quickly as she undid the last few buttons. She smiled at him as she shrugged out of the blouse, letting it fall in a heap around her feet.

She stood there in her bra, facing him, her arms at her sides. She felt a little vulnerable, but it was the *good* vulnerable. And then there was her need, growing.

His face darkened a little. "Sorry about that bruise." She glanced at her arm and then met his gaze. "It's healing. It doesn't hurt. Stay focused, Alex."

He nodded. "Take off your bra, Emelia."

She complied, feverish with anticipation. She dropped her bra at her feet.

He smiled, surveying her breasts, and her desire intensified.

He balanced the brush on the stool and took off his shirt.

*Finally*, she thought as she admired his muscular physique. She smiled at him.

"Stay right there," he said. He grabbed the brush and walked up to her. She thought of the tantalizing nearness they had shared when they had their first kiss here in the studio. This was so much better than that. He pressed the brush to her chest.

The soft bristles tickled her skin, and the wet coolness of the paint made her shiver. The paintbrush was like a little tongue exploring the sensitive skin of her chest. She suppressed a moan.

He stepped back. Emelia glanced down at herself. She had expected something schmaltzy like a heart, but it was another irregular splotch of the blazing orange, like the ones on the canvas. Alex bent, placing the brush into the can on the floor and then stood again. Then he carefully pulled her into an embrace, chest to chest. His powerful arms felt good against the skin of her back. His skin was cool, as always, but now she could feel his hardness pressing against her. She closed her eyes as she let herself get lost in the delicious moment.

Alex stepped back and, opening her eyes, Emelia could see that he had a matching splotch on his chest now, slightly smudged but easily distinguishable. "We will always share this connection, Emelia." His words were intoxicating, and the dampness grew between her legs.

"Stay right there," she said. She bent and gathered up her shirt and bra and folded them into a makeshift cushion at his feet. Then she knelt in front of him. She opened his belt and unbuttoned his jeans. She hungrily unzipped him and yanked down his jeans and underwear to reveal his erection. "Well now we're getting somewhere," she said. "Are you ready after all this time, Alex?"

"I am, Emelia."

She began. Alex gasped as she took him into her mouth. Again, there was a disconcerting moment. His flesh was so cool. But she was so carried away now that it didn't matter. The coolness gave way to the warmth of her mouth, and Alex moaned as she continued. His hands found the sides of her head as she sped up. His body trembled, nearing the edge, and Emelia knew he could hear the wet sounds of her mouth on him.

He moaned her name. *Yes, baby, yes,* she thought, increasing the tempo even more. Then he stiffened and arched his back, pushing into her mouth. "Oh Emelia! *Oh!*"

She leaned back, breathing heavily. His legs were shaking. His face was raised, and his eyes were closed, as he savored the moment. She glanced toward the stool nearby. *My turn.*

*"Whew!"* he said. Emelia got to her feet and went to the stool.

He watched her, smiling, as she reached under her skirt and removed her now-damp panties, letting them slide down to her ankles. She stepped out of them, raised her skirt enticingly, and positioned herself on the stool with her legs open and inviting.

He got on his knees in front of her. "I want this to be good. Tell me what to do to make it good."

Emelia reached out, gently slid her fingers into his hair and drew his face between her legs. "I will. And I know it'll be good."

He was responsive to her instructions and yes, it was good. *Very good.* She gently rocked her hips, savoring the building sensation. She pushed herself against his mouth as the moment became inevitable. "Alex!" she cried. "Yes! *Yes!*" She closed her eyes and arched her back, clutching his hair, lost in the heat and satisfaction of that final moment.

As he leaned back, his lips glistening, she brought his face up to hers and kissed him, tasting herself in his mouth. She caught sight of the painting behind them, bathed in the glorious yellow light from the windows. *Conflagration*, it would be called. Her heart swelled. *I know he'll finish this one. Because of me.* She had tears in her eyes.

*I am the muse. Come back after so long.*

# 25
—·—

O range light played across the ceiling of Alex's bedroom. He lay under the cotton sheet, staring at the ceiling. Round two, coitus, had not gone well. The body temperature thing was too much for Emelia when it came to body-on-body contact. She had started crying and they had to stop.

Emelia was nude, and sat hunched in a chair at the desk across the room, speaking on her phone. "Melanie, be sensible. You *have* to *sleep*. That's an order. There is Ambien in your go bag. Take one and get a fresh start in the morning."

Silence while Melanie replied. Alex suppressed a sigh.

"We all know the urgency," she said into the phone. "There is nothing any of us can do tonight, and you're no good to the investigation if you are exhausted and making mistakes. Listen. Sleep tonight and we will have a margarita tomorrow. Okay?"

More silence. Then, "Good. Get some Z's. Okay, good night."

Emelia laid her phone on the desk and walked over to the bed. She saw his face and said, "Alex, don't be upset." She crawled onto the bed and continued up until she slid into his embrace with the sheet between them. She whispered in his ear. "Baby, I came *so* hard upstairs. You did so great. I almost fell off the stool."

"Me too," he said, holding her closer. "I'm glad it was you after so long."

"That makes me so happy." She kissed his cheek. "Let's coast on that for a little while, okay? We're both smart. I'm a scientist. My job is figuring stuff out." She licked his neck. "I predict we will have to do a *lot* of experimentation." She gave a playful little moan.

He chuckled and leaned to kiss her.

Plaintive whines from underneath the bedroom door interrupted the moment.

"Um, they usually sleep here on the bed with me," he said.

She rolled off the bed and went to the door. She opened it and the dogs burst in, leaping on the bed in delight. "The gang's all here!" she said, jumping back on the bed.

Once everyone was settled, she lay sandwiched between Alex and Midnight, and he lay sandwiched between her and Dizzy.

They finished out the night with the rest of *Duck Soup* on the big screen TV mounted on the wall. Alex relaxed as she dozed in his arms. *Sleep now, my beautiful one.*

Early in the morning, Alex stood in the living room in front of the window next to *Poe's Lament*. Edgar gazed in eternal dismay at the dropped piece of paper, and Alex gazed at his reflection in the glass, his heart thumping and his hands trembling.

*He's planning to kill 600 innocent people*. Alex sighed. By opposing Titus, he was going into certain danger, and perhaps certain death. Which wouldn't have meant as much back when he was just a vigilante vampire, artistically blocked, and had just one old man who loved him. Now there were so many lives at stake. And that number included Emelia.

He knew with certainty that he was in love with her. She was so beautiful, *so smart*, so optimistic. He had opened up a new world for her, and she had revived feelings that he had shut out so long ago. And somehow, she had single-handedly reignited his artistic passion. He could see *Conflagration* completed in his mind. It was just a matter of adding paint to the canvas. He knew it would perhaps be his greatest work, and he also knew he'd give it to her when it was completed, a token of his thankfulness that she had entered his life. And, as the light of dawn gathered outside the window, he knew there was no going back. Not now.

He stared into space beyond the window, not seeing. He desperately wanted to shield her from the evil to come, to preserve her life above all else. Grasping at straws, he thought he could ask her to teach him how to use the VPD so he alone could track Titus through the Deepest Shadow. He dismissed the thought: she would never agree to that. *We'll catch him together, you and me.*

He'd said it so casually then, perhaps to get closer to her. She'd even said it back to him. *No, she is committed.* And she probably wasn't thinking about dying a painful, gruesome death in Titus' hands. Maybe in front of Alex's eyes. He pushed the horrible thought from his mind with mindfulness.

The light outside the window had taken on a pink quality as sunrise approached on the other side of the building. He turned to the statue and said, "Edgar, what can I do?"

"You can get your girlfriend some break... fast!" Emelia said, her voice pitched low and masculine.

He turned and saw her in the hallway; the white cotton sheet wrapped around her. She was smiling, and Midnight and Dizzy were standing next to her. When she saw his face, she rushed over in a rustle of cloth. There were orange stains on the sheet, transferred from the paint they had not washed away last night.

"Alex, what's the matter?" she said, wrapping his naked body in the sheet along with hers. "Still worried about last night?"

"I was thinking that Titus is very, very dangerous, and I was worried about you. What if he is waiting to attack us in the Deepest Shadow? I might be able to fend him off, but you're so much more...fragile than me. Emelia, I can't bear to lose you after I only just found you." A tear rolled down his cheek.

"Oh, sweet Alex!" she said. She pulled him over to the couch and they sat, still wrapped in the sheet. She kissed away the tears on his cheeks. "You are so magnificent and caring. And so brave to want to protect and preserve me.

"Listen to me," she said, "I once dated a guy who knew how to build sandcastles. Not silly little kid's bucket sandcastles, but big sculptures made of sand like you'd see in those sand sculpting contests. He'd sculpt these amazing things, but then the tide would come in and wash away the whole thing. After just one day."

She looked at him, more vulnerable and beautiful than ever. "It made me sad, but he just smiled at me. He said, 'Some beautiful things are fleeting, and we must love them for the time they are here. Look! The beauty is still all there, in every grain of sand. Just transformed.'"

She held his face in her hands. "You and I may be fleeting in this dangerous endeavor, and so we must love each other while we are here. I want to be by your side even if the worst happens. And then, if we must, we will transform together. You and me, Alex. No one can take that away from us."

It was suddenly so important to say it. "Emelia, I love you."

Her eyes were wide and so very beautiful. "I love you, Alex."

They kissed and held each other for a long time.

Firearms practice at the private indoor range. Maxie Bright, his hand on the switch, rolled in the target and shook his head. He regarded Alex. "See? Good tight grouping but off to the left of the target. Is something distracting you?"

"Sorry, Maxie," Alex said as he reloaded the magazine on his KelTec. "I just found something amazing and now I am worried Titus will take it away."

Maxie nodded. "Would this thing happen to have long beautiful legs and a killer smile?"

"Yes indeed."

Maxie's elusive smile made a return engagement. "There is nothing like a daaaame," he sang. He clapped Alex on the shoulder with a beefy, tattooed hand. "All your secrets are safe with Maxie. Spill it."

Alex took a deep breath and told Maxie about Emelia and the VPD that could track Titus.

Maxie whistled. "Dating a human. Tricky. Jonas'd flip if he found out. But he won't."

"Thanks, Maxie."

"So your girl has a device that can track Titus?"

Alex nodded.

"And she wants to be part of the hunt for this maniac, thick or thin, right?"

"Yes," Alex said.

Maxie whistled. "I know a thing or two about women. I presume you know she ain't gonna quit on it, no matter what you say."

"You presume correctly," Alex replied.

"Well, there it is, see?" Maxie said. "That's all the more reason to stay focused. You gotta use your hypnotist tricks to see to it."

"You're full of surprises, Maxie. How did you know that?"

Maxie laughed. "Jonas has a bigger mouth than he cares to admit. But don't be mad. You know I'm right. Right?"

"Yes. There are things I can do."

"Work on 'em, then. Her survival and yours may depend on it. In the meantime, I'll get you shipshape on firearms."

Maxie walked over to a small cooler and took out a couple of beers and brought them over, plunking one down on the bracing shelf by Alex. "Let's take a break and talk, man to man."

"Is alcohol a good idea?" Alex asked.

Maxie's smile decided to stay for a bit. "It's just these two, and one ain't gonna hurt you. Or me!"

They opened the cans and clinked them together. A tattoo on Maxie's forearm showed two dice with seven pips showing and Maxie's name in an arch over them.

"You ever bowl, Alex?" Maxie asked.

"A few times in the distant past."

Maxie quaffed beer. "Man, when I was in the service, I was a bowling *machine*! I won so much fucking money. Wanna know my secret?"

Alex smiled and took a sip of beer. There was just something about Maxie he really liked. "Tell me."

"Well, bowling and beer go together like beans and rice, see? But, and it's a big but: only to a point. If we were playin' for money, I'd buy a few pitchers of beer for the guys. But I'd only ever have one while they went to town. I'd nurse that sucker like it was my last beer until Judgment Day. It loosened up my reflexes *just enough* to roll like a king, while they started to roll like court jesters. And then the money just rolled in. Those pitchers were just kinda a business expense.

"Anyways, my point after this long-ass story is that you need to do what you can do to stay calm and focused even when the bullets are flyin'. Even when your girl is in danger. For me, it might be a beer or a shot. *One*. For you, hell, it could be one of your hypnotist Jedi powers, see?"

Alex nodded. "You're a piece of work, Maxie."

"You don't know the half of it," Maxie said with a twinkle in his eye.

He regarded Alex for a few moments. "Man to man," he said, "I like you, Alex. You're putting your ass on the line for all us cowards. I've been thinkin' a lot about that. I got some ideas that may give you an edge against this Titus. And I'm damnwell gonna share 'em."

"Please do," Alex said.

Maxie's smile came and went, and he nodded. He talked for a long time and Alex listened carefully to every word.

# 26

That same afternoon, at the hotel, Emelia peered over Melanie's shoulder as she used her laptop to load the newly rewritten code into the Void Particle Densitometer. On a nearby laptop, Rick Emerson, on a Zoom call from the tech lab at CDPR, watched. The desk in Melanie's hotel room was littered with paper coffee cups, electronic tools, scribbled notes, and a small, framed photo of her two cats that her husband had sent her. Once the code was loaded, Melanie put the VPD into diagnostic mode. A red LED on the device blinked rapidly. "Fingers crossed," she said. On the laptop screen, Rick held up crossed fingers on each hand. Emelia crossed her fingers. Finally, the red LED winked out and a green LED next to it glowed green. "That's it!" Melanie cried. Rick said, "Good job, slick!"

Melanie turned to Emelia. "It's gonna work. Now we can create distinct profiles of particle trails and assign identities to them. Then we can store those in memory and compare them against a fresh particle trail. Resolution on the trails should be sharper, too, with less scatter."

Emelia put a hand on her shoulder and squeezed. "Good job, Mel."

From the laptop, Rick said, "I'm gonna do testing with a couple of live sprites at the lab here. We'll have results later today and email a report." Rick looked over his shoulder. "Somebody is here to say hello," he said. Then CDPR director Mark Petrovsky leaned into view. He was smiling. "Well, well," he said. "Melanie saves the day! Do I need to FedEx a bottle of champagne?"

The two women laughed. "It's gonna be margaritas and Emelia is buying," Melanie said.

"You've earned it," Petrovsky said. "I'll buy Rick a margarita here for his role in this."

Melanie smiled and mimed holding up a margarita glass. "Here's to you, Rick."

Rick held up an imaginary glass and said, "Here's to you, Melanie!"

"Good job both of you," Petrovsky said, putting his hand on Rick's shoulder. "We're gonna sign off here so Mark can set about testing. Keep me informed."

Everyone said goodbye and the Zoom call ended.

Emelia hugged Melanie from behind and whispered, "Girl power."

Melanie reached up and squeezed Emelia's arm. "Girl power," she said.

Emelia yawned when she pulled into the driveway at Alex's house. She had an updated VPD in the trunk of her car and, before her margarita date with Melanie, she had reluctantly attended another briefing with the FBI where a sour Jack Crain (was he *ever* not like that?) had groused about Behavioral Analysis slow-walking their psychological profile of the Vision Killer. "He appears and disappears and there have been no witnesses except for a kid," Alison had said out in the hallway after the briefing "He's a phantom. They're stumped."

"Huh." Emelia said. Privately she thought, *Well, Jack, at least I know his name. And how he gets around. And that he leaves a particle trail that can be tracked. By a device I have in my possession. I'd love to share all that with you, dearest Jack, but hey,*

*I'm just a lowly slug from the CPDR. Good luck*! Pettiness was not generally her style, but in this case, it felt pretty good.

There was an awkward small-talk moment between her and Alison where she really wanted to ask if she had spied on her the other day, but she blew that off. Alison was under considerable strain working for that asshole of a boss.

Then she drank celebratory margaritas with Melanie, the hero of the day! Emelia was delighted to see her happy. She was going to make a fine investigative agent. Emelia made a mental note to ask Mark to put through the promotion soon.

Using the fob Alex had given her, she opened the gate, pulled inside the fence and parked. She wanted to surprise him if possible. She looked up at the building. Sunset was fading into night, and the lights were on in the upper two floors. *This is my boyfriend's house. And I have a key!* She opened the passenger side of her car and pulled out a large, bulky shopping bag from *Everything Bed and Bath* and a smaller bag with a change of clothes, toiletries, and—she giggled happily.

She went to the door and used the key attached to the fob as quietly as she could, but the canine alarm squad responded with a fusillade of barking at the top of the stairs. Oh well. At the top of the stairs, she greeted Dizzy and Midnight (Midnight got extra kisses, of course). There was no Alex to be seen. Faint 40s music drifted down from upstairs. *He's in the studio! He's painting!*

Her pulse quickened. She got past the baby gate and stepped through the hall into the alcove by the kitchen. She gasped.

On the kitchen counter were plates and bowls. Cutlery. A set of pots and pans, including a cast-iron skillet. Utensils. Cloth napkins and paper towels. Plastic containers with lids. Dishwashing soap, dish towels and a drying rack. Sourdough bread! Dry goods, including a box of her favorite cereal. A coffee grinder, expensive coffee beans and a mug emblazoned with *HERS*. She went to the refrigerator and opened it. Food! Milk, eggs, orange juice, and a bowl of grapes. Plastic wrapped, thick cut steaks. Butter and other condiments. Broccoli, potatoes and a few other produce items. Front and center was a six-pack of The Devil's Hopyard ale.

She shut the door, grinning, and her first thought was *I know a vampire who's getting laid tonight*!

A few minutes later, after dropping off her items in the bedroom and dispensing treats to Dizzy and Midnight, she took off her shoes and socks and crept up the spiral staircase. The music was louder now, a song about dancing the jitterbug in the rain. She eased past *Experiment in Reds* (it bothered her somewhat less now) and peeked around into the studio.

He stood shirtless, in jeans and bare feet, in front of the canvas with a wide brush. He painted rapidly, intensely focused on the canvas as he worked. Emelia touched her hand to her heart, holding her breath. *Jackson Williams at work*!

"Alex?" she said, but it only came out in a whisper, such was the depth of her emotion. He didn't seem to hear.

Then he stopped, took a few steps back and surveyed the canvas. He saw her and smiled. "Are you my girlfriend?"

She put a finger to her chin as though she were thinking it over, teasing him. And then with an exuberant laugh, she said, "That I am," and rushed into his embrace. It was short-lived as she turned to look at the canvas, her mouth agape.

His splotch had evolved into an angry collision of oranges, deep reds, and yellows, spiked through with roiling threads of black, suggesting oily smoke or black lightning. The smell of fresh oil paint was strong.

"Oh, Alex," she said, turning to him with a huge grin. "It's so beautiful."

He still had his arm around her, and he gently squeezed her. "So I'm guessing you like it."

She put her hands on his bare chest. "There is no guesswork involved," she said. She kissed him deeply, feeling heat between her legs again.

"Sorry about downstairs. Didn't have time to put things away," he said, smiling.

She laughed and play-slapped his chest with her hand. "Such a wonderful surprise! We don't have to order out for pizza again!"

She glanced at the canvas again, noting how lonely her splotch on the right side seemed. *He'll fix that*, she knew. Soon the splotches would be joined in a gestalt of blazing colors, girded by black lightning, so vivid you could almost feel the roiling heat.

"I don't know how this stuff works," she said, looking up at him. "Are you done for the day? Do I need to leave you alone for a while longer?"

He smiled and kissed her on the forehead. "I was done for the day when you caught my eye. I think I need a little downtime with my beautiful scientist girlfriend," he said.

A smile lit up her face. "Your scientist girlfriend has a surprise or two for you, it turns out. Come downstairs, Mr. Jackson Williams."

He grinned and followed her downstairs.

Ten minutes later, Alex stood at the entrance to the short hallway leading to the bedroom. "Ready yet?" he called. He drained the last of his Chilean wine and set the glass on a side table.

"Just a moment longer," she called out. His sensitive ears picked up cloth rustling. "Okay, come on in!"

He walked in to see her nestled in a too-short orange lace nightie on top of a large white electric blanket. The lush aroma of her freshly applied perfume swirled in his nostrils. She held the blanket's control in her hand. He took a step toward her, but she said, "Stop right there, mister." He stopped.

"Go into the bathroom and take a very hot shower. Me, I'm going to um," her hand slid down between her legs, "get warmed up while you get warmed up. Hurry back."

"All hail science!" he said, stripping out of his jeans. He ran to the bathroom while she got herself started.

A little while later, he slid into bed with her. The blanket on top of them was warm, and so was he. She felt the shimmering heat between her legs and hungrily pulled him on top of her. As he gripped her with his powerful hands, poised and ready, she surrendered herself utterly to him. "Oh! *Alex*!"

# 27

The next morning, Emelia sat on the couch, feasting on steak and eggs, sourdough toast and a small bowl of grapes, along with fresh-brewed coffee and orange juice. Serving as a tray was an antique wood panel Alex was planning to use for a project sometime. He sat in a small chair nearby and watched her eat, smiling. She held up the *HERS* coffee mug and kissed it before taking a sip. "I'm so happy," she said.

"That makes me very happy," he replied. "Sorry I forgot to get a tray. Thought I thought of everything."

She ran her fingers over the dark, stained wood. "*This*. This is the tray I want. It's my cup of stars."

"Quoting my favorite book again. If I weren't already in love with you—"

"But ya are Blanche, ya are," she said, imitating Bette Davis.

"Whoa," Alex said. "Hill House and Baby Jane! My head is spinning."

"I am *not* going to quote *The Exorcist*," she said with a laugh.

She took another bite of steak. "This is perfectly cooked," she said. "How do you still know how to perfectly cook a steak after 90-plus years?"

He laughed. "Actually, I was terrified. I didn't know what to do. YouTube university to the rescue."

She held up her juice and toasted him. "Yay YouTube!"

She ate a few more bites and stopped. "I'm so full. Can't eat a breakfast like this every morning if I want to keep my figure for my hot vampire boyfriend. But after a workout like we had last night—" she winked at him.

Alex laughed. "Hail science." He glanced down at Dizzy and Midnight, who were sitting quietly at his feet, watching Emelia. "I think we might find someone to finish your breakfast."

She nodded, taking another sip of coffee. "I've got an idea for the crime scene today."

"I'm all ears."

"So, Melanie and I will go in an official capacity in the afternoon and see what we can find with her VPD. I expect to find a trail from Titus. No interference from you, because you haven't been there yet. And the improved VPD would account for that, anyway. We should be able to follow Titus' trail to wherever he came into the house."

"And then?" he asked.

"Come back with you after nightfall. There is an abandoned house two houses down. Go into the Deepest Shadow there and pick up the trail from there if we can. What do you think?"

"Sounds great," he said. "But there is just one hitch."

She popped a grape into her mouth. "What?"

"I gotta feed. I've put it off and I can't put it off anymore."

She frowned. "Isn't it possible to—do *that*—during the day?"

He took a deep breath. "Bad guys tend to be easier to find at night."

She nodded. "Not a conversation I expected to have over breakfast."

"Sorry," he said.

"Alex don't be sorry. It was just a comment. You've been so amazing and attentive to my needs. I need to learn to accommodate yours, as well."

"Thank you. I know a few rough-and-tumble places where I might luck out during the daylight hours, but I've also got practice with Maxie and Sun today." He glanced toward the staircase. "Kinda hoped to get in a little painting time, too."

She nodded. "Definitely don't want to get in the way of that. My splotch is lonely."

He winked at her. "Not for long."

She clapped her hands.

He smiled at her. Then he took a deep breath. "Emelia, it's probably kinda crazy to ask you this since things have gone so fast, but—" he trailed off.

"I'm not *quite* ready to marry a vampire, if that's what you're thinking," she said. Alex's eyes widened. That hadn't occurred to him.

"No, no," he said. "So here it is: Maybe you can save See Deeper a little money and, just for now, maybe you can stay here instead of the hotel. I've got an office with a fancy computer and wifi that I rarely use."

She said nothing but got up and took her tray into the kitchen, followed by the two dogs.

*Crap.* He went after her into the kitchen, where she was feeding bits of scrambled eggs to Midnight and Dizzy.

"Maybe I shouldn't have—"

She wiped her fingers on a cloth napkin. "It's okay. That's just kind of a big step."

She must have seen his crestfallen expression and came over and put her arms around his neck. "My love, I know you've been lonely for so long. Too damn long. And if I'm honest, despite the thing with Alison, I have to say that I've been lonely too. It's like that silly meme: 'I work with supernatural creatures all day and I come home to a cat.'"

"You have a cat?"

She laughed. "No silly. That's just the meme. Besides, if I did, Midnight and Dizzy would never forgive me."

He chuckled at that. She pulled him to her and kissed him. "Neither of us knew we'd be falling in love but now it's happened," she said. "It's been a six-day crazy whirlwind for both of us. Just give me a few days to think about it, okay? I've got a few practical things to suss out."

"Absolutely."

She kissed him again. Her gaze met his. "Alex, don't get me wrong. I am over the moon that I met you."

He nodded. "Me too. I keep asking myself how I got so lucky."

"Same. But we may have to tiptoe a little bit to figure everything out, okay?"

"That's fair."

She pulled her phone out of her pocket and glanced at it. "I'm supposed to have lunch with Melanie at noon," she said, regarding him with a devilish grin. "But that leaves just enough time for you to take a hot shower. Whaddaya think?"

"I think cleanliness is next to godliness," he said.

"Well, warmth certainly is, in our case. Get going, mister. I'll be waiting under the blanket."

Night had fallen in one of Houston's poorest neighborhoods. The humid air was oppressive. Mosquitos and crane flies buzzed. The street man only known as Jacla was beating a dog with a stick in an empty lot.

"You don' bite me," he slurred, his breath thick with alcohol. *WHACK!* The dog, tied by a length of rope to a chain-link fence pole, yelped in pain.

"I teach you!" *WHACK!* The dog emitted a piteous, ululating whine.

Somewhere someone yelled out an open window. "You stop that Jacla! Leave that poor dog alone!"

"I show you!" Jacla yelled back and raised the stick again as the dog flattened itself on the ground, whining. A hand gripped his wrist and squeezed it like a vise.

"Ow!" Jacla said. With his free hand, he pulled an ice pick out from his tattered leather belt and twisted toward his assailant. "I stick you, fuckah!" he cried, and drove the pick into the man's midsection. It went deep, and he pulled it out and stabbed again and again. It felt weird, like stabbing a cardboard box or something. *Not right.*

The hand gripping his wrist snapped it like it was a twig. The cracking sound was muffled and wet. Jacla was so boozed up it took a moment for the awful shooting pain to register, white-hot in his wrist.

Jacla screamed, but another hand clamped over his mouth and through the pain, he felt himself being dragged through the lot, kicking and struggling, to the remains of an old brick-and-concrete foundation. Panicked, he tried biting the hand on his mouth, but that was weird, too: like biting into a sponge. His vision spun with the pain and fear, but then there was a new pain, lancing into his neck like two ice picks.

Jacla's eyes rolled and as the hand came away from his mouth, he emitted a slobbering, gurgling sound. He began to feel faint. The pain in his neck subsided, and he writhed, trying to get away. He glimpsed a mouth with lips and sharp teeth slicked with blood. His blood. Then he heard the voice.

"If you ever hurt an animal again, *ever*, I will come back. And it will be so much worse next time. Understand?"

Jacla, at the edge of fainting, nodded and said something that sounded like *gugh.*

The man released him and strode off in the direction of the dog.

In the darkness of her hotel room, Emelia dialed her phone. She wiped tears from her cheeks. A male voice answered. "Emelia?"

"Yes Mark. Were you asleep?"

"No. Up late reading. Sandy already went to bed. Everything okay?"

"Mark, it's important for me to tell you I am going to be tendering my resignation from See Deeper soon. Not now. Not in two weeks, but soon."

"I'm listening, Emelia," Mark said, his voice grave. "Tell me what I can do to fix this, and I assure you I will fix it posthaste."

"It's something really big. It's so big, the gravity is pulling me away from See Deeper. I have a chance to help stop the killer. I think we will be able to do it."

"We? CDPR?"

"Yes and no. I can't say more. Whether I succeed or not, there will be no more See Deeper for me."

"Are you implying what I think you're implying?"

"Yes. If I succeed and our bad guy is stopped, you will know. On that day, my resignation is activated. If I fail, there will be no need for a resignation."

"This is above your pay grade, Emelia. Are you sure?"

"Yes."

Mark was silent. Probably thinking furiously.

"There's one more thing, Mark."

"I'm listening."

"However it goes, I would like for you to promote Melanie Sanders to Investigative Agent, effective immediately, if possible."

"Consider it done. Tomorrow. I'll FedEx a badge and the papers. She kicked ass with that code."

"Yes. Between you and me, it's been a little bumpy for her and a little bit of that is my fault."

"Is Melanie in any danger?"

"No. Part of the bumpiness is because I am shielding her." *Well, it's partly true.*

"Good," he said. I wouldn't want to lose two—" He went silent. Emelia bit her lip to avoid sobbing.

She took a deep breath and said, "But that has nothing to do with the promotion. She's sharp, responsive, and dedicated. Good eye for details. Like someone else we know."

"You've got that right, Agent Cord." It was what he always said when she hinted at what they both already knew.

"If we succeed, I want her to know that she and Rick played an important role in that. If I—" she paused. She didn't want to say *fail* again. "If I don't make it, please tell her I believe in her."

"Emelia, listen closely. I can pull some strings and get you 24/7 protection," he said. "Do you need Dr. Chavez out there? Or Mike Wilkinson from Quantico? Tell me how I can help you and I will move heaven and Earth."

"They're already in motion, Mark. I am going to FedEx the papers tomorrow. Please sign and seal them."

"Consider it done—" He was silent for a moment. "Emelia, why do you have to leave See Deeper if you stop the killer?"

Tears rolled down her cheeks. "Because, Mark," she said. "'Because' is the only word I can use. You've been the best boss anyone could ever ask for."

"Heaven and Earth, Emelia," he said, almost sternly. "Just say the word."

"I can't," she said softly.

"You are the finest agent I've ever had. Never forget that. If conditions change, let me know immediately, day or night. Otherwise, keep your head down if you can."

"I will. Thank you for everything, Mark. My love to Sandy, okay?"

"Yes. Goodbye, Emelia. And good luck."

"Goodbye Mark. Thank you."

There was silence on the line. Emelia let herself weep for a little while, and then she slept.

Night had given way to a foggy morning when Verna Pilkington unlocked the front door to the Montrose Animal Shelter. Through the window she saw that somebody had left an animal out on the sidewalk. She shook her head. It happened from time to time. She called out, "Middy! Can you come help me?"

Middy Astor was a student at Rice University and sported a red mohawk and lots of tattoos and piercings, but Verna didn't care. She was wonderful with animals, gentle and loving.

Just as Middy joined her, Verna opened the door to see an underfed black mongrel—whippet and who knew what else—cowering on an old couch cushion. The dog was tied to a nearby water spigot and there was something white underneath a corner of the cushion. As Middy reached for the dog, it emitted a frightened whine. "It's okay, girl, it's okay," she said, gently stroking the shivering dog.

Verna pulled the envelope out. Written in sharpie on the outside was, *Please take care of this poor girl. She needs medical attention and lots of love.* Verna gasped when she opened the envelope. It contained five crisp $100 notes.

# 28

— • —

N ight was just drawing its mantle over the green expanses of Houston when Alex and Emelia set out.

Earlier in the day, Alex had trained with Sun and Maxie, and Emelia had celebrated with Melanie over her new promotion to Investigative Agent.

They had reunited in the late afternoon for energetic love-making under the electric blanket, and then supper at an expensive Italian restaurant. Now, clad in nondescript dark clothing and sneakers, they drove to the location of Titus' latest killing spree as the last vestiges of twilight fled. A comfortable silence settled between them as Alex eased the car down the street. The VPD was in the footwell by Emelia's seat.

"There it is," she said. The murder house came into view, cordoned off with police tape. "The abandoned house is just up here."

As they pulled up, two houses down, Alex saw a blackened hole gaping in the shingled roof. Clearly, a fire had occurred. The street was quiet, and Alex parked on the opposite side of the street from the house.

Alex wore a shoulder holster with his .22 KelTec under a light jacket. It was loaded with silver bullets. Maxie had given him a second holdout pistol, a .38 revolver, also loaded with silver bullets, and Emelia had it in a side pocket of the leather VPD case. Alex knew she'd had basic firearms training in Quantico, and he was glad she was armed. There was no knowing what they'd find.

They exited the car and walked across the street to the abandoned house. A smell of burned wood and plastic hung in the air as they walked along the side of the house. A flimsy-looking lock hung from the hasp of a gate in the redwood fence. Alex broke it easily, and they went into the backyard. There was a partially filled swimming pool choked with floating debris from the fire, and a gaping hole in the rear wall of the house. Next to the hole was a set of sliding patio doors.

"A bit safer to go through here," Alex said. He tried the doors and one slid open along its track. They peered in, and a wafting smell of cinnamon candies mixed with the burnt smell and the musty scent of water-soaked furniture.

"I've been wanting to experience the Deepest Shadow again," she said.

"Well, you're about to. Watch your footing."

They went in slowly, and Alex switched on a small LED flashlight. They were in what must have been a den. To the left was a heap of blackened debris, but this side of the room was basically intact, with a couple of easy chairs and an upended coffee table. The interior of the house was overwhelmingly dark.

"We'll transition when I switch off the flashlight. Are you ready?"

"Yes. Just let me get the VPD turned on."

"Wait until we're in," he said. He gently gripped her elbow and clicked off the light.

A swirl of the cinnamon-candy smell enveloped them, and Emelia gasped as the room dissolved into the vast, bizarre space of the Deepest Shadow. Alex guided her forward across the spongy ground and once they were fully in, he glanced back to see a large, irregular gray splotch that was the opening from the den.

"Switch it on," he said.

Emelia flipped a couple of switches and there was a *beep-beep* sound as it powered up.

"Ready," she said. They walked to the right, passing gray rectangles and squares as well as irregular patches.

"House number one," Alex said as they continued past gray shapes on the right. There was a slight break and then more gray shapes. "House number two," he said.

Another break and as they neared the murder house, Emelia paused and glanced at the VPD screen. "I'm getting a signal," she said. "It's very faint."

They moved up and she said, "Slightly stronger but still pretty weak. The particles degrade over time."

"Can you track it?" Alex asked.

"Alex, he used the ruined house just like we did!" she said. She showed him the flickering image on the display screen. The thin line, barely visible, stretched from a gray rectangle at the murder house and trailed off to the left back to where they'd come from.

"I'm getting an indicator of a second trail but it's not showing up on the screen. Probably just too faint. He backtracked, I think."

Looking up from the machine, Alex saw a cluster of glowing dots in the open area of the Shadow. They undulated but it was clear that they were getting closer. There was a *whup-whup-whup* sound and Emelia saw it closing the distance between them. It looked like a massive, velvety black eel spotted with bioluminescent patches. Tendrils streamed from its head, and as it neared it opened its jaws, which were lined with glowing bluish teeth.

"It's coming for us!" Alex said, turning toward a gray rectangle and tugging at her elbow. She resisted for a moment, pressing a button on the VPD. Then they ran across the spongy ground as the *whup-whup-whup* sound grew louder behind them. It was almost upon them as they crossed the threshold into what seemed to be a closet. As the huge thing gnashed its jaws just beyond the threshold, a strange oily smell enveloped them. *Its breath*.

Suddenly, everything changed as Alex flicked a switch and light illuminated the room. The portal into the Deepest Shadow and the eel-thing were gone. They were in a small, narrow broom closet, with a broom, mop, bucket and shelves lined with cleaning supplies and neatly folded rags. A vacuum cleaner stood in a corner near the door. Emelia opened her mouth to speak, but Alex put a finger to his closed lips. "*We're in one of the neighbor houses,*" he whispered.

They waited as the oily scent and the cinnamon-candy smell faded, giving way to aromas of pine and citrus from the cleaning supplies. There was a faint sound of activity and a man's voice said, "—Somebody there?"

A tense moment passed as they waited. There was a soft sound of footsteps on carpet.

The doorknob twisted and the door opened.

"Shit!" the man said, stumbling back across the hall. Emelia was as startled as he was. *What the hell do we do now?* Alex took her hand and pulled her forward as he stepped toward the man. "Hi!" Alex said. "We didn't mean to startle you there."

The man's eyes were wide. "Who the hell are you? How'd you get in there?"

"It's the funniest thing," Alex said, and in an instant Emelia's fear evaporated. She knew she loved Alex, but in this strange moment she was prepared to follow him to the ends of the Earth. To do anything he asked of her. Some rational sliver deep in the back of her mind wanted to resist, but it was impossible.

"I'm Bud Tomkins and this is my wife, Janet Tomkins," Alex said, holding out his hand. "And you are?"

"Bill Veevers," the man said, shaking Alex's hand. "I'm kinda confused about this."

"That is completely understandable, Bill," Alex said. "We don't want to take any more of your time, though. Can you take us to the front door?"

"I guess I can," he said, confusion still clouding his features. "This way."

Emelia, still more enamored of Alex than she ever thought she could be, followed eagerly as Bill led them down the hallway and through his living room, which had a large tank of tropical fish. The evening news was on the television. They passed through another short hallway, and Bill unlocked the front door for them. He opened it, and Alex and Emelia stepped through. She couldn't stop grinning. *He's so smart.*

Once they were outside, Alex said, "Hey, Bill. Thanks for everything. You may want to go catch the rest of the news. Don't forget to lock up."

"Um, okay then," Bill said. He watched them for a moment and then closed the door and locked it.

As Alex led Emelia back to the car, she said, "I love you so much."

"I know," he said with a sigh. "I swore I wasn't going to do this. No choice, though."

"What?" she said as they arrived at the car.

"It's the charisma pheromone, Emelia," he said, holding the door for her.

"Well, it's *great*," she said.

Twenty minutes into the drive back to EaDo and Alex's house, Emelia suddenly said, "O—kay, *that* was an interesting experience. I think I'm back."

"Sorry about that," he said with a sigh.

She took his free hand with both of hers. "Baby, don't fret. I know you had to do it to get us out of there. You just exude that from your pores?"

He nodded, glancing at her. "Still love me?"

She laughed and squeezed his hand with hers. "Not as much as I did five minutes ago, but still very much. What on Earth was that thing in the Deepest Shadow? Did Titus send it?"

"We just call 'em shadow monsters. They seem to be indigenous to the Shadow. I'm pretty sure Titus has to avoid them like we do. They're just wild animals, like some of the critters you've studied. They don't often come out to the fringe like that. It must have spotted us and homed in for a snack."

She let out a slow breath. "Here be monsters," she said. "Well, that was a good little shakedown for the VPD. I was able to tune out your trail and actually save the signature of Titus' trail. Melanie is a goddamned genius."

"Indeed." He let out a sigh.

"What is it?" she asked.

"Think, my beautiful scientist. If Titus used the ruined house to get in and walked over to the murder house and then backtracked to escape—"

"Fuck," she said. "He's going to be a lot harder to track with the VPD."

Alex nodded. "Probably drove there in a car like we did."

"Well, this is just one data point. It's not a trend yet. He left a much longer trail from Lennie's house. Plus, running around in the open is exposure for him. They released the sketch from the description from that little boy who saw him at the carnival, and it's been all over the news. He's definitely distinctive looking."

"You said the particles degrade over time," Alex said. "Do you think there'd still be a trail from Lennie's closet?"

"I don't know. Seems doubtful but Melanie also amped up the sensitivity with the new code. We could try it."

"Then we're going to head straight there," he said, suddenly taking a corner a little too fast.

"What about our slithery friend with the glow-in-the-dark teeth?"

"It's rare that they come that close to the fringe. He probably moved back out into the distance once his dinner evaporated into the real world."

She squeezed his hand with hers again. "Once more unto the breach!"

Gialdo Botalli forked pasta and a bit of veal into his mouth. He smiled thinly. It was from Very Best Pasta just half a mile away. It was owned by Cambodians, and it had been a pleasant surprise to find they made excellent Italian dishes. *Who knew?* A few other men lounged in chairs around the table, their assault shotguns on the table. They looked bored. One of them, Heller, was smoking. Ordinarily Botalli would complain, but it helped mask the vague smell of mold and rot that permeated the entire lair. That's what he called the place. It had been designed with a basement—lunacy in Houston—that often flooded despite the recently installed sump pump. That accounted for the moldy side of the smell. But the rot? Well, there were locked rooms he and the other men were not allowed into. The smell of rot seeped out from under the doors. He did not ask about them. He did not want to know.

His employer was rich and seemed to be involved in some sort of criminal activities. Judging by the fifteen guards hanging around, who did not exactly seem to be law-abiding types, his employer expected trouble. To Botalli it all added up to a lair. As he lifted another forkful from the plate the intercom in the wall beeped and the thin, reedy voice of his employer said, "Botalli, office."

He wiped his mouth and stood. Heller glanced over. "You gonna eat the rest of that?"

Botalli paused. "It would be unwise for you to touch it, Mr. Heller."

Heller shook his head slightly. "S' just gonna get cold."

Another man next to Heller with a bald head and prison tattoos on his arms and face, said, "Heller, how long you been here?"

"Five days, punk, what's it to you?"

The bald man, who referred to himself as Clackerball, started to rise, a switchblade gleaming in his hand. Botalli raised a thick knobby finger, and Clackerball sat back down.

"Mr. Heller," Botalli said, "we will accommodate your relative newness here only to a degree. Clackerball—he does not care for the honorific of 'Mr.'—was prepared to perhaps give you an impromptu colostomy for such a remark."

"Damn skippy," Clackerball said, still fingering the switchblade.

Botalli nodded. "It is not wise for we who are in Titus' employ to engage in disharmony. Unless you care to end up in one of those locked rooms, I advise you to exercise restraint."

"Still gonna get cold," Heller muttered in quiet defiance.

Botalli looked at him with steely blue eyes. "Unwise."

Botalli closed the door to the office after entering. He didn't care for much of the lair, but he liked this room. It was decorated with old tapestries festooned with Roman iconography and scenes and decorated with careworn Romanesque pillars and statuary. The smell of old dust and earth, not entirely unpleasant, crowded out the pervasive smell of rot in the rest of the place. Sitting at a modern oak desk with a computer, a cell phone and four of the silver daggers known as *sescespitas*, was Titus Seneca.

He looked unutterably old, skeletal and frail, but Botalli knew this was an illusion. Titus was immensely strong and dangerous, perhaps because of ancient magics that Botalli and his ancestors on the great peninsula could only comprehend in feverish dreams. Titus waved a clawlike, liver-spotted hand at the chair in front of the desk. "Sit."

Botalli bowed slightly and sat. Titus regarded him with rheumy, bloodshot, pale blue eyes. Then Titus reached beneath the desk and came up with three shotgun shells. He dropped them on the aged felt pad that topped the desk. "Recognize these?" he asked.

"I do," Botalli said. "The silver buckshot shotgun shells we procured."

At that, Titus laughed, and Botalli found it to be a most disconcerting sound. He maintained his composure, nevertheless.

"Yes, yes. Silver. A bane to the man who hunts me. In fact, a bane to me, as well. But you did not know that, eh?"

Botalli cleared his throat. "I feel that my generous compensation in your employ also suggests that I abstain from being too inquisitive."

"Wise, Botalli," he croaked out. "Wise, indeed. What was the test you mentioned?"

"The supplier told me a magnet would reveal the non-ferrous nature of the pellets."

Titus nodded. "Yes, I recall now. Non-ferrous."

He fell silent, and Botalli thought it best to remain silent himself.

"There is a better test," Titus said finally. He picked up one of the *sescespitas*. "Silvered blades on these," he said. He held the index finger near to the blade. "I can feel the heat of it. I can sense the poison it has for me."

Botalli nodded silently. He *was* wondering what kind of man could be harmed by silver, though. He remembered the werewolf phobia ruse he had laid out to the ammunition salesman. Was it a ruse? Or—.

The finger hovered over the gleaming metal. "Were I to touch the unalloyed silver, it would raise a painful blister, you see. It would take a long time to heal."

Botalli nodded silently. *Composure is essential.* He had begun to feel a black sliver of fear somewhere deep inside him.

Titus set the dagger down reverently. Then he picked up one of the shotgun shells and effortlessly broke the plastic cylinder open and spilled the gleaming, spherical pellets into his left hand. "Hmph!" Titus said. "No heat, no pain."

*Let him make his point fully.* Botalli stiffened, fighting to remain composed. *You are in the company of death.*

Titus broke the other two open, handled the pellets, and then dumped them unceremoniously on the desk. A few rolled off onto the carpeted floor.

"Well, Botalli, what do you think?"

"I would say with certainty, sir," he began, "that you are right in your assumption. I believe the vernacular term is 'swindled.'"

Titus laughed again, and this time Botalli could not suppress the fearful shiver that wriggled down his spine. "Yes, swindled, indeed! But it matters not! Do you know why?"

Botalli cleared his throat again, wishing he was not so suddenly thirsty. "No."

"This man, this one who seeks me, he will be expecting silver to be employed against him when he comes. But it will be this harmless metal, whatever it is."

Botalli was unsure how a man could survive shotgun pellets of any kind, but better not to ask undue questions. He was still in dangerous territory, having been the one who was fooled.

"It is *delicious*!" Titus said. "As he fights his way to me, he will be perplexed and confused. And imagining his machinations to avoid the deadly silver pellets amuses me to no end!"

Botalli, who had always been scrupulously careful, analytical and cunning, was just starting to process what Titus meant by *fights his way to me.* He briefly thought of Heller and Clackerball. And the others. And himself.

"I can scarcely wait to see his face when we finally meet! Delicious!"

Botalli risked a smile and nodded.

"Ah," Titus said, still smiling that yellowed, decayed smile as he played with the loose pellets with his fingers.

"If I may, sir," Botalli said. "The man who deceived us—"

"Oh yes. I trust you will pay him a visit. I leave the *harshness* of that visit up to you. Retrieve the silver if you can. That is all."

Botalli stood and bowed. He hoped Titus would not notice he was sweating. Then he turned and opened the door. He didn't think there was a sound worse than Titus laughing, but he heard it behind him. *Giggling*.

The lights were on at Lennie's house. Alex guessed it was an oversight. But then, it still hadn't been that long since the murders. Alex used the key Lennie had given him so long ago and opened the door. Once they were inside, Emelia went to the living room. Alex followed, laboring to not look at the bloodstains on the carpeted floor. He came up to where she was standing in front of *Sunlight on Boughs*, gazing at the painting. She turned to him. "Where we met." He nodded and smiled at her. She embraced him and he held her for a few seconds. As they parted, she said, "Let's go."

They went down the hallway to the coat closet. The light was still on. Alex closed the door behind them. He put his hand on her elbow. "Ready?"

"Yes. Fingers crossed for a trail."

"Right." He reached up and clicked off the light. The familiar cinnamon candy smell swirled around them.

"No giant eels, if you please," Emelia said as they crossed the threshold into the Deepest Shadow. They walked a little way forward and Alex scanned for luminous dots in the distance. There were none.

"Light up the VPD," he said. She did, and they stared at the screen as she made adjustments to the controls.

As Emelia turned with the device, a flickering line appeared on the screen. "Damned if that isn't it!" Emelia cried out. "Very faint, but the pattern matches the signature I captured earlier tonight."

"Let's go," Alex said, and using the device as their guide, they made their way along a wide, curving path, with the threshold of gray shapes off to their left. They walked for a long way, and Alex periodically glanced off the right to the middle of the Shadow, vigilant for shadow monsters. "Signal is a little stronger now!" Emelia said. "Two trails now. Coming and going."

"Quite the distance," Alex remarked. "I guess we know now why he's using a car to get around."

"He's refining his methods," Emelia replied.

They continued for a while longer and the trail curved toward a large, vaguely rectangular splotch ahead. "That's it," Emelia said.

"Somewhere outdoors," Alex noted. As they neared the threshold, he said. "Take out your pistol, Emelia. Check it."

They paused while she did so. "Be ready for anything when we transition," Alex said.

"Okay."

They crossed, emerging into a blind alley between two buildings. There was some sort of awning above that cast enough shadow at night to create an opening. Alex drew his pistol, and they moved forward, their feet clicking on the concrete pavement. As they emerged from the alley, they saw they were in an industrial area with a street running perpendicular to the alley they had emerged from. The buildings were dark and there was no traffic. Streetlights cast enough light to see by. Emelia put her pistol back in the pocket on the leather case and lifted the

VPD, scanning. "Got something!" she said. Alex held his pistol at the ready as Maxie had shown him. "Lead the way."

"Slightly stronger signal. Still two tracks. He used that alley all right."

They crossed the street. "It's leading to the door of that building," Emelia said. Just across the sidewalk was a nondescript, apparently abandoned building. Double doors of wood and glass lay ahead of them. The interior was dark, but there was something white taped to the glass on one of the doors. They approached and saw it was a note.

In blocky black handwriting, the note said. *There you are, my friends. I warned you, and yet here you are. Know that I am old and I see far. Very far. Devices help me see even farther. It is a wonder. But now I know you must be eliminated. Perhaps later, or perhaps now.*

At that moment Alex saw a red light through the glass and saw the tripod-mounted camera pointed at the door. A beeping sound reached his ears.

"Emelia! Run!" he shouted, shoving her off to the right, toward the concrete facade of the building. At that moment the brightest light he had ever seen blossomed behind the glass. In the moment before the detonation shockwave reached him, his only thought was *I'm sorry, my love.*

# 29

For a long moment, there was nothingness. Consciousness roiled, diffuse and indistinct. No thoughts, only sensations. Floating, swirling, shapeless. A slow sense of what? *Coalescing*. Molecules of thought playfully danced around each other and came together. The first reluctant thought was only two words: *Not dead*.

An emotion blossomed through the haze, the smoke, the fleeing *dissolution*. Fear swirled around the second thought: *She's dead*. There followed an unutterable sadness. But now, drawn together as if by some strange gravity, particles collided, stuck and attracted more to them. Vapor reluctantly gave way to semi-solids, and then solids. A faint sense of *thump-thimp—thump-thimp*—it was his heart beating. He was a *he* again. His name was *ahhhh-lecks*. Alex.

It all happened quickly now. A sense of *forming*. Hearing returned. *A woman crying*. It was somehow a happy sound to him, that voice, and he rejoiced. *Not dead. Eeeee-meee-leee-ahhh.* Emelia!

Moments later, Alex was aware of being on his knees on the sidewalk. He opened his eyes and saw glass and chunks of debris strewn in front of him on the street. He felt her arms holding him up and heard her sobbing and saying, "You're alive!" over and over. His vision sharpened to see her face, scratched and bloody but intact. Somewhere a car alarm beeped.

He was himself again, and with Emelia's help, he got to his feet. Knowing she was alive was the best thing in the world, and he embraced her. She embraced him back. It was then that he realized the explosion had shredded all his clothing and he was quite nude.

Somewhere there was the sound of a police siren in the distance.

"Alley," he said, the words rough against his newly reformed vocal cords. They retrieved the VPD, its strap broken, and his pistol, also intact, and he also got a small, nondescript spray bottle that had somehow survived the blast as well. He rummaged through the scraps of his clothing and got his keys, his phone and his wallet. He put the items into pockets on the battered VPD case, and then the two of them stumbled, limped, and hobbled back to the alley. As they neared the darkness and the threshold, they paused and held each other again.

"Are you all right?" he asked her.

"Yes, I think so," she replied. "Scraped my knees pretty bad, I think. I stumbled after you pushed me, but I think it protected me from the blast. A little scratched up here and there."

She looked at him, her eyes wide. "You were a gas."

"What?"

"After the explosion, there was just white vapor hanging in the air in front of the door. Like white smoke, but after a little bit then it began to contract, to draw in on itself. It shaped itself into a human form and then you were back. Oh, thank goodness you're back!" She embraced him.

"Gonna have to ask Maxie about that," he said, holding her gently.

The siren grew louder. "Let's go," he said, leading her back to the threshold.

Once inside, after a quick scan of the distance for shadow monsters, Alex, though still lightheaded after the explosion and his reformation, picked Emelia up and cradled her in his arms. She in turn held the VPD, which, after a quick check, seemed to be somehow undamaged, and guided them back along the faint, flickering trail to Lennie's house. They emerged in the coat closet and Alex set her down carefully after turning on the light. She glanced down at her knees. Her black jeans were torn, and the abraded cloth was wet with her blood.

"Hold on a sec," Alex said. "You have a chip of glass embedded in your eyebrow." He reached up and took it out, hating that it made her flinch. Blood welled up and Alex dipped his index finger in his mouth. "Hold still," he said and dabbed saliva on the wound.

"Whoa," Emelia said. "It doesn't hurt anymore."

"Can you walk?"

"Barely. My knees are throbbing."

He put an arm around her and helped her through the door into the hall. They went a little further down and found a bathroom with old-fashioned green ceramic tile and a friendly aroma of potpourri. He helped her sit on the edge of the tub. "Be right back," he said.

Alex made his way further down the hall and found what must have been Lennie's bedroom. A quick search yielded sweatpants with pockets and a T shirt. None of Lennie's shoes fit him. "It's okay, buddy," he said, thinking of his lost friend. "This'll do. *Gracias.*"

He went back to the hall bathroom and found Emelia leaning on the edge of the sink and looking at herself in the mirror. She turned and saw him and nodded. "Let's get those jeans off," he said.

"Yes, sir!" she said with a smile, reaching down to undo her belt. Alex couldn't help but admire her. Joking around after nearly being blown to bits.

She unbuttoned her jeans and slid them down. "Ow, ow!" she cried as the cloth passed over her knees. As she stepped out of them, Alex retrieved the small spray bottle from the VPD case. He spritzed his open mouth a couple of times and put the bottle back in the pocket.

"What's that?" she asked. She had sat back down on the edge of the tub. Her knees were badly scraped.

"A special solution from a vampire pharmacist. Stimulates saliva production."

"Another surprise from the world of vampires," Emelia replied. "You guys think of everything."

Alex knelt in front of her. "This will hurt a bit at first. It'll pass quickly though. Are you ready?"

She nodded. Alex put two fingers into his mouth and wet them with saliva, which was flowing freely now. She hissed as he dabbed the scrape on her left knee. He put his fingers back in his mouth and he could taste her blood. *Something else I vowed would never happen*, he thought as he dabbed her left knee again.

"Yeah, that's it," she said. "It's not hurting now."

She watched in amazement as the blood clotted and in moments the scrape had completely scabbed over. Alex repeated the procedure with her right knee, and it, too, scabbed over quickly. Then he got a washcloth from the stack on the counter and wet it with water from the sink. He washed her face and neck to clean away dirt from the explosion and noted a few small cuts and contusions. He dabbed saliva on them, and they rapidly faded.

"Okay, this is gross, but completely fascinating," Emelia said.

Alex laughed. "We need you presentable for your next FBI briefing," he quipped.

"Yeah, I'd never hear the end of it from Alison if I showed up injured," she said.

She glanced down and saw that the scabs on her knees had loosened and fallen away, revealing pink healed skin underneath. "Damn!"

"Dr. Alex to the rescue. Can you stand?"

She stood and marveled at her transformation in the mirror over the sink. She was essentially unhurt now. "I expect I will be a bit stiff and sore in the morning," she said.

He nodded. "Nothing a few ibuprofens won't fix." He gathered up her jeans and rinsed the blood out of the knees with water from the tub faucet. He then dried them as best as he could with a towel from the rack by the tub.

"We're interfering with a crime scene," she said casually as she looked at the pink splotches on the towel.

"I don't think they're going to learn anything else from this crime scene," Alex said.

Emelia put her jeans back on. "Much better!"

She inspected her face in the mirror over the sink. "Wow. I think I'm okay."

He walked up and embraced her. After a brief kiss, he said, "You're more than okay."

"Thank you. Did you know that was going to happen to you?"

"No. I'd never heard of that happening, like, ever. But then vampires don't get blown up that often, I'm guessing." He was silent for a moment. "I was sure I was a goner. I'm hoping Maxie might have heard of that phenomenon."

She leaned her head on his shoulder. He felt her shiver, and he held her a little tighter. She met his gaze. "My shock at all this is wearing off. I thought I'd lost you. It was horrifying. I mean, right at the moment the bomb went off I thought that was it for both of us. But then I realized I was still alive, and I'd have to face life without you. It was awful. But here you are, thank goodness. Thank goodness!"

Her expression became grave. "He's very serious about killing us, Alex. He had that whole setup ready to go on the outside chance that we'd somehow track him to that building. He's fucking smart. Dangerously smart."

Alex reached up and stroked her hair as she put her head back on his shoulder. Words failed him. He was having a lot of trouble getting past that word she had uttered: *Us.*

The next morning, Alex sat in the meeting room of the Compound with Bardru and Maxie. Across the table sat Jonas, Clint, and Tessa.

Alex had already explained what had happened, leaving out any details about Emelia. He'd made sure Maxie would likewise not say anything about her presence.

Jonas said, "That's quite the story. It's amazing you're still here with us."

"Nobody is more amazed than me," Alex said. He turned to Maxie. "Tell them what you told me this morning, Maxie."

Maxie's transient smile was nowhere to be found. "Well," he said, "Based on what Alex told me, he had an experience that matches a story I heard about from one other vampire. He was fighting in Afghanistan and holed up with a machine gun crew in a reinforced bunker. They took a direct hit from an artillery shell—whether it was pre-sighted or just bad luck, I dunno, but pow! The position was pretty much obliterated. But the vampire described what Alex described. He reformed after the hit and his crew was blown to smithereens. But he survived.

Maxie took a breath and continued. "So, the thing about most ballistic weapons is that they kill or wound with percussive kinetic energy. A bullet is a tiny thing, but it hits you and delivers a shock of kinetic energy and that kinetic shock is an important part of the damage. It causes systemic shock to tissues and organs beyond the actual path of the bullet or fragments. And explosives are even worse. The pressure wave can burst your eardrums, rupture your lungs and scramble your brains in your skull even in a near miss, and that's not counting the chunks of shrapnel.

"So bullets, well, I'll admit I've done a couple of experiments along these lines—if you shoot a vampire with a bullet, it passes right on through, but there is a little puff of white vapor that trails the bullet, but then—" He paused for a moment.

"Go on," Jonas said quietly.

"Well, it's the damnedest thing, Jonas. The white vapor gets sucked back into the hole, and there's no hole anymore. It's like the percussive shock vaporizes a bit of the vampire's flesh, and then the vapor reconstitutes itself, healing the wound. Unless the bullet is silver. That's another kettle of fish, see?"

Jonas nodded. "So a very large percussive shock, like that of an artillery shell or a bomb, might actually vaporize the vampire's entire body and then it just reforms?"

Maxie nodded. "That's the idea. It matches what that Afghanistan vet told me and what Alex experienced. Alex is lucky to be here, having taken the brunt of that explosion head on."

Jonas turned his gaze to Alex. "We're glad you're okay."

Alex nodded. "It was definitely a surprise. Glad to still be here."

"This Titus is playing for keeps, Jonas," Maxie said. "But one thing—"

"Go on."

"There's an extra bit of good news out of this, aside from Alex still being with us, see? The explosion destroyed the camera before the shockwave hit Alex, so Titus couldn't see the aftermath. He didn't see Alex reconstitute. There's every chance that for now, he thinks Alex bought it. That may help us somehow. I'm not really sure how much, but it's something."

"Good analysis, Maxie." Jonas said thoughtfully. "Hopefully it will give us some kind of advantage, at least for a bit."

Jonas turned to Alex. "You know I'm the one that has to ask the tough questions, right?"

Alex smiled. "You wouldn't be Jonas if you didn't."

Jonas smiled and nodded. "Alex, are you still committed to help us?"

Alex thought of Emelia, and how she looked, battered and bloody after the explosion. "Jonas, I've never been more committed than I am now. I mean to stop Titus, whatever the cost."

Jonas stood and came around the table. Alex stood as well. Jonas reached out and shook Alex's hand. "I know you and I have locked horns a time or two. But now we know what you're up against, and how high the stakes have become. If you make it through this, the Collective will see to it that you never want for anything ever again. That's my solemn pledge to you."

"I'll do my best," Alex replied.

Jonas nodded and clapped him on the shoulder. "That's all we can ask. Thank you."

# 30

It was late afternoon, and Alex was feeding the dogs. As they munched on kibble, Emelia came up the front stairs of Alex's house. She was dressed for work: a dressy white blouse, dark gray slacks and a matching blazer. She stepped over the baby gate and said, "Where's my four-legged welcoming committee?"

Alex went to her. "Feeding time overrules welcoming guests," he said, leaning forward to kiss her. He surveyed her for a moment. "You look like a million bucks. No one would guess you almost got blown up yesterday."

She smiled at him. "You look like a million bucks yourself. No one would guess you *did* get blown up yesterday!"

They came together for a languorous kiss. Alex felt so lucky to have her in his arms. As they parted, he asked, "How did the FBI briefing go?"

"Well, it was very interesting for a change. Someone anonymously leaked a psychological profile of one Titus Seneca and linked him to the bombing. I'm assuming that was your Collective."

"You assume correctly. The leadership decided to do it after I met with them. Our HPD guy Clint helped us make it untraceable. How did Alison's boss take it?"

"You mean the prick?" she said with a sigh. "Jack *stay-in-your-seat-and-shut-up-Emelia* Crain?"

Alex laughed. "Wow."

"Yeah. He pooh-poohed it. I made the mistake of asking if there was a Behavioral Analysis profile yet and he gave me a glare that could have melted titanium. They *still* don't have one. Alison told me they have four agents trying to run down the provenance of the leak. That's more than they have at the bomb scene. Crazy."

Suddenly, there was a flurry of wagging tails and furry bodies brushing against Emelia's legs. She greeted the dogs and dispensed kisses until they settled down a bit.

"Crain's running this thing like the Keystone Cops," she said. "Alison privately told me that the FBI regional director is getting involved after the bombing. His name is Robert Cantrell and, according to Alison, he *does* believe that the profile is 'of interest' and he also thinks the bombing is related. So he's probably going to overrule Crain."

"Eventful," Alex said.

"Blowing up a building will do that," she said. "Do you want to hear the finale of my day?"

He smiled silently.

"Alison Martin made a Hail Mary pass at me. She deployed the phrase 'rock your world, baby.'" Emelia sighed.

Alex came up and embraced her. "Did you tell her you have someone to rock your world already?"

Emelia frowned. "No, I didn't want to hurt her. She's lonely and navigating in man-infested waters and she has a prick boss and lost her sweetheart not too long ago. It makes me sad. I shut her down as gently as I could. But of everything that happened today, that made me the most upset."

Alex led her over to the couch. She grimaced as she sat.

"Can I cheer you up with an ibuprofen and beer cocktail?" Alex asked.

"Pretty please with kisses on top?" she asked. The two dogs jumped on the couch on either side of her and nuzzled her. "Okay, this is a bit better," she said, laughing.

"You need some pampering. Can I make you some dinner?"

"Yes please. Something light. Cheese and crackers and fruit and ibuprofen and beer on my cup of stars tray."

"Anything for you, my Merricat."

She smiled at him. "Light on the arsenic, if you please."

Later that night, Emelia walked through the revolving glass door and saw Melanie waiting at a small table in the piano bar Classico. Melanie had a martini going, so Emelia waved at her and ordered a martini at the bar. The pianist had just started a piece that was interesting and repetitive when Emelia sat down. Melanie glanced over at the pianist, and then back to Emelia. "That's Philip Glass he's playing," she said. "Never thought I'd hear that in a piano bar. It's called *Metamorphosis*."

Emelia smiled as she sipped her martini. "I like it." She looked Melanie in the eyes. "Gotta say some serious stuff."

"Uh oh," Melanie said.

Emelia reached out and touched her arm. "There is no easy way to say it except to say it. I'm resigning from See Deeper."

Melanie gasped. "Why?"

"That's the hard part. I can't say why. I've already talked to Mark about this. I tried to prepare you for some of this, but I'm in uncharted waters. That bomb attack in west Houston?"

"Yes?"

"It was meant partially for me."

Melanie's eyes were wide. "What? How—how?"

"It's okay. I'm okay. It was a close call. But part of the reason you might be feeling left out on this particular investigation is that I've been working to shield you from some very bad stuff."

"Maybe I can help," Melanie said.

"You already have in some respects. The new code, *your* code, for the VPD played a role in my tracking the bad guy doing the mass killings."

"He sheds void particles?" She paused for a moment. "That was his trail we picked up in the murder house."

Emelia nodded. "Clever girl. And that's one reason I'm shielding you. He tried to kill me with that bomb."

"But that trail just ended in a closet." Melanie observed.

"Yes. Yes it did."

"But you can't expand on that. For my safety."

Emelia squeezed her arm and nodded.

"Have you talked with Mark about this? About the attempt on your life?"

"I sent him an email, yeah. Look, I can't say much more about the particulars. I feel terrible about keeping you in the dark, but there is a silver lining on that dark cloud."

"I still want to help you, Emelia," said Melanie, her jaw set with determination.

Emelia took a deep breath. "I know you do, Mel. But your destiny is different from mine. His next attempt might succeed."

Melanie went pale. "My destiny?"

"Yes. As I said, I'm resigning. But I've also planted seeds for you to take my place at See Deeper."

"What?" Melanie cried.

"Easy, easy" Emelia said, patting her arm gently. "You're going to spook the pianist, and I like this song."

Melanie's cheeks reddened.

"I'm resigning or, well, let's not talk about the other possibility. You're a valuable asset to See Deeper and now you're a full-fledged Investigative Agent. You deserve it. Mark is going to ask you to take over the trainee training segments I oversaw. I have full notes and guidelines prepared in my office for you to use. How well you do with that has a bearing on how quickly you become the next Senior Investigative Agent."

"You can't be serious about this."

"I am serious about it. You're smart and capable and brave but adding another person to this equation ups the risk factor exponentially. Whatever happens with me, there will be other investigations, other encounters with the supernatural, and those are for you. That's what I mean by your destiny. See Deeper needs you. Mark will back you 100%, I promise. You can't seize this day, here and now, but you can seize all those days to come."

"I still want to stay here in Houston. I want to support you any way I can. Maybe the hunt will break in our favor."

Emelia smiled at her, but her heart was breaking. "Stay, then. I still need someone to drink martinis with at the end of the day. But a day may come when I won't be here at the end of the day. I'm going to say this once, tonight, and it will have to suffice on that day."

"Emelia, please don't." Melanie was on the edge of tears.

"Goodbye and good luck, Agent Sanders. Not for tonight, but in case that day comes. Now let's get another martini and listen to some wonderful music."

Melanie sniffled and wiped her nose with a cocktail napkin. "Girl power."

Emelia's broken heart rallied. "Girl power."

They raised their glasses and clinked them.

It was 2:23 am when Emelia made her way up the front steps in Alex's house. The lighting was dim, and it sounded like the television was on. She saw a black shape, nebulous and indistinct at the baby gate at the top. Two gleaming eyes regarded her, and she was aware of a black tail wagging behind the shape.

"My sweet girl Midnight, did you wait up for me?" Emelia said as she neared the dog. "Is your dad home?"

She stepped over the gate and went through the hall. A movie was playing on the television. James Mason, in his role as Captain Nemo, was steering the *Nautilus* through an underwater cave. Alex was asleep on the couch with Dizzy snuggled up against him. *My men*. She watched them for a moment.

Alex's eyes opened and he softly said, "Hey."

She had learned that was the way Southerners, and especially Texans, greet people. "Hey," she replied. "Did you, um, get something to eat?"

He nodded. "I lucked out. Been home for a while."

She came up and knelt by the couch. She leaned in to kiss him and hesitated.

"I brushed my teeth," he said. He still looked sleepy.

"My thoughtful man," she said and kissed him.

Alex sat up, and Dizzy emitted a grumbling sound as he shifted.

"You okay?" he asked, rubbing his eyes.

"No," she said. "I told my boss that the gravity of all this was pulling me away from the best job I've ever had and the best people I've known, and now I just feel lost."

"You had the talk with Melanie?"

The best she could manage was a weak nod.

He stood up and took her in his arms. He was shirtless and she rested her head on his shoulder. His arms felt so good around her. A thought hovered just at the edge of her awareness, but she couldn't place it. Then she stepped back and glanced down. He was wearing jeans, and his feet were bare. It had proven to be his official mode of dress for—

She glanced at the spiral staircase. "Have you been working?'

He smiled at her.

"You've been painting!"

In a rush of excitement, she rushed to the stairs and hurried up, her shoes ringing on the metal stairs. It was dark but she knew the switches to hit at the top to light up the alcove and the workshop. She gasped and stopped in front of *Conflagration*. Angy, looping swaths of fiery orange and red paint connected the original two splotches and had expanded around them both, all threaded through with twisting, oily black lightning. The painting was a full a third of the way to completion.

She could almost feel its glaring heat inside her; there *was* heat inside her, roiling and seemingly unquenchable, and as Alex came up, she reached up and hungrily kissed him.

"Make love to me," she said, her voice urgent. "Now."

"No electric blanket," he said with a laugh as she wriggled out of her blazer.

She kicked off her shoes and yanked at the buttons of her blouse. "We'll figure something out."

# 31

—·—

They both slept in after the night's exertions, and Emelia woke at 11 a.m. to a delightful savory smell in the air and a distant sizzling sound. It wasn't bacon, and it didn't smell like breakfast sausage. She was alone in the bed. Apparently even Midnight had succumbed to the aroma and abandoned her.

She threw on some pajamas from a previous night and made her way to the kitchen. There she saw Alex stirring the crumbly, orange-tinted meat sizzling in the frying pan, and it all came together.

"Chorizo!" she said. Alex glanced over at her.

"No," he said. "*Fresh* chorizo. And fresh tortillas! And freshly made salsa. All gifts from my housekeeper, whom you still have yet to meet. She is thrilled that I have apparently come to my senses and am eating at home. I'm making chorizo and eggs for you."

"I can't wait!" she said.

As she sat on the couch with her tray and her brunch, under the watchful gaze of the two dogs, Alex asked, "Got everything you need?"

She smiled and said, "Yep. What if, and this is just a theoretical, mind you, but what if I can't eat all of this and I, um, *accidentally* feed some to Dizzy and Midnight?"

"You can do an experiment to prove your hypothesis," he said with a smile. "However, if the proof ends up being some rather frightening dog farts later today, well, such are the perils of scientific inquiry."

She laughed as she saw him heading to the staircase. "Are you going to work?"

"Maybe," he said. "We'll see. Enjoy your brunch."

After her leisurely brunch, watching the late-morning news, which featured a terse statement from Jack Crain and a follow-up statement from FBI Regional Director Robert Cantrell about the FBI's commitment to finding the bomber, Emelia debated giving her leftovers to the dogs, who had not moved an inch.

She succumbed and as they happily gulped down chorizo and eggs and tortilla bits, she decided to sneak up and see Jackson Williams at work on *Conflagration*. As she ascended the staircase, she made a mental note *not* to jump him again. *A man's gotta work*.

He stood in front of *Conflagration* in jeans and bare feet but also a cotton pullover. *He's out of uniform.* His arms were crossed, and he stared at the painting like someone in an art gallery might.

"Figuring out what comes next?" she asked.

He turned and smiled. "Not exactly." He beckoned her over. When she joined him, he held her by the shoulders and pointed her so that she faced the painting. "Take a deep breath."

She did. "And another nice deep breath." She complied and then he said simply, "What do you see?"

"Angry colors. Heat. Liquid lightning, I think."

"Good. That's very good."

"Now, what do you see in the unpainted sections of canvas?" he asked.

"Just white. Gesso, I think?"

He shook his head. "Tsk. Don't see what is there. Try to see what *should be there*. Use your imagination. What's lacking?"

"More angry colors. More heat. More black lightning."

"Better." He walked up and pointed at a thin, ribbon-like swath of red that reminded her a little too much of a hue from *Experiment in Reds*. Then he moved his finger down to the white surface beneath it. What belongs here?

She was starting to get it. She let go of her analytical mind and leaned into intuition.

"It's too red: cooling down. You need to heat it up with yellow or orange," she said.

He turned to her and said, "Yellow or orange? Which?"

She let her intuition swirl. She took in the rest of the painting: that already existing interaction of colors.

"Yellow is too hot," she declared. "Orange is transitional. No, wait. Yellow. The yellow has to threaten to consume the red and make it orange and maybe red doesn't want that. Opposition."

"Very good, Emelia Cord," he said as he came up to her.

A nervous laugh escaped her. "I'm not real certain where...that...came from."

He took her by the shoulders and kissed her on the forehead. "I am. Follow me."

"I've been thinking a lot this morning about a few things," he said as they threaded their way across the space. "I've been learning a lot from Sun and Maxie, but I've also picked up from them what it is to teach."

They came across a tidy little area, with a few of the waist level tables. There were cans with clean brushes and a few fresh palettes, and natural light spilled down from a skylight above. There were fresh tubes of paints in a crazy riot of colors laid out. A can of thinner nearby. And the centerpiece was a prepared blank canvas on a cherry wood easel. It was chest height to Emelia.

She turned to him, shaking her head. "I—I couldn't."

He took her by the shoulders again. "But ya already did, Blanche," he said, mimicking her impersonation of Bette Davis from a while back.

Her hands trembled. "I'm not—"

He put a finger to her lips. "You are giving up your career for me. I know it's your choice, but it's an enormous responsibility to bear. So maybe I can help you make a career change. Maybe I can unleash something that's already there in your subconscious. You may be a scientist, but you're fiery and passionate, as well. That's what it takes to make art. There's science to it, as well, and you have that too. Let me teach you to draw out the passion and a different way of seeing for you.

"I can't," she said, pulling back. He held her tight. She returned his gaze.

"Then sleep on it. A few nights. I've planted the seed. That's all I ask."

"But you've been to school for this. You have talent."

He nodded. "You can go to school. Any school you want—I'll see to it. You can learn to harness your natural talent. And you'll have two esteemed coaches to help you."

She looked confused. "Two?"

"Max Ellis and Jackson Williams."

Her eyes were wide. "I'm not sure I could ever have your talent for this."

"Maybe not. But you can learn to become the artist that is already inside you. With your own talent and passion. It may be similar to what I do or it may be something more amazing and mysterious and thought-provoking than you ever imagined. And it will be you. Yours. When you first set a brush to the canvas of *Conflagration*, I said, 'look at you, being an artist.' Believe those words, Emelia. *Believe*."

It turned out to be a slow workday, so among other things, Emelia checked out of the hotel and moved into Alex's house. She told him she'd thought about it, and she was ready. He helped her set up the office and even moved the large painting *Topsy Turvy IV* in to decorate one of the walls. They made plans to buy some additional furniture, including bookshelves, for the office when time permitted.

"What about your house in Atlanta?" Alex asked.

She shook her head. "I haven't thought that far ahead," she said. "Still reeling from the newness of all this."

"I understand. At least you're saving See Deeper some money."

At that, her expression became downcast, and she stared forlornly at the floor. Alex rushed to her and embraced her. "I'm so sorry."

"It's hard," she said, her face buried in his shoulder. "I'm grieving, I guess."

He held her close. "While you were picking up your things, I arranged a surprise for you."

"Oh?"

"Well, you know there are other vampires in Houston, right?"

She nodded.

"Well, this evening you're going to meet two more!"

Her blues had fled, and she seized his arm. "One is your uncle! Bar— Bar—" she trailed off.

"Bardru. That's right. The other one is a big surprise. As big a surprise as I could think up for you."

"Oh, Alex! I can't wait."

At that moment Midnight came in, awkwardly dragging a jet-black doggie bed with her mouth. She came up to Emelia with the bed hanging from her mouth. "Aw, Midnight!" Emelia said as she took the bed from her and slid it under the desk so it would be by her feet when she was sitting in the chair. Midnight happily plopped down on it, becoming nearly invisible in that black-dog-on-a-black-bed way. Emelia got on her knees and kissed Midnight's head. "What a sweet girl!"

Before the anticipated meeting, Alex, already dressy in black suede slacks and a dark gray long-sleeved pullover, took Emelia shopping, and she picked out a tight retro cotton sundress with a summery red hibiscus motif at a resale shop in Montrose. She came out of the changing room and twirled for Alex. "Oh *yeah*," he said.

She looked at herself in the mirror. "The fit is perfect, but it's a *little* short," she said, tugging at the hem. "But damned if I don't feel sexy as hell in this."

He came up and put his arms around her waist. "You are sexy as hell, in or *out* of that."

She laughed and twisted to kiss him.

In the jewelry case, they found a necklace of polished irregular red stones and a matching bracelet. She put them on and said, "*Experiment in Reds*. How do I look?"

He grinned. "Like a million bucks."

As they drove, the failing light of the sunset illuminated towering thunderclouds in the east, and they glowed red, orange and purple as white threads of lightning coursed through them. The thunder was muted but rolled by, inevitable. After Emelia had a quick nosh at a little Cuban eatery in Montrose, Alex drove them to an office building in Neartown. An Art Deco sign outside said The View. A valet parked the car as a cool breeze swept past from the approaching front.

Then they rode an express elevator to the top floor. They emerged into a classy nightclub with white linen on the tables, and a spectacular view of the Houston skyline through banks of huge windows. 40s music played softly in the background. Hearing the music, Emelia turned to Alex and said, "Is this your doing?"

He shrugged and smiled. "A happy coincidence, maybe?"

She laughed. "I'll bet."

"Ready for your surprise?"

She took his arm. "More than ready."

He led her along to a row of tables near the bank of windows and Emelia spotted two men, one older and thin with pomaded hair, and one seemingly middle-aged, balding and heavyset, conversing. They both wore black suits and ties, and they stood as the couple arrived at the table. They both smiled and the middle-aged man whistled when he saw Emelia. She blushed.

"Emelia Cord, this is Bardru Valeska, my uncle."

Bardru took her hand and gently kissed it. "I am so very pleased to finally meet you," he said, smiling.

"Surprise time," Alex said, turning to the middle-aged man, "Emelia Cord, meet Maxie Bright!"

With a broad grin, Maxie took her hand, but instead of kissing it, he raised their joined hands and twirled Emelia around underneath. She laughed in delight.

"I've heard so much about you both!" she said. "It's such a wonderful surprise to meet you!"

Alex laughed, regarding Maxie in his dark, somewhat ill-fitting suit. "Maxie, that's the most dressed-up I've ever seen you!"

"I clean up okay, I guess." He cocked an eye. "Besides, it's fer *her*, not you!"

More easy laughter between them.

"Sit! Sit!" Bardru said, gesturing to the table.

The drinks, fine wines for Bardru and Alex, and beers for Maxie and Emelia, flowed in abundance. There followed many stories of Bardru's exploits in Russian circuses and the American West, as well as Maxie's stories of his naval career.

Emelia hung on every word.

"So there we were aboard the *USS Canacker*," Maxie said. "It was peacetime, except for rumblings between North and South Korea that never amounted to nothin.' We were in the Philippine Sea, and it was dead summer. Hot as hell, see? So the captain dropped the anchor and announced Swim Call. Sailors in tropical waters love Swim Call. Great way to cool off."

He quaffed beer. Emelia smiled at him. "Anyways, you know who else loves Swim Call? The goddamned sharks, that's who. So you gotta have a shark watch. Plink at 'em with a semi-auto and they'll run. I was off watch, so I damnwell wanted to swim with the other guys. So they got another gunner's mate to be shark watch: a striker who had just made his rate. This guy's name was Albert Courtner. but nobody called him that. He had some weird condition where his hands constantly shook. So everyone called him 'Shakey.'

There we were, going on deck with our towels and swim trunks and the bosuns had already rigged a cargo net over the side. Suddenly word spread like lightning that Shakey had pulled the duty for shark watch. He actually came out on deck with a big dumb smile on his face and the rifle shaking in his hands. Suddenly we were all looking at each other and people were muttering and shaking their heads."

Maxie smiled and winked. "Sure enough, five minutes later the call came over the loudspeakers. 'Now hear this: swim call has been cancelled.'"

They all laughed. "Splendid story!" cried Bardru. He raised his glass. "A toast to shark watch!" More laughter as they clinked glasses.

At one point, Emelia took Alex's hand under the table and leaned close to his ear. "Thank you so much for this, baby."

A sound of distant thunder rumbled against the windows as Maxie asked Bardru for another story.

## 32

The storms passed in the night with very little rain, and the next day, Sunday, September 1, arrived with cool temperatures and mostly sunny weather. It was a perfect day for the Fiesta de los Colores, a Hispanic/Latino festival celebrating its tenth anniversary. The fiesta had traditionally been held on about 12 acres of open fields near the eastern edge of downtown Houston. The lot had attracted numerous developers hungry to take advantage of so much prime real estate so close to downtown, but it was owned by the recalcitrant Reyes family and was the site for many lucrative festivals each year. Fiesta de los Colores was no exception, and it was in full swing just after 1 p.m. when Titus Seneca climbed like a great spider over a back fence near a storage building. He stood in an alley, surveying the brightly colored banners known as *papel picado*, and the crowds milling about various vendors and food stalls.

"*Incipiat*," he said and strode forward.

Alex and Emelia were in the office at his place, trying to get the wifi working after a brief power outage when both their phones rang almost simultaneously. Jonas told Alex, "He's out in the open, killing people at a festival!" and Alison told Emelia

"Our bad guy is on a rampage! He's killed four cops and several civilians. 2390 Pinto Street!"

They got their firearms, extra magazines and ID lanyards, then hurried down to Emelia's car. Sirens sounded in the distance and four helicopters were hovering just east of downtown. "Shit!" Emelia said, glancing in that direction.

"Hurry!" Alex said, and she got in on the passenger side. The gate opened as Alex placed the battery-operated light bar Clint had given him on the dashboard.

"Wish we had a siren," Emelia said.

"I'll just honk the damned horn," Alex said, pulling out onto the street.

Alison called again and told Emelia what to say to get past the police cordon. Alex was roaring down streets but slowing if there were other cars or pedestrians.

"Alison said she and the FBI don't know what to do," Emelia said. "They and the police have shot him dozens of times, including with riot shotguns, and he's still up. SWAT is on the way. He's leaving a trail of bodies wherever he goes."

"600 soon." Alex's voice was grim. "They don't have the right ammunition."

"Alex, if we kill him and they dig silver slugs out of him, what then?"

"Shit." Alex handed her his phone. "Hit the speed dial for Jonas and hand it back to me."

She did, and Alex explained the problem to him. "It's my call," Jonas said. "No time to call a meeting of the Collective. Some of the leadership are here. "If you get a shot at him, take it." There was a brief silence and then another voice.

"Alex, it's Maxie. Remember your effective range: ten meters. Thirty feet. Remember your breathing and your stance. If it comes to it, remember your training from Sun."

"I will." He hung up and glanced at Emelia. "They said to take the shot if I get it. Something else, Emelia, and it's extremely important."

"Tell me." She saw people who had fled the festival running wildly down the sidewalks now on either side of the street. Women, children and even some of the men were crying.

"*He knows what you look like.*"

"The camera," she said.

"That's right," Alex said. "I know you are firearm-certified, but don't take any shots unless he starts coming toward you. He can kill you with his bare hands. He's fast too, so fire all your shots if he starts to approach you. Torso shots. Try to stay close to me. We're just going to play it by ear but defend yourself no matter what."

"I will."

The police cordon was ahead. Faint gunfire echoed, even though the windows were up. "Emelia," Alex said. "This may be it for one or both of us today. If I don't make it, I love you."

She put her hand on his leg. "I love you too. I'm hoping this isn't our time to transform."

He turned and nodded. "Me, too."

At the cordon, before waving them on, the HPD lieutenant said, "Nothing is stopping this guy. I know that sounds crazy but it's true, so believe it. Bullets and shotgun rounds—nothing seems to work. Coupla guys tried to tase him and got torn apart. We've got a National Guard helo on the way. Don't take any stupid chances, okay?"

Alex nodded and drove up to park behind a line of police cruisers with their lights going. Civilians were still streaming past as they got out of the car. "*Demonico!*" a wild-eyed man shouted as he passed. "*Demonico!*"

It sounded intermittently like a shooting range. There were intervals of relative quiet and then a barrage of cracking reports. They heard shouting. And screams.

"My god, Alex," Emelia said as they hurried forward.

Bodies lay ahead. Some were festival-goers and some were cops. The beaten down grass of the festival ground was stained with blood. As they neared, they saw a dead man in a tan jacket with an FBI badge. His throat had been cut and a pistol lay near his hand.

They hurried toward the gunshots. As they got closer, they saw some people huddling in a stall selling musical instruments. Emelia pulled Alex to a stop. She punched a few buttons on her phone and shouted, "Run," into it. "*Correr*," a female voice said back.

She waved at the people. "*Correr! Correr!*" she yelled, and Alex joined in. The group broke cover and ran toward the cordon.

They continued past more bodies. It was quiet and then another round of cracking reports. "He's moving from cover to cover, it sounds like," Emelia said. "They're pot-shotting when he moves."

Alex nodded. Now they were close. Clusters of police and SWAT riflemen huddled at some of the stalls.

"We've got a problem," Alex said during a lull in the shooting.

"We can't get near him," Emelia said, finishing his thought. "We'll get shot all to hell in the panic fire."

The sharp, sweet smell of cordite hung in the air. Alex and Emelia tried to get a little closer when Emelia's phone rang. She answered it and then turned. Alex followed her gaze and saw a blonde woman huddled with a few riflemen and FBI agents with pistols. The blonde gestured for them to come closer.

"It's Alison," she said, just as a figure, lean, skeletal and pale, dressed in tattered rags of clothing, darted from cover ahead. Gunfire erupted around them, and Alex pulled Emelia down to the ground. Bullets whizzed past them, and one hit the ground not far away, sending up a plume of gray dirt." Several people were shouting, "Ceasefire!" and they heard a woman's voice. "Emelia! Cover! *Cover*!"

The figure, which had an almost ridiculous fringe of long white hair spilling down from a large bald spot on the head, vanished behind a supply truck as bullets spanged into the body of the truck and shattered the windshield.

Alex's mind reeled. *TELL THEM TO STOP*! rang through his skull in a voice he'd heard before in the Deepest Shadow. Someone was shaking him "Alex!" Emelia said. "Come on!" He came to his senses and there was a lull in the shooting. Emelia pulled him up and they ran for the cluster of law enforcement agents with Alison. They hunkered down when they arrived, and Alison admonished Emelia: "What were you *doing* out there?" Then Alison's gaze fell on Alex, and recognition flickered in her eyes. Her face went pale. *Great*, Alex thought.

Alison seemed to regain her composure. "He's rabbiting," she said. "His plans to kill as many people as possible with his bare hands—well, he had a couple of weird-looking daggers before, but snipers shot those out of his hands—anyway, his initial plans have collapsed. Most of the civilians have fled or are hiding. If any cop gets near him, he kills them. I think he's headed toward that parking garage." She pointed to a four-story garage at the edge of the festival grounds. "Maybe he's got a getaway car stashed there.

"Communication is all fucked up," Alison went on. "This guy plowed through our forward command post and busted them all up. Captain Legroue of HPD is dead. As you saw, there's a ton of panic fire every time he moves. People are completely freaked. Emelia, who *is* this guy?"

Emelia shook her head. "I don't know," she said. "We've been trying to find out."

"There he goes!" someone shouted, and another insane fusillade began. Titus ran and both Alex and Emelia saw the yellowish puffs of vapor as bullets passed through his body. They retracted as even more appeared from separate hits. He staggered more than ran, such was the effect of so much gunfire on his body. But he continued, nearing the fence that separated the festival grounds from the parking garage.

"How can he stay up!" Alison cried out. "This is *fucked*." Emelia glanced at Alison and her eyes were wide.

"Easy, Alison," Emelia said and put her hand on Alison's arm. Alison shrugged her arm off and cast a withering glance at Alex. *Jesus*, Emelia thought. *Really*?

They watched as cops and agents displaced and ran to new cover, their heads down, trying to pursue Titus, who now scrambled over the fence like some great, ragged insect and plopped down the other side. It was utter chaos. Some people were yelling "ceasefire" but the panic fire continued, and Emelia gasped when they all saw what looked to be an FBI tactical agent go down as he tried to displace. "Christ!" Alison shouted. "That's Saunders!"

A bullhorn-amplified voice crackled from somewhere. "Man down! Man down! Cease your goddamned fire!" a commanding voice shouted. "Displace and take positions closer to the parking garage!"

Without so much as a glance at Alex or Emelia, Alison jumped up and started running along with the other officers in their huddle. They were making their way toward the garage.

Alex and Emelia hurried after them, but they heard a moaning sound off to their right. A heavyset woman in brightly colored clothing rolled over on the ground. She was holding her neck and blood covered her hand and had stained her blouse. Emelia saw Alex turn and run faster than any Olympic athlete she'd ever seen. Breathlessly, she ran after him and saw he had kneeled next to the stricken woman. Her heart swelled when she saw him dip his fingers into his mouth and start swabbing her neck with his saliva.

By the time Emelia arrived, huffing and puffing, the woman was sitting up and genuflecting. "*¡Milagro! Dios te bendiga, mi hijo!*" she said and hugged Alex. He kissed her tenderly on the head and helped her to her feet. Then Alex took Emelia's hand, and they started off toward the parking garage as the woman shouted, "*Gracias, mi hijo!*" after them.

"She looks like my housekeeper," he said as they hurried along. "I thought it *was* her for a moment. Either way, I had to help," he said.

Emelia squeezed his hand. She hadn't thought she could love him more than she already did, but she realized she was wrong. "You did good, baby," she said breathlessly.

As they neared the clusters of officers and agents, there was an odd moment of relative quiet as it became clear to all that Titus was *climbing up the outside wall* of the parking garage. To Alex it was surreal, like some insane, small-scale version of *King Kong.* A loud *thup thup thup* sound came from overhead and a dark green helicopter swooped overhead. The side hatch was open, and they saw a soldier with a rocket-propelled-grenade tube on her shoulder braced there.

"Hold your fire! Hold your fire!" the bullhorn voice shouted. "Chopper on the scene! Hold your fire!"

Titus was fully nude, now, the last scraps of his clothing having fallen away. As the helicopter looped around for a shot, Titus stood on the whitewashed top wall of the parking garage, his emaciated frame silhouetted against the sky in a grotesque display of defiance. His face was a mask of rage. As Emelia and Alex neared, Emelia said, "His *genitals!*"

Alex's superior vision had already caught it. Titus' genitals were grotesquely malformed, fused and twisted into a bulbous, distorted dangling mass that could only be described as *monstrous.*

Alison ran up to them from somewhere. "Take cover—helo's gonna take a shot."

The telepathic voice rang in Alex's head again. "*I SEE YOU NOW!*"

Alex shuddered and saw that Titus was staring directly at him, Emelia and Alison.

"C'mon, you idiots," Alison said and loped off to a cluster of cops in a spot of cover nearby. Alex and Emelia joined them as the helicopter hovered in position. The RPG fizzed away from its tube and struck Titus in the chest. The explosion was bright and loud, and fragments of concrete rained down.

Smoke swirled and Titus Seneca was gone.

# 33

—·—

There were cheers and high fives. The commanding voice on the bullhorn said, "Stand down. See to the wounded!"

Amid this, Alex's gaze met Emelia's. His expression said it all. *He's not dead*. She nodded and said, "Go."

Alex sprinted off toward the fence, running slower than he could, so as not to draw more attention than he already was.

"What's your HPD boyfriend up to?" Alison asked.

"Is this really who you are?" Emelia asked. "I feel sorry for you."

"Whatevs," Alison replied, turning to high-five her colleagues again.

At the fence, Alex looked up. Sure enough, a yellowish mist was drifting down the front of the parking garage. Alex climbed over the fence and ran toward the front of the parking garage. He saw the entrance blocked by two HPD cruisers with lights going. A gravel road led away toward some industrial buildings a couple of blocks away. The mist glided down to ground level, and no one paid attention but Alex. He trailed the mist as it drifted down the road.

Alex frowned. Titus should have reformed by now, but maybe he had had an ability to stay in this form longer somehow. The industrial buildings were just ahead now, and Alex saw a dark blue town car parked on the street near one of them. The yellow mist swerved toward it. Alex drew his pistol; 16 shots in the magazine and one in the chamber. *This is my chance*. He was close enough now to see that the windows of the town car were partially open: common enough in the heat of late summer in Houston.

The mist began to flow through the window. Alex said nothing. He was sure Titus knew he was there, but this wasn't the time for heroic utterances. He raised the pistol and set himself in the stance Maxie taught him. He was about ten feet from the window as the mist swirled and began to coalesce.

Things happened quickly. The car's engine roared into life, even though Titus still seemed to be mostly a mist. Startled, Alex fired three shots as the mist took on a vaguely human form. The driver's side window shattered. The silver slugs *sizzled* through the mist, leaving black trails, two of them smashing through the passenger window and Alex staggered, his eyes rolling up in their sockets as an unearthly howl of pain racked his mind.

The car started to pull away and Titus was still mostly a mist! Reeling, Alex took a few steps forward and emptied the magazine into the car. His aim was wild now, but a few shots were still close enough to hear that sound, like flies crackling to death on the screen of a bug zapper, as slugs passed through Titus. He was aware of a distant bullhorn-amplified voice far away saying, "Who the hell is that? Stand down right now!"

The screaming in his head was inescapable, seemingly endless and hammering off the bones of his skull. He staggered again, vision blurred, clicking the emptied pistol at the window as the car slowly pulled away.

For a moment he glimpsed Titus, scarred by the passage of the bullets, his mouth agape and still screaming, but from his mouth now, gripping the wheel of the car and then it roared off down the street, spitting a cloud of dust and gravel.

Alex collapsed to his hands and knees into the gravel road, acrid dust swirling in his eyes and nose and mouth. He heard what he thought was a distant voice in unutterable pain say, in almost a whisper, "*Not enough.*"

Alex rose, cried out, and hurled the pistol after the receding car, hurtling away. *Not enough*. He collapsed again.

Emelia waited by the car, staring at her phone and the *Where-RU* app. He had called her phone and told her he'd meet her there. She watched the blip indicating Alex's phone moving closer on a side road on the app. She looked up and saw him coming down the side street, disheveled and covered in dust but alive and unhurt. She rushed to him and embraced him.

"Alex, thank god you're okay!" she said, holding him.

"Not okay," he said, his voice raw.

"Are you hurt?" she cried.

"He got away." He shuddered in her grasp. "Seventeen shots and he got away!"

She held him tightly. "Alex, just relax for a minute. I know you did your best. I know it." But the dismay and defeat in his face was heartbreaking.

He took a deep breath and seemed to relax a bit. "Kiss me," she said. He kissed her, and she could feel the tension leaching out of his body. When they broke, he said, "Thank goodness you're still with me."

She hugged him tight. "I am, baby, I am. Today was not our day. Thank goodness. Thank goodness!" she said, almost in tears.

He seemed to be recovering his composure. "I hurt him. I don't know how bad it was, but he was scarred when he formed. The bullets passed through the mist, but they still damaged him. There was a sizzling sound. His voice screamed in my mind and I lost my aim and missed with several shots."

She looked at him, resolute. "You wounded him. That's something, Alex. If you face him again—no! *When* you face him again, he'll be weakened."

He sighed. "Maybe."

"Of all the people fighting him today, you were the one that hurt him. *You alone*. And you saved that woman's life."

He nodded. "Do you mind driving us home? I need to call Jonas. I'm still a little rattled."

"Of course." She took his arm and led him around to the passenger side of the car. His hands were shaking when he gave her the keys. Hers were not. She steadied his hands in hers and met his gaze. "It's not over. We're going to stop him, Alex. You and me."

Alex sat on the couch with an untouched glass of wine in his hand. The huge television screen was showing nonstop news footage of Titus' rampage. It had made national and international news. The civilian body count was 96, and the law enforcement toll was 34. 22 injuries of varying severity. Numbness had settled over Alex. He had talked to Jonas and there was a meeting at the Compound tomorrow morning.

Emelia came in from the kitchen and popped open her beer. She stood behind him. "152 people," he murmured.

"No!" Emelia said, reaching for the remote and switching it off. "Don't torture yourself like this! He was aiming for 600 and, thanks to law enforcement and you, he fell far short. The death toll would have been 153 if not for you helping that poor woman. And you hurt him. You weakened him. He had to flee."

He finally took a sip of his wine. "He was already fleeing."

She came around and regarded him with a stern look. "Stop it. None of this is your fault. If we'd tried to stop him sooner, I'd have been shot to pieces and who knows what would have happened to you. In a way, you lucked out. There were no cameras on your confrontation. And the secret of how to kill vampires is still safe."

He managed a weak nod.

Still not satisfied, she whistled. Alex's eyes widened. He didn't know she could whistle. Midnight and Dizzy came running in, their claws skittering on the polished concrete floor. She bent down and patted the couch cushion next to him, and the dogs happily obliged, jumping up and licking his face. He laughed as he petted the two dogs.

He looked up at her, dodging dog kisses. "You're so amazing."

She smiled at him. "All in a day's work. Drink your wine. You and I have some business to attend to in the bedroom."

A little while later they made love with a furious intensity. It was a release they both needed after such a harrowing day. As they lay together exhausted and sated, he ran his hands over her sweaty body. Emelia had noticed that before. "Not complaining, but why do you do that?"

He smiled. "Before you came along, I hadn't touched a woman for so long. It's a tactile thing. A kinesthetic thing. My hands are hungry, and you feel so good."

"Makes sense," she said. She writhed under his touch. "Take your fill of me, my love, but be prepared if I need to satisfy *my* hunger as a result."

More whining from under the door. Emelia crawled on top of Alex, laughing. "Doggies are going to have to wait a bit!"

The next morning, Alex stood at the lectern in the main hall at the Compound. The leadership of the Collective occupied part of the front row. Alex told the story, omitting details about Emelia. Maxie sat at the end of the row, next to Bardru. Maxie nodded at him approvingly.

"That's it," he concluded. There was a smattering of applause. Jonas stood and approached the lectern. He shook hands with Alex and addressed the group.

"It was a horrible thing, and a tragic loss of lives, but we were lucky. Our secret is safe, thanks to Alex and Maxie. And our enemy is presumed by the authorities to have been destroyed. Even more importantly, Titus has suffered some measure of damage and may be weakened.

"Clint called me early this morning, and aside from some 'who, what and why' follow-up investigations, both HPD and the FBI are calling it closed. Tessa, can you come up here, please?"

Alex stepped down and sat next to Bardru, who smiled and patted him on the arm.

Tessa took a sheaf of papers up to the lectern and spoke. "I think I speak for everyone when I say thanks to Alex for his intervention with this Titus."

Another smattering of applause and Alex nodded.

"Well," Tessa said. "HPD recovered the fragments of one of the unusual daggers Titus was using. We have a photo from Clint if anyone wants to see it. It has a silver-plated blade, and the pommel guard is two bulbous objects resembling testicles. It's an old type of dagger with sexual connotations, known as a bollocks dagger in England, but he was heard speaking Latin, and he referred to it as a *sescespita*."

She cleared her throat and continued. "Most of you have read my profile, and it seems that a few of my assumptions have been confirmed. The uncensored video of him once his clothing was shot away shows a severe genital deformity that is likely to be a part of his psychopathology. Several victims early on had their eyes gouged out which is why he is called The Vision Killer, and it's likely he does that out of a feeling that the victims have somehow seen his deformity, at least in his perception.

"Later, snipers shot the daggers out of his hands, as Alex reported, and he began to kill people with his bare hands. But a few times he physically gouged out eyes with his fingers. One thing that did not happen during the prolonged attack was him feeding on anyone. So there are no APES bodies among the dead. Another grim stroke of luck.

"I plan to revise my profile of him based on the new evidence, but he appears to be conforming to my original profile for the most part. I will make that profile available to Alex and anyone else here who desires a copy.

"In conclusion, I think after this defeat of sorts for him he will lay low and lick his wounds. I don't think we can expect another public attack for a while."

Tessa was silent for a long moment. "This last part is especially important. Alex, be aware that you have hurt him and given his nature I do expect him to strike at you somehow. You must be exceptionally careful. He's attacked you once with the explosives and I do think he will attack again, and perhaps soon. That's all I have."

She stepped down and it was silent in the hall.

Jonas stepped up to the lectern. "Thank you, Tessa. I know Alex will exercise caution. We've reached a critical stage in this, and the stakes are high. We'll have to be vigilant."

Alex, sitting in the front row, could not help but notice that Jonas was once again looking directly at him when he spoke those last words.

## 34
— · —

Shotgun practice with Maxie the next day. "If this guy has henchmen or guards or what-the-hell-ever, I figger they'll have riot shotguns. And if you do some of what we talked about in our important conversation of not so long ago, you will end up with one. They're safer to use inside a structure and less likely to shoot through walls. 'Course that depends on the loads and the walls."

Alex showed Maxie a disarming move specifically for a rifle that Sun had taught him. From his armlock, Maxie grunted and said, "Man I gotta meet this Sun. He sounds like a badass!"

Alex laughed. "I seem to be surrounding myself with guys like that," he said, releasing Maxie and clapping him on the back. Maxie's smile famously appeared and fled. "Hey, I really enjoyed meeting your lady. She's a pistol, no pun intended."

Alex smiled. "She was delighted to meet you, too. That Shakey story had her in stitches even on the way home. Meeting her changed everything. I just hope we both make it through this."

"Sure. In service of that, I have a little surprise for you." He went over to a wooden crate and picked up what looked like a dismantled wetsuit. "Know what this is?" Maxie asked.

Alex shrugged. "I'm not sure."

The smile came and went. "This," Maxie said, "is the start of some full body Kevlar armor. I got the idea from those bank robbers in North Hollywood in 1997. They wore whole damned suits they'd cobbled together from cut-up bulletproof vests, so I'm making one for you."

Alex came over and examined it. "Ain't much to look at now," Maxie said, "but if those mooks have silver loads in their shotguns, this could save your life. There's video of those bank robbers running around and taking multiple hits from pistols, shotguns and even rifles and still staying up. You need an edge when you find out where this Titus hangs out and this could be it."

"Good thinking Maxie."

Maxie nodded. "Yeah, well, you know."

Alex let Maxie take measurements of his body with a seamstress' measuring tape.

Maxie scribbled the figures onto a page in a beat-up spiral-bound notebook. "This'll help. I'll bust ass to get this done, but I can't say exactly when it'll be ready."

Alex clapped him on the shoulder. "I know you'll bust ass. Just let me know."

There came a moment of silence between them as they regarded each other. Then Maxie spoke. "I started all this because Jonas and the fat cats in the Collective were paying me a pretty penny."

Alex was silent, letting him speak. "Anyways, after the other night when I met your Emelia and Bardru—well, I'm just sayin' it ain't about the money anymore, see?"

Alex put his hand on Maxie's beefy shoulder. "I feel the same, Maxie."

Maxie's elusive smile decided to stay a bit.

Alex emerged from double glass doors onto the faded wooden deck at the Cityscape Café. He went over to the table where Bardru was sitting with a smile on his face. Two glasses of dark red wine were on the table. Alex sat down and shook hands with the older man. Bardru did not immediately release his hand. "It has been a long time for us, a long time as uncle and nephew, eh?"

"92 years," Alex said, sitting.

"And yet we are both as fresh as your lovely Emelia, are we not?"

Alex laughed. "Yes!"

It was Bardru's turn to laugh. "She is good for you. I saw it the other night and I can see it in your eyes today."

Alex nodded. "I'm so grateful, Uncle."

Bardru drew himself up. "I am weary of that term."

"Uncle?"

"It does not adequately convey our journey," he said. "It is outdated."

"This is a surprise," Alex replied. "Is everything okay, Bardru?"

Bardru took a deep breath. "The last time we were here, we talked about that line from *The Wolf Man*. 'The way you walked was thorny, through no fault of your own,'" he said.

"We did. And it has been, of late."

"And in the doing of all these things, have we not grown even closer?"

Alex smiled. "We have."

Bardru nodded. "Am I not like a father to you?"

Alex reached across and took Bardru's hand. "There is no 'like.' You *are* a father to me."

"Good. Then I would like to make it official. I have no children, and my own family is long-ago passed. I know it is a foregone, but I would just feel better, more complete, if I could call you 'son' instead of 'nephew.' To truly be able to say that."

Alex's heart swelled, even more so because he could see that Bardru clearly shared the feeling. The older man's eyes brimmed with tears.

They both stood and embraced. Alex said what Bardru needed to hear. "Thank you so much, Father." In saying it, he realized it was what he needed to hear as well.

Bardru held him tightly. "My son," he said.

It was late in the afternoon. Alex stood facing Sun in the dojo.
The smaller man's face was uncharacteristically grave. He took
a deep breath and spoke. "Today we will talk about yin and
yang." He pointed to the symbol painted on the wall opposite
the portrait of Bruce Lee. "What does that signify to you?"

Alex looked at it briefly and turned to Sun. "Forces in opposition. Or harmony."

"Ah!" said Sun. "So close to understanding it. This may be
the most important conversation we ever have."

Alex, who had developed a deep respect for Sun during their
training and their conversations, nodded, listening.

"I know who you seek. How could I not after the other day?
And if he were truly dead, as everyone is saying, you would not
be here to train, correct?"

"That's correct, Sun."

"And I have an intuition about your true nature." He smiled.
"Westerners are oh so practical, and they eschew the supernatural, even as they secretly fear it in the silences of the night. And
for the most part the world acquiesces. Science this and science
that. Which I am fine with, for the most part.

"But when it comes to yin and yang, there is science and then
there is the supernatural. Yes?"

Alex stared at this phenomenal little man in his baggy business suit. "Yes," he replied.

"Good. Have you ever heard the term *Jiangshi*?"

"No."

"Americans with a penchant for Hong Kong movies know them. They are Chinese vampires."

*Holy shit*. Sun must have seen the change in his face and smiled. "Ah! How close am I to your true nature, Alex?"

Alex held up his hand with index finger and middle finger extended and touching. "This close, Sun."

"So and so. I have been paid handsomely to train you, and I intend to earn that pay. But there is an important lesson you must learn. The *most* important lesson."

"I am ready, Sun."

Sun scrutinized him. "I wonder. Do you think you have fully embraced the yin and yang of your nature?"

Alex thought hard for a moment. "I'm not sure."

"I submit that you have not. Unlike your Western vampires, *Jiangshi* are not torn between humanity and monstrosity. They are just what they are: creatures of pure yang energy, no longer balanced by yin."

He demonstrated a rigid, hopping movement, arms extended in front of him before flowing back into his normal, fluid movements. "*Jiangshi* are feared not because they drink blood, but because they have lost the harmony that makes us human. They are frozen in one state, eternally unbalanced."

Sun's eyes narrowed as he studied Alex. "You fear becoming a monster, so you partition yourself—human techniques here, vampire ferocity suppressed. But by refusing to blend these aspects, you create the very imbalance you fear. Your enemy, this killer who is still with us despite being blown up, he has no such conflict. That will be his advantage over you. That is why he will defeat you."

Suddenly Sun emitted a piercing shriek and launched himself at Alex. His first kick crashed full force into Alex's jaw, and he whirled, smashing a fist into Alex's groin. More lightning-fast blows followed. Such was the fury of Sun's attack that Alex reacted in an electric surge of surprise and anger. "No!" he roared and lashed out, striking Sun near the shoulder. There was an audible *crack*. The small man flew back several feet and landed in a heap on the mat. Horrified, Alex rushed over to him.

He saw Sun smiling as he slowly raised himself into a sitting position. He grunted as he reached up and gingerly touched his collarbone, which was surely broken. "Now Alex!" he cried, his dark eyes bright. "I saw your fangs! Now you understand!"

Alex was shocked. He could easily have killed Sun. He helped his teacher stand. "Now take me to the hospital," Sun said quietly, hand on his collarbone.

Emelia met Alex's gaze in the emergency room waiting area at St. Luke's hospital downtown. She had rushed over when he called her. He told her what happened.

"I could have killed him," Alex said, still in shock after a half hour.

"I think he knew that," Emelia said. "I think it was the point. Alex, you know who Robert Oppenheimer was, right?"

He nodded. "The scientist behind the atomic bomb."

"That's right. Do you know what Oppenheimer said after the first atomic bomb test? 'Now I am become Death, the destroyer of worlds.' He quoted the *Bhagavad Gita*—a text about a warrior's duty to act despite moral doubt. Oppenheimer didn't create the bomb because he wanted to destroy; he did it because he understood that sometimes terrible power must be wielded by those who comprehend its gravity. He embraced his role not because he wanted to, but because he knew what would happen if that power fell solely to those without conscience."

She was trembling and her eyes were wide. She moved closer and put her hand on his face. "Your ability to kill isn't your curse, Alex: it's your responsibility. What makes you different from Titus isn't that he kills and you don't. It's that you understand the weight of taking a life. Jellybean taught you that. You carry that burden with you. That's why you must be the one to stop him—because unlike him, you'll never take pleasure in it. You'll do what needs to be done, and then you'll find your way back to yourself. Back to me." They embraced there, standing in the waiting area.

He felt a huge swell of emotion. "I love you, Emelia," he said, with deeper certainty than he had thought possible.

She looked at him, with those gray-green eyes he'd encountered so long ago. "I love you, Alex."

## 35

The next morning Emelia forbade Alex from turning on the television. He called to check on Sun, who was taking the day off but sounded cheerful. "I'll trade a broken collarbone for your integration of yin and yang any day," Sun had said over the phone.

After their call, Alex sat with Emelia at the computer as she ordered bookshelves and a better chair for the office. Midnight was curled up in the bed by Emelia's feet, and Dizzy had plopped down in the doorway.

"I feel restless," Alex said. "Wanna go do something?"

She smiled. "I'm a little tired. My ambitions are leaning more toward taking a nap between two dogs."

"And after your nap?"

She frowned. "Against my better goddamned judgment, I agreed to meet Alison later this afternoon. She's being reassigned out of Houston now that the Vision Killer case is closed. She wants to quote—apologize for being a bitch—unquote. Her exact words."

Alex cleared his throat. "That's a little party I plan to skip."

"Smart choice. I barely want to go myself. Maybe it'll be some closure for us. Bleh."

"Well, then, I am going to go take a bottle of expensive wine to my new dad. It's been a while since I've been to his museum of a condo."

Emelia hugged Alex. "I'm so happy for you and Bardru. He was sooooooo nice to me the other night."

"It caught me off guard—the father thing," Alex said. "But now that we talked about it, it seems natural as hell. Plus, he loves you to death. He told me, 'She rescued you from Silana, more surely than I ever did.'" He gazed at Emelia. "You have, you know," he said, smiling at her.

She put her hand to his face. "And you've opened up an amazing world for me." She yawned. "Nap time. Midnight! Dizzy! Let's go!"

A little while later he stole into the bedroom and watched her sleep for a few moments. Then he took off his shirt and shoes, and ascended the spiral staircase. He stood for a few minutes in front of *Conflagration*. Then he went and got four cans of paint: red, orange, yellow and black. He lined them up in front of the nearly completed painting and then grabbed a can of brushes. As he dipped a flat brush into the orange paint, he said, "It's time."

An hour later he set a thin brush charged with black paint into the can. He stepped back and looked at the painting. For him, it was complete, down to the Jackson Williams signature in black ink at the lower right corner. Pride flooded through him. Then he whispered, "No." He grabbed the thin brush and recharged it with black paint. Then he walked around to the back of the canvas and wrote on the frame with the black paint. *For my beloved Emelia*.

Emelia woke and stretched luxuriously. Dizzy grumbled and rolled over onto his back. Sounds drifted in from the living room.

She said under her breath, "You are in so much trouble, mister." But when she peeked in at him from the hallway, he lounged on the couch with a glass of wine, watching a movie. She recognized it: *Fists of Fury* with Bruce Lee. She turned and said, "Off the hook," and went back to take a shower and get dressed.

When she emerged again, the TV was off, and he was tying his sneakers. She came up to him, the two dogs walking alongside her. The sunlight was golden as it spilled through the window, illuminating *Poe's Lament*.

"Not looking forward to this," she said. He stood up and kissed her on the forehead. "Some things gotta be done." He went to the kitchen and got his bottle of wine, decorated with festive twirls of ribbon. They went down the front stairs and as they walked to their respective cars, Emelia said, "My love to Bardru. Any message for Alison?"

He laughed and then sighed. "Best unsaid."

"Fair enough. Meet back here later?"

He smiled and hoped he didn't look too much like the cat that ate the canary. "Yep."

She came up to him and regarded him. "You seem awfully happy."

He kissed her on the forehead again, "Well, I've got myself a dad now."

She cocked an eyebrow. "I wonder if that's it, mister."

He opened the driver's side door of her car. "I'll see you this evening."

"Well, it's a sure bet that your meeting will be happier than mine," she said and climbed into the car. "Love you, baby."

"And you are my beloved Emelia, of course!"

She laughed. "You nut. I'm outta here."

As her car disappeared down the street, Alex glanced up at the third floor, anticipating a very happy reunion when she got back. "Journeys end in lovers meeting," he said as he walked to his car.

Emelia saw Alison standing in front of the tavern called, ironically enough, Happy's.

As she walked up, Alison said, "I didn't know if you'd want to go in."

Emelia sighed. "I kinda don't."

Alison nodded. "Understandable. I just want to say I'm sorry for...for that day. My blood was up because of the strangeness and I kinda lost it. But that's no excuse. I'm terribly sorry, Emelia."

Emelia didn't want to kick her while she was down. "So you've been reassigned?"

Alison's face brightened a bit. "Yes, to Norfolk, Virginia. I'll be out from under Jack Crain's thumb."

"That's got to be a huge relief."

"You have no idea. It'll be a fresh—" Alison's eyes grew wide.

A figure in dark clothes and a floppy black hat darted up to them. His old, old face was marred by a long, twisted, black scar. Long white hair spilled down around his shoulders. Alison reached for her shoulder holster as he said, "Good evening, ladies."

Without warning, Emelia's surprise and fear melted away. Alison relaxed, and her empty hand withdrew from her jacket. Emelia *knew* what was happening as he said, "Will you please come with me?" That tiny sliver of her mind screamed for her not to comply.

"Sure," Alison said calmly.

"Okay," Emelia said, knowing she had lost the battle.

"This way," Titus said, gesturing to a black sedan nearby.

# 36

— · —

D ark clouds were scudding across the sky and stormy weather was threatening as Alex parked on the street. The stairs creaked beneath his feet in the large quadruplex that contained Bardru's condo. He stopped at the door. It was slightly ajar. "Bardru?" he called out, his pulse quickening. No answer. He grabbed the knob and swung it open.

The place was a wreck. Books and antiques were scattered on the floor. Bardru's expensive kneeler had been thrown through the large painting of Christ.

Alex gasped. Bardru was stuck to a wall, unmoving, his head hanging down. He stepped closer and saw that Bardru had been crucified, his arms stuck to the wall with two of those strange daggers that Tessa had referred to as *sescespitas*. A third had been thrust into his chest. Whitish vapor drifted up from Bardru's flesh as he sublimated.

Alex collapsed to his knees. Titus. Titus had done this.

His thoughts immediately went to Emelia. But she was with Alison, the FBI agent, in a public place. He'd call and check on her in a bit. He felt numb.

He forced himself to stand, and pulled the daggers from Bardru's hands, supporting the body, which felt frighteningly light, and taking it to his bed. Awkwardly he swept some books off the bed and gently laid Bardru down. He removed the dagger from his chest and tossed it away. One book stood undisturbed nearby, on a small table: Bardru's Rembrandt Bible. Alex took the volume and laid it near the body. He retrieved a golden cross from the floor and placed it on Bardru's chest, arranging his silver-scorched hands over it.

Alex had abandoned religion long ago but had always respected Bardru's Catholicism. Anguished, Alex wondered what an atheist could possibly do or say in such a moment. And then, like a ray of sunshine appearing through a dark cloud, the words from his faraway youth came to him. He stood over his father's dissipating body and spoke, his voice breaking.

*Our Father, who art in heaven, Hallowed be thy name. Thy kingdom come, thy will be done, On earth as it is in heaven. Give us this day our daily bread, And forgive us our trespasses, As we forgive those who trespass against us. And lead us not into temptation, But deliver us from evil.*

Then Alex leaned down and kissed Bardru's forehead. The mist-wreathed flesh felt like shifting sand beneath his lips. Alex stood, hands clasped, tears streaming down his face. He glanced around and decided to at least tidy up the chaos. He replaced books and tomes on their shelves, righted the tumbled furniture, antiques and statuary. He leaned the torn painting against the wall where Bardru had been pinned. When the room had been restored, thoughts of Emelia suddenly became urgent. He glanced back at the bed. Bardru was almost gone now, and the vapor hanging in the room almost smelled like incense.

Tearfully, Alex went to the door and gazed for a long moment at the body. "Goodbye, Father," he said sadly. Then he closed the door.

Back out on the street, an uncharacteristically cool breeze rustled Alex's hair, and a few large drops of rain fell here and there.

He speed-dialed Emelia. It rang and rang and then he heard her voice. *Hi there. This is Emelia Cord. Please leave me a message, and I promise to get back to you as soon as I can. Thanks!*

"Call me immediately—it's an emergency," he said. He also sent her a text saying the same thing.

He hurried back to his car, dread coiling in his gut.

Emelia came to, feeling dizzy, in a brightly lit room. She was restrained, her arms and legs strapped to a vertical cross-shaped wooden rack. She vaguely remembered being forced to breathe chloroform or something in the car along with Alison. The thugs in the back of the car had groped her, fondling her breasts and crotch and laughing as she lost consciousness. But her clothing was intact, and she didn't feel as if she had been violated. She despaired about how long that might last.

The air in the room was heavy with a sour-sweet, rotten smell. As she glanced about, she saw a table directly ahead that was strewn with surgical instruments and clamps, and rusty surgical saws. It was not a heartening sight. Off to her right, Alison was strapped to a similar rack, head lolling forward, but still breathing. She was still clothed as well. A third rack sat empty beyond Alison.

"Alison," she whispered. "Wake up. Come on, Alison!"

Alison's head stirred and her eyelids fluttered. "*Huh-melia*?" she slurred.

"I'm right here. We're in big trouble."

Alison regained her senses and glanced around. "Oh shit," she said. "Did they drug us or something?"

"Something like that," Emelia said.

"Those fuckers were feeling me up before I passed out."

"Same here. How tightly are you strapped up?"

Alison tested the leather straps holding her. "No good," she said. "Emelia, look at that table. What are they gonna do to us?"

"This is important," Emelia said. "At Quantico you did the mental toughness segment right?'

"Yeah."

"Me too. This is going to be the acid test of that for both of us, I think."

"Fuck, Emelia. This is the real world. They're gonna rape the shit out of us and cut us up."

"C'mon" Emelia whispered. "We don't know that for sure. Let's take the situation minute by minute like we were trained."

"Look at that table! You know they're gonna do it."

"No, we don't. You're letting your imagination run away with all this. Master it. We have to survive this somehow. We have to help each other if we can."

Despair clawed at Emelia. Alison kept saying "*Fuckfuckfuckfuck....*"

The metal door at the opposite end of the room slid open with a metallic thump.

# 37

A lex texted Maxie. *How soon on that suit?*

Maxie's reply: *Bustin' ass. 4 hours of sleep last night. Estimating 24 hours or so.*

Alex's shoulders sagged. Helplessness bore down on him. Outside the house, sullen rain fell in fits and starts. Alex paced. He tried Emelia's number again and again. Nothing.

*It's my fault.* I brought her into this and now who knows what that monster is doing to her. If she's even still alive. His thoughts turned to Bardru and he shuddered. *Goddammit.* How had he ever had the pure *hubris* to think he could go up against Titus? To expose the people most important to him to this danger?

He paced some more. Who could he even talk to? He didn't want to slow Maxie down. He was going to need that suit soon. Jonas? A nonstarter. *Hey Jonas, Titus has my human girlfriend who knows the secret to killing vampires.* Sun? He didn't know enough about the actual situation. He went into the office and sat down at the desk. *Think!*

Somehow, his thoughts drifted back to his hypnosis mentor, the esteemed hypnotherapist James Wilcox. On a fine fall evening, they had taken a break from training and were conversing over snifters of Jameson Irish Whiskey.

"I always tell my clients that whenever faced with something insurmountable, the first thing you do is convert the *problem*, this big, monolithic problem into a *process*. How do you eat an elephant? The old saying goes: one bite at a time. What's step one? What's step two? The monolith will tumble."

What is step one? he wondered. He calmed himself and thought. The answer struck him. Talk to the *right* person. And there was a right person!

Titus Seneca walked across the room to Emelia and Alison. He wore silk pajama slacks and a wife-beater T-shirt. He seemed impossibly thin, and the pale flesh was almost translucent. As he approached, Emelia saw the scars Alex had inflicted on him. They resembled linear black bruises on his face and neck, as well as his upper chest and right elbow.

He smiled. His teeth looked brittle and rotten. "Yes," he said, raising his spindly arms. "You see what he did to me. The pain is constant, as will be *his* when he arrives."

Alison stared at him. "How can you still be alive?"

He laughed, a phlegmatic bubbly sound.

"Oh, I am more tenacious than most."

Emelia's phone, which sat on the table amid the nasty things, buzzed and rang.

Titus picked it up. "A marvelous little device. So many devices to understand for someone like me. I suppose this is the one who seeks you?" He held the screen up so that Emelia could see it. The screen displayed Alex's name. Emelia said nothing. She fought to stay calm. He had to know she was missing by now.

"Tsk," Titus said, placing the phone on the table. "Such defiance. I've seen it so, so many times before. It will wither in time, as always."

He strode over to Alison and reached up to handle a lock of her blond hair. "So lovely. I was blonde myself when I was a boy. But that was so, so long ago."

"You'd better let us go," Alison said. "The FBI is going to be searching for you."

"Indeed?" he replied. "They said on the television device that I am dead, so why would they be searching for me?"

Alison glanced over at Emelia, who shook her head, her expression resolute.

"In any case, there is work to be done. It is in my nature to hurt. I have hurt thousands of people in my time. Now I must, alas, hurt one of you. But which one should it be? You are both beautiful to my eyes. Oh! And it is about the eyes, of course. You have both *seen* me."

He picked up one of the daggers with the testicle-like hand-guards. "Mmm. The *sescespita*. It will solve that for one of you and the other will be cleansed in the watching, I think. But who will lose her eyes and who will watch? It is a delicious conundrum. There is pain in the doing and pain in the watching. We must maximize both. But there is also pain in the anticipation, as well! We must not be hasty. That is why all these delicious tools are spread across the table. For you to look at and wonder which will be used and what will be done to whom, and when.

"Oooh," Titus said, picking up a bulbous, pear-shaped device with a screw and a handle sticking out of the smaller end. "Such a naughty little bauble. Inserted into the vulva, easier for the matron, but a bit more challenging for the virgin. Or into the anus: that can be entertaining as well. Once firmly in place, crank, crank, crank." He twisted the handle, and the screw caused the valves of the bulb to expand in sections, opening like a horrifying metal flower. "So very naughty."

Sound erupted from Alison's throat: raw terror, rising and falling.

"Don't give him the satisfaction," Emelia said. "C'mon, be tough. *Tough*! You are a Special Agent for the FBI."

Titus laughed that horrible laugh again. "I am learning much about the two of you, even from this brief chat." He set the terrible device on the table and came near to Emelia. She steeled herself. He leaned close to her neck and sniffed. "Oh yes, much strength runs in the sweet red elixir in those veins. To taste that rich, red pulsing strength. To feel it pouring from your neck and coursing down my throat. Oh! To savor that strength as it ebbs from your body!" She shuddered as his tongue slithered up her neck, cold and wet like a slug. She closed her eyes. *Alex, find us, please, please, find us.*

It was 9:45 at night at Desdemona, the bar where he had had his first serious conversation with Emelia. Large drops of rain from the storms rolling across the city were pattering on the roof. He sat where she had sat, as if some stray molecules of her intellect had somehow remained there, like a trail of void particles. He had a notebook and a Sharpie with him. He used mindfulness to quell the gnawing fear that Emelia was dead somewhere, or, worse yet, that she was still alive and he was doing terrible things to her.

He dialed his phone. A female voice answered, "Tessa Cavatore."

"Tessa, it's Alex. I need your help," he said, his voice shaking.

"All right. Take a deep breath first."

He did.

"Now take another deep breath."

She was the expert. He did so. "Okay."

"Now tell me what you need."

"Tessa, when you work with your clients, whether vampire or human, you guarantee them confidentiality. That's what therapists do, right?"

"Yes," she said simply.

"I need for this conversation to be confidential. I'll pay whatever your going rate for therapy is, but I desperately need your confidential help. *Please.*"

"Alex, try to stay calm. Two things: to reassure you, everything on this call, and even any subsequent calls will be 100% confidential. Two: you've done so much for us already that we are in your debt. I will do my utmost to help you, and it won't cost anything."

"Thank you," he said. He took a deep breath. "Okay. Titus has, I'm pretty sure, kidnapped or possibly killed someone very important to me."

She gasped. "Oh, not Bardru!"

The words were like a blow. He had to take a moment to regain his composure. Fighting back tears, he said, "He already killed Bardru. This is a different person. We were supposed to meet but she never showed up. I think Titus has her. You were right—he struck at me, very hard. Please help me."

"Oh, Alex, I'm so sorry. Okay, try to stay calm. Listen to me: he is methodical, and he is clever, but he has his own needs that compel him to act in predictable ways. We need to stay focused on the possibilities they present."

Alex wiped tears from his eyes. "I'm listening."

"I hate to ask you but how and in what condition did you find Bardru?"

"He was crucified against the wall in his condo. The place was a mess. There must have been a struggle. He lost. I—" he trailed off.

"Okay, thank you for telling me that. You know this already, but Titus' aim is to hurt you. Not just physically—that attempt may come later. But also, psychologically. He's a sadist. The crucifixion is a desecration, a debasement of Bardru's faith. He knew you'd know that, so it was the ugliest, most hurtful way to harm you psychologically."

"It worked pretty well," Alex said. "I am hurting."

"I know. More than any time since this started, you have to be strong. I will help you if I can. You think he kidnapped this other person?"

"Unsure," he replied. "She's just missing."

"Have you checked her home?"

"She had moved in with me."

"Okay. I assume you are involved with her?"

"Yes."

"Okay. I can't be certain, but for the moment I think she may be alive."

"How?" he asked.

"Think about it. He could have just killed Bardru, but he took the time and trouble to crucify him, knowing that you would discover him at some point.

"Titus wants to maximize your suffering thinking about this person you love in his clutches. He wants you to agonize in the *not knowing*."

"Well, that is one hundred percent happening. It's killing me."

"You can't let it kill you Alex," she said. She spoke very deliberately "*You. Must. Be. Strong*. It's her only hope of surviving this."

"But what can I do?"

"Wait for him to contact you."

Alex shook his head. "Why would he do that?"

"To *gloat*, Alex. He's got the upper hand. He wants to hear you beg or plead or grovel. It's his nature. Think about it. He could have blown you up at that building the minute you walked up but he *left a note*. He taunted you in the Deepest Shadow and bragged on himself in the process. He wrote a taunting message in blood at that one murder scene. He even taunted you after you hurt him following the rampage at the festival."

Alex thought back. *Not enough*. For the first time since leaving Bardru's condo, hope flickered.

"Still with me?" she asked.

"Yes."

"For now, always carry a notepad and pen. Use a recording app on your phone. Be ready for his call, day or night. He may say something useful because of his massive ego. You've got to listen closely."

"Should I give him what he wants? Beg, plead, grovel?"

There was a silence. "I'm going to give you this advice with a strong warning that it may backfire. Are you ready?"

"Yes, Tessa."

"Don't give him what he wants. But you need to be crafty in the way that you do that. There was an Austrian psychologist named Wilhem Stekel who said, *the worst sin towards our fellow creatures is not to hate them, but to be indifferent to them: that's the essence of inhumanity.*

She went on. "He expects you to cry and grovel, but if he hears you being indifferent, he may grow so angry that he betrays something important you can use."

"Or just kill her outright. That's the backfire, right?"

"I hate to say this Alex, but you need to hear it to completely comprehend what I am saying. He *is* going to kill her. That's in his plan. But he wants you to play the game. To suffer as much as possible *before* he kills her. I'm so sorry to be this blunt, but you're gambling with a madman. If he doesn't kill her outright, she may survive longer as he tries to figure out another way to get at you."

"Tessa, this is really difficult to hear."

"I know, Alex. But the situation requires some difficult assessments and thoughts. My heart goes out to you. We really aren't supposed to say that in therapeutics, but I do feel that way. However, I do have something hopeful to tell you."

"I'm all ears."

"When you're acting aloof and indifferent, say these exact words. 'Hell, I don't even know if she's still alive.' Repeat that back to me."

He took a deep breath. "Hell, I don't even know if she's still alive."

"Good. That may stimulate him to let her speak to prove it. Then you'll have some proof that she is still alive at that moment."

"Okay."

"Alex, I can only imagine how hard this is for you. You may speak the words that cause him to kill her. But you may also speak the words that prolong her life and give you more time to find her. It's a crapshoot, but sometimes the dice come up boxcars. And so I can leave you with that thought, here is a possibility: he may *tell you where he is* at some point."

"Why on earth would he do that?"

"So he can trap you and hurt you physically like you have hurt him. So he can kill your lover in front of your eyes. Again, it's his nature. He is bent on revenge. Revenge on you specifically. It's not a certainty that he'll do that, but I do think it's possible."

He sighed. "Thank you for being honest with me, Tessa. It hurts but I need to hear it."

"I'm sorry it hurts. Now, what do you say when he taunts or gloats?"

"Hell, I don't even know if she's still alive."

"Perfect. If I think of anything else I will call you, okay?"

# 38

—·—

"**G**oddamn," Alison said. "I have to pee so bad."

Emelia had been drifting into and out of fitful sleep. Her arms felt numb. She flexed her fingers rapidly. *What time is it?*

"They never show this shit in movies," Alison grumbled. "I don't think I can hold it."

"Like you said hours ago, this is real life," Emelia said. "I have to go myself. Pee and get some relief. It's literally the least of our worries, right now."

"Oh god that's so much better," Alison said. Emelia did the same and felt the warm urine soaking her jeans. It *was* a relief. She remembered snorkeling in Cozumel while on a college trip. *Diver's delight.*

"Any idea what time it might be?" Alison asked.

"Night, I think."

"What do you think he's going to do to us?"

"I'm trying not to think about it. Minute by minute, remember? Right now, we're alive, we're unhurt, and our pants are soaked."

Alison laughed at that, but her laugh was high and tinged with hysteria.

"Easy, Alison. We have to try and keep it together."

"Easier said than done."

"Alex is likely already trying to find us."

That unhinged laugh again. "How? We're somewhere in a city of millions of people. And that's if they didn't take us out of Houston while we were knocked out."

Emelia sighed. "Is there *any* possibility that the FBI is looking for you?"

"Unlikely. The immediate case is closed. I was supposed to be at a reassignment briefing tomorrow, er, this morning, I guess. But even if I miss that they may not think anything is wrong for hours, or even days."

Emelia wanted to mention that Alex had been working on his reach, but she realized she might have to explain what that was to Alison, and it just wasn't worth it. She wasn't exactly being a paragon of optimism. Had she slept through her goddamned mental toughness segment at Quantico?

Emelia shifted, testing the leather straps holding her arms. The worst thing was that Alison was probably right about what was going to happen to them.

*Stop it, Emelia.* Minute by minute. Think things through. Observe. Watch for mistakes or weaknesses in their plan. Plan for contingencies. Be strong. Survive, even if they hurt you. *Survive.* She occupied her mind with that until she drifted off again.

Storms clamored all night as they swept along a stationary front that stretched for dozens of miles across Houston. It had been the longest night of Alex's life, yet he had somehow dozed off on the couch with his phone in his hand and woke when Dizzy and Midnight licked his face, wanting breakfast. He fed the dogs and laid back down, heavy with exhaustion. A few minutes later he fell into a deep sleep and jerked awake when the phone rang. It showed Emelia on the screen. He leapt to his feet and activated the recording app.

"Hello?"

It was the voice he'd only heard in his mind until now. "Are you Alex?"

"I am."

"Ah," Titus said. "We had a rather unpleasant first meeting the other day."

Alex steeled himself, thinking about his conversation with Tessa.

"I imagine you are worried about Emelia?"

It broke his heart to say it. "Who?"

"Games?" Titus said. "Is that how it's to be?"

"I'm just at a little bit of a loss, is all," Alex said, fearing that his words would end Emelia's life.

"Emelia will be at a little bit of a loss, too. Maybe I will give her to my men for a while. They are a rough lot, but I'm sure they will find ways to entertain her."

He scribbled on a pad in the office. *STILL ALIVE.*

"You say that, but hell, I don't even know if she's still alive." *PleaseberightTessa.*

"Fool!" There was a short, terrifying silence and then he heard Titus grumble some words to someone. His heart leaped when he heard the urgency in her voice. "Alex! Where are you? Where—*are*—*you*."

Titus came back on the line. "So pretty, and so unspoiled. That may change soon. Because of you."

Alex scribbled. *UNHURT.*

"All right Titus. What do you want me to do?"

"You need to learn respect. I have some, *erm*, work to do with these two lovely ladies. Perhaps I will use the camera on this phone device and send you some pictures of my handiwork later. Then we will see how bold you supposedly are then, eh?"

The call ended. He looked at the time. He'd slept until 3:45 p.m..

Titus tossed the phone back on the table. He scowled at Alison and Emelia. "He thinks to outwit me," he said angrily. "That will end badly for him, and for *you* as well!"

He rifled through the torture tools on the table, laughing. Alison's breath came in short gasps, and Emelia's heart hammered in her chest.

"So much to choose from, and yet," he said, reverently lifting the *sescespita*. "This old friend has served me so well. He caressed the bulbous shapes at the base of the gleaming blade.

"He is so erect. So eager to penetrate. But whom? Who will suffer his *thrusts* and who will be the one to watch? Perhaps you ladies can help me choose."

"Do it to her!" Alison spat out. Emelia reeled in shock. But beneath the shock was a sad realization. Titus had fully broken Alison.

"Please don't hurt me," Alison blubbered. "I'll do anything. I can find out where Alex lives and tell you. Just—just, not me. Please."

Titus laughed. "Alison, do you think I don't already know where he lives?"

An icy chill slithered down Emelia's spine.

"Please," Alison said, weeping.

Titus stepped over to Emelia. He lifted the gleaming blade until it was level with her eyes. "And you," he said almost sympathetically. "Will you betray her to me, as well?"

Emelia clenched her jaw, staring into those red-rimmed gray eyes of his. She refused to speak.

He waved the gleaming *sescespita* inches from Emelia's face. "The decision has been made!"

He quickly stepped over to Alison, who had already begun to scream. He grabbed her hair and plunged the blade into her eye. "*Accipe phallum meum!*"

Emelia squeezed her eyes shut, near to breaking herself. The screaming wasn't the worst of it. It was the scraping sound of the blade against the bone of Alison's eye socket. And Titus. He was humming merrily.

At 5 p.m., a lull in the storm ended in a wind-driven patter of rain against the window.

Alex took several deep breaths and listened to the conversation for perhaps the fiftieth time. It was what Emelia had said and the way she had said it. It was heartbreaking to hear her say, "Alex, where are you?"

But then it was curious to hear her repeat it. "Where—*are*—*you.*" There wasn't an uptick in her tone in that second sentence. *It wasn't a question.*

He felt a chill. *It was a statement. IT WAS CODE!*

He paced. He held the phone to his chest. *My love, what are you trying to tell me?* Tears streamed down his cheeks. It was some kind of forest-and-trees thing, he knew, and he cursed fate that he wasn't as smart as her.

Then he froze mid-step in the living room. His dogs whined, sensing his distress. He closed his eyes, took two deep breaths and opened his eyes calmly. Then he began to scroll through the screens showing the apps on his phone.

He saw it. *WhereRU.*

The *sescespita* clattered on the table. Alison was moaning hoarsely. Emelia opened her eyes. Titus appeared, his face close to hers.

"Your strength is why you can still see right now. That may change, later, but—" Emelia shuddered as his hands slid around her waist, like a lover's would.

He whispered, clasping her to him. "I must drink of this strength. I must—"

Emelia winced at the sting of his fangs. *Survive*, she thought as he suckled at her neck. *Survive*.

The man sitting in the dark sedan yawned. He spritzed water on his face from a small spray bottle to stay awake. During a lull in the rain, he became alert when he saw activity at the three-story building he was watching. The gate swung open, and a red Miata backed out and roared away. He waited ten minutes as he had been instructed, then leaned over to the device in the seat next to him. He extended the silvery metal radio antenna, flipped a toggle switch and then pressed a red button on the device.

A bright flash illuminated the windows on the third story of the building. Then, as the wind picked up and rain started to pelt the sedan, he drove off.

The beast was born in a bright, noisy flash. For the moment it had the three things it needed to survive. Oxygen from the air, fuel from the canisters attached to the device and heat from the initial detonation. It roiled in the drawer in which the device had been hidden, dark orange and belching black smoke. The drawer and the ones around it were delicious fuel and it swirled up, healthier and healthier. As it grew it came across an unfamiliar can, metal and rectangular. It caressed the can in its fiery embrace and the can swelled and suddenly burst, spewing more fuel everywhere. The beast devoured it. It embraced a red canister, which also burst, but the powder inside it wounded the beast! But not enough, for nearby was another of the rectangular cans full of nourishing liquid fuel.

As it grew it found squares and rectangles of wood and cloth and paint, which it began to consume, ignoring the brief pain of another red canister bursting. Too little to stop the beast now. Then it encountered a rectangle that reflected its own colors: orange and yellow and red and black. It swirled around it and began to consume it. Had it been sentient, which it was not, it might have seen words on the frame that said in black paint: *To my beloved Emelia*.

Had it had sensory organs, which it did not, it might also have heard the howling of dogs.

# 39

— · —

The storm had worsened when Alex arrived at Titus' hideout: the *WhereRU* app linked to Emelia's phone had led him there. It was dark now, and gusts of wind drove shoals of rain that clattered on the hood and windshield of Alex's car. He parked down the street and jogged down to the wall surrounding the compound.

He took a moment and concentrated, extending his *reach* out in search of Titus. Alex cried out and staggered back. The presence in the compound blotted out everything in a gigantic, stinging, blinding glow. It had to be him, but locating his exact position was going to be impossible.

After taking a few moments to recover, Alex stepped close to the wall. He leapt up and easily gained the top. He pulled himself up as rain lashed at him. It was a large, rambling, two-story structure with floodlights illuminating the grounds around it. Some windows had been boarded up and others carefully bricked shut.

Glancing around, Alex saw what he was looking for: power lines from a transformer on a pole sloping down to a service mast on the roof. To protect the wires from falling branches, the wires were bundled with a braided steel cable. Alex leaped from the wall and grabbed the cable bundle and climbed hand over hand to the service mast. With his fingers, he managed to separate the electrical cables from the steel cable, and using all his strength, he yanked the cables hard. They snapped with a great actinic flash of blue-white light. Blinking his eyes, he saw that his hands looked misty for a moment and then reformed. A normal human's hands would have been burnt to stumps. The floodlights around the compound had gone out.

*Well, they know I'm here.* He climbed down until he was hanging from the eaves and dropped to the wet lawn below. The shadows were deep, and he could smell cinnamon candy. Walking around the perimeter, he found a sheltered alcove where a door had been bricked up. It was dry so he reached into his pocket and produced an object in a plastic sandwich bag. It looked a bit like a flip phone. He unwrapped it, flipped it open and tapped the screen a few times. The device beeped and Alex set it down in a corner of the sheltered area. Then he went back out into the rain and followed the cinnamon-candy scent.

Borglum shifted his weight from foot to foot. After what Mr. Botalli had told him about Mr. Titus not caring whether they died when the bad guy showed up and then seeing the bizarre video of Mr. Titus on the TV, he had almost bailed on this insane job. But he needed the money, and what guy could stand up to buckshot from a riot shotgun? Well, Mr. Titus apparently could, but he was special, Borglum supposed.

Sweating, he glanced down the long shadowy hallway near the front of the house. The battery-operated emergency lights had come on when the power went out, but they were few and far between. Borglum had guessed that the bad guy was here. But if he showed up in this hallway Borglum could get off several shots before he—

He tensed at the sound. It was familiar, but faint and hard to tell exactly what it was. "Who's that?" he called out. The sound went silent, and he took a few tentative steps toward the shadowed end of the hall. "I gotta shotgun and I ain't afraid to use it," he called out. *God damn this goddamned job*, he thought, as he took a few more steps. The sound was there again.

*Psss psss psss psss.*

Borglum recognized it then. It was what you said to get a kitty cat to come here. "What the fuck?" he said, moving a little closer. "You think you're funny?"

*Psss psss psss psss*, came the sound again and this time he whiffed a strange, sweet scent. Like candy or something.

"You ain't gonna be so cute with a mouthful of buckshot, motherfucker!" he called out. He was trembling. "Fuck this job," he said to himself and walked toward the shadowed end of the hallway. He'd run by and then get the fuck out of here.

*Psss psss psss psss.*

"Goddamn you!" he said. He rushed toward the corner, now panicked. *Get past it and out, fer chrissakes!*

He was almost home free when the cinnamon candy smell exploded in his nostrils, and he saw the man emerge out of the shadow.

Borglum raised the barrel, but the man reached out *so fast* and lifted the shotgun barrel toward the ceiling as Borglum pulled the trigger.

As the shot went off, Borglum felt the weapon twist in his hands, and his trigger finger snapped. Before he could cry out the man's fist struck him in the throat, and he heard a muffled crunch as his larynx collapsed. In a blinding moment of pain and disorientation, everything went dark.

In the gloom of the Deepest Shadow, the man twitched, helpless in Alex's grasp. *Intercept the threat, invade the enemy's space and strike hard*, Sun had said.

Now Alex sank his fangs into the gurgling man and drained the blood from him. *Go in with a full stomach*, Maxie had said.

The man slumped. Alex took the shotgun and let go of the body, which vanished. He'd be lying dead somewhere in the house now, Alex knew. He raised the shotgun and ejected a shell. He held it in his hand. No feeling of warmth. He broke it open, and the silvery pellets spilled out onto the ground. He put the back of his hand close to them. No warmth. His skin touched them. No burning pain.

"Huh," Alex said. He thought of something Maxie had told him. *They may not all have silver shot, but you can't assume that everyone won't. Ya kinda gotta think of all possibilities, see?*

He racked the gun, chambering a shell. He thought of the movie *Die Hard*. "Now I have a shotgun," he said quietly, moving along the gray shapes of the compound's shadow-openings.

Konnick yelled out, "Shot fired! He's in the house!" He peered around a doorway in the gloom. "Hey, Borglum, you there?" No answer.

He raised his shotgun, which had a bright LED flashlight attached to the barrel and shined it down toward the corner. "Borglum, you better sing the fuck out iffin you don't want to get shot!"

There was something ahead on the floor. Konnick crept forward toward it, shotgun at the ready. His mind reeled when he saw what it was. A pair of legs, but they disappeared into the wall just below the knees. That's all there was: some dead legs embedded in a wall. There was a swirl of cinnamon candy smell, and Konnick saw a man emerge from the shadows, back to him, just a yard away.

He raised the shotgun and fired. It struck the man in the right shoulder and should have knocked him down, but he whirled, and Konnick thought he saw a patch of mist on the man's right chest.

It seemed like slow motion. As he racked the shotgun for a second shot, the man stepped offline and entered Konnick's guard, grabbed the action of the shotgun with his left hand, controlling it, and punched him in the chest with his right hand. The man's fist smashed through his sternum and ribs, crushing his heart and lungs. In the last moment, Konnick realized the man's fist was *inside his chest*. He dropped to the floor.

Heller and Clackerball were by the front door when another of the guards ran around a corner with a shotgun in his hands. "Coming in—don't shoot!" he said, running toward them. "Borglum's dead!"

"What the actual fuck?" Clackerball said, as the man came up to them. "That fucking dumbass. What happened?"

"Wait a minute," Heller said raising his shotgun. "This guy's soaking wet."

All at once Heller and Clackerball relaxed. Clackerball lowered his shotgun an inch. Even though they knew this guy had to be their target, he was somehow *trustworthy*. "Uh, are you actually working for Mr. Botalli?" asked Clackerball.

Alex smiled at them. "I am."

*"Above all else,"* Maxie had told him, *use your charisma pheromone to even the odds.*

Watson had snuck away from his post to grab a quick nip from the bottle he kept stashed in the breakroom. Okay, maybe two nips now that the guy was on the premises. Things were getting crazy. He'd heard shots. *Just need a little liquid courage,*

he thought, chugging bourbon. He stashed the bottle again and saw Heller and Clackerball in the doorway. "What's the codeword, Watson?" Heller asked, his shotgun leveled at him.

"Are you off your goddamned rocker?" Watson replied.

"Wrong answer," Clackerball said, raising his shotgun. They opened fire.

# 40

Titus came over to Emelia. Her eyes were half closed. She heard chaotic sounds of gunfire and shouts. *So weak*. Nearby she still heard hoarse, shallow breathing from Alison. Titus grinned and she could smell the sour, rotten stink of his breath. "He's coming for you, Emelia," he said.

"A—lex," she said, a tear running down from the corner of her eye.

Suddenly she saw the blade of the *sescespita* near her face. It was smeared with Alison's blood and gore.

"I can't decide if it's better for him to find you temporarily unspoiled, or—" he said, sliding the flat of the tip down her cheekbone.

She snuffled. "Take me but...leave him," she whispered.

"Oh, but I already took so much of your precious blood. That *strength*. That sweet, delicious blood," he whispered in her ear, licking his lips. She closed her eyes, wishing for death. For her transformation, even if Alex didn't make it in time. *Please*.

Alex crept through the silent, maze-like structure in the dim light. Most, or maybe even all the guards were dead or had fled. He came around a corner, shotgun in hand and encountered a tall, well-dressed man holding up his hands.

"Please don't fire until I've had a chance to speak," he said in a cultured Italian accent.

Alex nodded. "Are you Botalli?"

"Very good," he said with a smile. "But that matters less than finding your friends. I can help you in exchange for my life. I am unarmed. I'm done with this business and this place. I just want to get away. But first I will show you where they are."

Alex nodded again. "Okay, but if this is some trick, I can kill you before you bolt. Very fast reflexes."

Botalli smiled and lowered his hands. "Indeed, sir. Follow me."

Shotgun at the ready, Alex followed him through several rooms and down two staircases. They ended up at a metal door. "He calls this the Salon," Botalli murmured. "It is, I must warn you, a misnomer."

Before either of them could react, the door slid open and Titus pounced on Botalli, screaming "Betrayer!" Alex got a glimpse of Emelia inside and dashed past them as Titus slashed at the tall man with the *sescespita*. Botalli's screams dissipated into gargling coughing sounds.

Emelia hung on the bondage rack, eyes closed and for a moment Alex thought she was dead. Without thinking, he set the shotgun down on the nearby table, scattered with surgical tools and...worse things. He lifted her head, and her eyes opened. "Emelia!" he cried. Her eyes widened, and she said "No!"

Titus was upon him, and for the briefest moment he forgot his training. He pulled the pistol from his jacket pocket, but Titus batted it out of his hand.

As they grappled, Alex realized he was immensely strong. Titus hurled him backwards and he crashed into a table, shattering it. Then Titus was upon him, choking him with both hands.

*Sufficient skill can overcome an imbalance in strength*, Sun had said. Alex reached up and drove his thumbs into Titus' eyes. With a cry, Titus reached up to protect his eyes and Alex drove both fists into Titus's chest, and the ancient vampire reeled back. Alex rolled and regained his feet.

He saw the KelTec near his feet and lunged for it. But Titus leaped at him and struck him with the full force of his shoulder. Alex flew back, crashing to the concrete floor. As Titus dove for the gun, Alex spotted the black scar running down his right arm to the elbow. *Target the weakness.* Alex rolled toward Titus and trapped his scarred right arm as Titus grabbed the pistol. With a cry, Alex hyperextended the elbow at the scar point. The ancient bone snapped with a wet crack, and Titus screamed.

But even as the pistol fell, Titus caught it with his left hand, pushed the muzzle against Alex's thigh, and pulled the trigger. The silver bullet bored into the flesh and burning agony exploded in his thigh.

Titus put the pistol in the waistband of his pajamas, grabbed Alex by the hair with his good hand and dragged him back to Emelia. He dropped Alex in a heap at her feet. Alex grunted and clutched at the wound in his thigh. It was like a burning ember.

Emelia cried out, "Alex!"

Titus took a step back. "Don't you make the lovely pair," he said. It's actually difficult to decide who to despoil first. Delicious!" He laughed a phlegmatic laugh.

*Pain*, Sun had told him. *You will experience it, and it will try to overwhelm you. But you must be the master. Summon what you need. It is in you.*

Alex visualized a twist dial that went from zero to ten. The searing pain in his leg was surely a ten, but in his mind, he began to mentally click the dial from ten, to nine, to eight.

"Are you trying to stand?" Titus said. He took another step back, the gun still aimed at Alex's face.

*Seven. Six. Five.* With a herculean effort Alex rose, stiff, and awkward.

"Delicious!" cried Titus.

*Four. Three. Three. Thhrreeeeee.* It went no further. *Damm it.....Two!*

He reached out with a trembling hand. "Watch him die now, Emelia!" Titus said, aiming the pistol.

A loud report sounded from off to the left and the pistol in Titus' hand shattered. Alex glanced over to see Maxie in a shooting stance, wearing the unfinished Kevlar suit held together with duct tape. It had been the last thing Maxie had said to him that fateful day. *Plant this and I will come a'running.*

Maxie pulled the trigger again, but there was a weak *pop,* and a puff of smoke issued from the action of the gun. "Squib!" he shouted to Alex. "No shot!"

Enraged, Titus coiled like a tiger, ready to spring toward the usurper. Alex spotted the bloody *sescespita* on the table. *Silver plated*, Tessa had said. He grabbed it and Titus turned toward him just in time for Alex to cry out and plunge the *sescespita* into Titus' eye socket in an electric surge of vampire ferocity. Using his last reserve of strength, he drove it in hilt deep and a sickening sizzling sound, like steak on a griddle, came from the socket. Titus convulsed, his head shaking and his limbs twitching as he emitted a clotted scream from his gullet. He went down and began to sublimate into a mist. Panicked, Alex found another *sescespita* on the table and drove it into Titus' chest over and over, the blade scraping against his ribs as it penetrated. But Titus was already still, the smoking body twitching from the dagger blows but otherwise inert. Dead.

Maxie was nearby. The pain flared in Alex's leg again. He felt dizzy. He pointed at Emelia as he collapsed. "Get her down from there," he said.

Maxie set about freeing her and Alex hissed at the pain in his leg. His skin was hot and sweaty.

Then he saw the most beautiful thing ever. Emelia leaned over him. She looked groggy but he heard her voice. "You found us. Oh Alex!"

He pointed at the table. "Forceps. Get the bullet out!" She got up, wobbling a bit and then knelt next to the hole in his slacks. A thin streamer of white smoke was issuing from the wound, like smoke from a lit cigarette. She looked at him and hesitated for a moment. "Do it, Emelia," he gasped. "Dig it out." She plunged the forceps into the wound. Through the pain, Alex saw Maxie checking on Alison.

Emelia felt resistance and closed the forceps. She drew the sizzling slug out of his leg and threw it away like the poison that it was. She collapsed over Alex in a faint. He patted her cheek with his hand. "C'mon, Emelia." Her eyelids fluttered. O—kay, she murmured sleepily.

"Alex," Maxie said. This woman is dying of shock. She's almost gone. Unless one of us does a push, she's a goner. Do you want me to—"

"No! Emelia cried. "It has to be Alex!"

"Buddy, it's now or never," Maxie said. He reached down with strong hands and lifted, supporting Alex near Alison's neck. Alex bared his fangs and sank them into her neck. He drained the last of her blood and did the push—an age-old *intent* that she live on as a vampire—into her as she drew her last breath. There was no more blood.

The punctures in her neck healed in seconds. *I did it*, Alex thought.

As he left Alison, knowing that she had another chance now, a chance at a different type of life, Alex saw that Titus had completely sublimated, leaving only a bitter-smelling yellow mist in the air. But this mist was inert and did not move or show signs of coalescence. It began to disperse, and Alex knew he was truly gone.

Alex paused, noticing something strange. A fleeting spurious energy, perhaps that which had given Alison life—human life in those final moments, had fled from her into him. It seemed almost like a tickle inside him. It triggered old, old memories of himself before Silana.

Emelia moaned. He saw her reaching for him. "Transform," she said softly.

"No!" he shouted. Maxie moved toward her, but Alex waved him off. Grimacing, he staggered into a sitting position and pulled Emelia into his embrace. She was limp, barely breathing. Her skin was cold.

"Not yet my love," he said, fighting back tears. "Use your mind. Figure it out! Find your way back!" He looked at Maxie, who nodded.

Turning back to Emelia, he held her in the embrace and closed his eyes, and his body tensed as he *willed* it to happen, pushing those last vibrant wisps of human life energy into her.

"Not yet, my beautiful Emelia, not yet," he said, eyes tightly closed. He felt the life force, that tickle, that *spark* from Alison ebb away from him and he sensed, more than knew, maybe because of her nearness and her humanity, that it had found its way to Emelia.

"Please," he whispered, kissing her forehead. *Please.*

A long moment passed. He could only hear his breathing and Maxie's. He felt panic rising in him. *No, no, no!*

She emitted another moan, and her eyelids fluttered. "Al-lex," she said in a hoarse whisper, and he could feel a little warmth returning to her body. The flickering eyelids opened.

"That's it, Emelia. Find your way back to me now. You know how to do it."

She nodded and her beautiful gray-green eyes met his gaze. Her arms moved slowly, embracing him.

Maxie was standing nearby; his cheeks streaked with tears. "That's it, champ," he said.

"Love...you," she said, and though it was weak, he knew it was not a goodbye.

"I love you too, my beautiful one. Stay with me now. I've got you."

She nodded and he saw a hint of a smile upon her lips. He held her, the tears coming freely now.

# 41

— • —

A lison Martin woke up and her hands went up to her eyes. *They were there!* It must have been some kind of horrible nightmare. She blinked, grateful that she could see. She was on a cot in a pleasant, sunny, but unfamiliar room. The sound of the ocean was faintly audible, as were the plaintive cries of seagulls. Palm fronds waved outside a casement window. She tried to sit up but dropped back onto the thin mattress. She was weak and dizzy, as if she hadn't eaten for a couple of days. A ragged hunger gnawed at her gut. Frightened and disoriented, she called out "H-hello?"

A middle-aged woman walked through the open door. Her graying blonde hair was done up in a bun, and she wore faded jeans, and a simple blue knit blouse. She carried a teacup and saucer, and the aroma, like some rich, exotic bouillon, was enticing. As she neared, the woman lifted the teacup and held it out to Alison. She grabbed it with both hands, and gulped down the warm red fluid. Alison was half horrified because she was certain it was blood, and then fully appalled that it tasted better than anything she could imagine.

The woman smiled and said in a pleasant Texas drawl, "You're gonna be okay, I promise. I'm Vanessa Stanton. You're in my house in Galveston, Texas. Two blocks from the beach. Don't be afraid, Alison. I am here to help you. To guide you through the change. Think of me as an aunt."

In Houston, Armando Villereal, the court-appointed executor of Leonard Salazar Ortega's estate, sipped his coffee and reviewed the list of beneficiaries to notify. One name on the list was Alexandru Stoica, who was to receive three oil paintings: *Sunlight on Boughs*, *The Canasta Game* and *Willows at Lake's Edge*.

It was a sunny, cool morning in Atlanta, and at the headquarters of the Combined Departments of Paranormal Research, Mark Petrovsky walked down the hallway toward his office. He saw Melanie Sanders carrying a sheaf of Emelia's training materials. As she neared, he smiled and said "Big day: your first trainees. Are you ready?"

She smiled, although her eyes hinted of sadness. "She made sure I'd be ready."

"Big shoes to fill," he said. "You got this, right?"

Determination pushed the sadness from her eyes. "I do."

"All I need," he said as she passed.

He continued down the hall and unlocked the door to his office. He spotted a postcard lying flat on the clear space of his desk amid the computers and monitors. It was picture side up and superimposed over the cover art for one of his favorite books, *The Restaurant at the End of the Universe*, fiery orange letters said *Greetings From...*

Puzzled, he picked it up and turned it over. There was no canceled stamp; indeed, nothing on the message side except, in looping cursive, the word *Because*. The letter "e" at the end had a circle drawn around it.

He stared at it for a long time. Then with a profound sense of the bittersweet, he bent and opened the safe near his desk and took out a sealed manila envelope. He paused as he held it, gazing out at the golden sunshine streaming through his east-facing office window. *You pulled it off, ace.*

A man with too-cool skin drove through a Houston suburb. His left hand rested on the steering wheel and his right hand gently held the left hand of a woman with vibrantly warm flesh. Two dogs with singed fur snoozed on a blanket in the back seat. The man braked hard. "I can't believe it."

Ahead, on the sidewalk, he saw a young woman in workout clothes walking along.

"What is it?" the woman holding his hand asked, confused.

"I'll explain in a moment," he replied, with a squeeze of her hand. "Be right back."

As the man exited the car, a cool breeze swirled past—the first herald of fall in Texas. Even so, there was a scent of magnolia blossoms from somewhere, drifting along with the breeze.

He walked with a slight limp toward the woman. Recognition flashed in her eyes. He knew her name was Jennifer, and that she was nineteen or twenty. He knew that she liked to go clubbing with her girlfriends.

She pointed at him as he approached. "It's you!"

He nodded. His stomach rumbled but he ignored it.

She studied his face. "I mean—I think I know you from somewhere, but I can't remember where."

It's okay, Jen," he said. "We all forget things from time to time."

"One thing I remember is that you helped me," she said. "But I don't know how."

"It's okay," he said. "How are you nowadays?"

She smiled. "Great! Ben—he's my boyfriend, well, fiancé now—he and I are engaged."

"Congrats to you both!" the man said, grinning. "Happy news."

"Very much so—" She paused. "—and I think somehow, it's because of you. You helped me. I don't know how, but—it was something important."

His mind turned briefly back to that night, and it suddenly seemed like a long time ago, given all that followed. "I'm glad you're happy, Jen."

A moment of silence settled between them. The wind blew strands of her blonde hair in her face. Then, as though she had caught a wisp of memory, like a bit of dandelion fluff tumbling on the breeze, "I could swear I know you."

"You knew me," he said. "But I'm somebody else now." He reached out and they shook hands.

"Thank you," she said, gripping his hand with both of hers. "Thank you—for everything."

"You're welcome. Bye now." He smiled and turned.

As the man approached the car, he saw his woman smiling at him through the windshield, and his two dogs, one black and one white, stared from the back seat, their tongues lolling happily from their mouths. An immensity of gratitude swelled in his chest: as big perhaps as the cool front that rolled slowly southward across hundreds of miles of southeast Texas.

# ABOUT THE AUTHOR

Dan Perez – writer, hypnotist, sculptor and performer, has written a number of short stories, novels and self-help books. His fiction usually falls within the genres of horror and science fiction. Dan is an active member of Horror Writers Association (HWA). Dan was founder of two influential workshops for fiction writers: The Gulf Coast Writer's Workshop and The Tale Spinners. Dan lives in Houston, Texas with his dog Thor and some colorful tropical fish.

# Bonus short story!

**G**et the free bonus story 'Salt Water and Second Chances' when you join my newsletter— follow Alex and Emelia to the Texas coast for healing, romance, and an encounter that changes everything. Subscribers get updates on new releases, behind-the-scenes content, and exclusive stories. To sign up, scan QR code or visit: www.dansbooksnews.com

**New book release alerts only:** Scan the QR code below or visit: www.dansbooksrelease.com  **Follow me on Facebook:** https://tinyurl.com/4ukjnza8

# ALSO BY DAN PEREZ

This is a collection of my nationally published short stories.
There are twelve stories consisting primarily of horror and fantasy tales. The thirteenth story is new, and it is a Halloween story
praised by celebrated author Ray Bradbury himself.

Witches, vampires, ghosts, and goblins lurk in thirteen tales
of the uncanny. A boy discovers what Halloween truly means
when monstrous creatures emerge after midnight. A dying
young witch goes on a desperate rescue mission. A cuckolded
husband's revenge scheme takes an unexpected turn. A criminal
learns of a book he authored—in the future. A ghost haunts a
neglected mansion—or does it? A downed vampire fighter pilot
discovers a terrible secret.

*The Pumpkinseed Necklace* collects author Dan Perez's horror and dark fantasy stories that were nationally published in the 1990s, including a short story praised by legendary author Ray Bradbury as "beautifully, evocatively written." These tales of unsettling places and things range from psychological horror to poignant supernatural fantasy, and are unified by their exploration of what happens when the strange and the terrifying breaks through into our world.

Scan QR code below or visit: https://a.co/d/ixV54ol

# ALSO BY DAN PEREZ

In the vast deserts of New Mexico and Arizona, divorced ex-cop
David Parker seeks a fresh start on vacation with his kids.
Chemistry with a captivating woman sparks hope, but when
three people are brutally murdered at a motel he stayed in along
the way, Dave realizes he's been framed. Now, he must go on the
run to clear his name and expose the real killer. Will the police
catch him, or will the razor-wielding murderer find him first? In
the high desert, survival becomes a deadly race against both the
law and a merciless predator. Gum is a pulse-pounding thriller

set along the dusty desert stretches of Interstate 40. And among the predators that prowl the desert, the deadliest is the one that walks on two legs.

*"Nongard and Perez have masterfully crafted a gripping psychological thriller that will etch itself into the depths of your mind, resonating with, perhaps, the same intensity as your own memories of the torturous road trips you took as a child."*
**-Chase Hughes** Author of *Six-Minute X-Ray* and the best-selling novel *Phrase Seven*

Scan or go to: https://a.co/d/efvCdYi

www.ingramcontent.com/pod-product-compliance
Lightning Source LLC
Chambersburg PA
CBHW052015240626
47153CB00006B/1824